My God, Scott Thought As Kati Walked In.

She's ten times more beautiful than I remembered.

The passage of time had added an astonishing poise and self-confidence to the youthful loveliness that had attracted him before. But it was her face that held his attention, making his pulse race. Her eyes were capable of reflecting a thousand nuances of emotion. In the old days he'd always been able to read her thoughts, but he guessed that she was more guarded now.

Scott had often asked himself if his memory had tricked him into recalling her as so beautiful. Now he knew that it hadn't.

NANCY JOHN
is an unashamed romantic, deeply in love with her husband of over thirty years. She lives in Sussex, England, where long walks through the countryside provide the inspiration for the novels that have brought her a worldwide following.

HONOR BOOK

Dear Reader:

Romance readers have been enthusiastic about Silhouette Special Editions for years. And that's not by accident: Special Editions were the first of their kind and continue to feature realistic stories with heightened romantic tension.

The longer stories, sophisticated style, greater sensual detail and variety that made Special Editions popular are the same elements that will make you want to read book after book.

We hope that you enjoy this Special Edition today, and will enjoy many more.

> The Editors at Silhouette Books

NANCY JOHN
Rendezvous

Silhouette Special Edition
Published by Silhouette Books New York
America's Publisher of Contemporary Romance

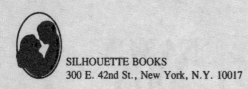

SILHOUETTE BOOKS
300 E. 42nd St., New York, N.Y. 10017

Copyright © 1985 by Nancy John
Cover artwork copyright © 1985 Robert A. Maguire

Distributed by Pocket Books

All rights reserved, including the right to reproduce this book or portions thereof in any form whatsoever. For information address Silhouette Books, 300 E. 42nd St., New York, N.Y. 10017

ISBN: 0-373-09219-9

First Silhouette Books printing February, 1985

10 9 8 7 6 5 4 3 2 1

All of the characters in this book are fictitious. Any resemblance to actual persons, living or dead, is purely coincidental.

Map by Ray Lundgren

SILHOUETTE, SILHOUETTE SPECIAL EDITION and colophon are registered trademarks of the publisher.

America's Publisher of Contemporary Romance

Printed in the U.S.A.

BC91

Books by Nancy John

Silhouette Romance

Tormenting Flame #17
The Spanish House #34
To Trust Tomorrow #57
Outback Summer #85
A Man for Always #115
Make-Believe Bride #192
Window to Happiness #262

Silhouette Special Edition

So Many Tomorrows #17
Web of Passion #38
Summer Rhapsody #75
Never Too Late #106
Dream of Yesterday #166
Champagne Nights #193
Rendezvous #219

Silhouette Desire

Night with a Stranger #119

For Helen and Andrew

Rendezvous

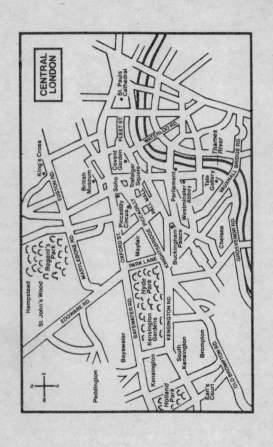

Chapter One

"Sorry, Bob, but I don't care for that guy you've picked as the model for our September issue center spread. . . ." While still talking into the phone, Kati Young beckoned the man who was hesitating in the doorway of her office to come in. "The blond girl is terrific, but not the man. You know I never object to the rugged look, but . . ."

"But not Cifbids?" her art director interjected.

"Definitely not Cifbids," she agreed with a laugh, running a hand through her dark wavy hair. "So you'd better come up with an alternative pretty quick, Bob. Like tomorrow."

That word Cifbids said it all. It had been coined eighteen months ago, soon after Kati had been promoted to the editor-in-chief's chair of *Rendezvous*. The sales figures for the up-scale glossy magazine for women had been sliding disastrously—largely, in her opinion, due to the general slackness from the editor on down to the most junior filing clerk. Kati, still only thirty, had been aware that her appointment was on a do-or-die basis, so she'd been determined to tighten things up right from the start. At her first briefing to the assembled staff she had kicked off with an edict on the subject of office dress.

"We have an image to project, and quite frankly you're not living up to it," she'd told them, using every inch of her five-foot-six stature to back up her new authority. "So from now on keep this in mind—Casual Is Fine But I Deplore Sloppiness." The initials of her phrase had been seized upon for an acronym which soon became a byword throughout Universal Publications, the magazine conglomerate that was housed in a sprawling Victorian building on London's Fleet Street. Cifbids denoted the pits in anything and everything. Sloppiness in dress, negative mental attitude, careless work . . . whatever. One bright spark whose brother was in the clothing business had ordered several gross of screen-printed T-shirts with the word blazoned in red across the front, and they'd sold like hotcakes. Prudently, Kati had awarded the garment her blessing. It was classified "okay casual."

Finishing her brisk phone call with the art director, Kati gave her attention to the lanky, fair-haired young man who was waiting to talk to her.

"Tim, the reason I wanted to see you was to give you my thoughts on your 'My Successful Wife' feature." She reached for a folder and spread its contents on her desk. "I like virtually everything you've done here. You've dug out some intriguing professions . . . the woman software designer is really great, and I love the small-town physician whose wife is a neurosurgeon. That man doesn't just accept her success; his genuine pride in her brilliance really shines through."

"Thanks, Kati." Tim raised his eyebrows questioningly. "But?"

"Yes, there's a but. Trouble is, Tim, one way or another all your husbands have come to terms with their wives' successful careers. Terrific, bully for them; I only wish it was always like that. But, sadly, we know it isn't. For every husband who happily accepts the situation, there must be quite a number who choke on the thought that the little woman outshines them in the success stakes. Find one or two of those, if you can. It won't be too easy. A man who admits to that sort of attitude is labeling himself a deep-dyed chauvinist. What are your own views on the subject, Tim?"

"How do you mean?"

Kati leaned back in her chair and crossed her long legs. "Suppose that you and Carol were married, and *you* stayed more or less at the same level, with modest salary increases, while *she* steamed ahead to bigger and better things."

"Like being made an editor?" he suggested, with a faint smile.

"Okay, that makes a good for-instance. How would you feel, Tim?"

He didn't rush in with a pat answer, and Kati approved of that. After a thoughtful silence, Tim said slowly, "I'd rather it was me who got the big job. But if it turned out to be Carol who had the gift . . ."

"Forget gift, and substitute hard work and dedication," Kati interrupted, her nut brown eyes sparkling.

"Whatever!" he said, gesturing. "If Carol had what it takes, then I'd wish her good luck. I'd envy her the success, yes, but I don't think I'd be resentful. I'd be pleased for her."

"Would you feel proud of her?"

"I'm proud of her already. It would just make me that much prouder."

"Either you're a diplomat, or a very rare breed of man," Kati said with a grin. "Oh, I've just had a thought, Tim. At a dinner party I went to the other evening they were talking about that woman barrister who's been hitting the headlines recently. You know, the one who won that big industrial espionage case."

"Verity Alexander, you mean?"

"That's she. I gathered from what I heard that the husband doesn't relish being known as Mr. Verity Alexander. He's just a small-time criminal lawyer. See what you can dig up there, Tim."

"I'll get on it right away." He gathered up the papers and returned them to the folder. "Thanks a lot for the ideas, Kati. You're dead right, of course—as ever."

She gave Tim a sharp look, always alert for sarcasm, but she saw that he meant it. Kati had never lost a sense of thankful surprise that the men under her in the hierarchy at U.P. showed so little resentment of her authority. She was good at her job, no question, but that didn't automatically earn a woman the respect of men. However, she'd always been careful to be constructive and never put anyone down without good cause. She expected a great deal of her staff, but never forgot that they were people with personal problems to contend with. She took pride in the fact that they felt they could confide in her—not necessarily as their boss, but as a friend with a sympathetic ear, and whose opinion they valued.

Tim paused at the door and glanced back at her. "By the way, have you heard about the troubleshooter that the firm is appointing?"

She nodded. "There's been talk for the past few weeks of taking an efficiency expert on board. It won't be too soon, I say. Things at U.P. need tightening up."

Tim's eyes widened in surprise. "I wouldn't have expected you to take that attitude, Kati, not after the miracles you've performed with *Rendezvous*. I saw the last quarter's sales figures the other day. Seventeen percent up on a year ago. It's fantastic."

"It's a good start, Tim. But that doesn't mean we can get complacent and sit on our butts. So what's the latest about this troubleshooter we're going to get? Has something come through on your hotline from the chairman's secretary?"

"Carol never tells me anything that's really confidential," he said defensively. "This . . . well, it'll be public knowledge any time now. When Mr. Channon was in the United States last month he met this guy and offered him the job of executive coordinator on the spot."

"Oh? So our new broom is an American?"

"No, he's English. Apparently he took off for the United States a few years ago and landed a big administrative job in TV."

"Which is supposed to make him an expert on magazine publishing," Kati commented dryly.

Tim laughed. "I guess the end-product is all the same to those top management guys . . . magazines or marmalade. Anyhow, Carol reckons that we'd all better watch out for thunderstorms. Mr. Channon was really excited about the appointment. He thinks it will mean a big turnaround in U.P.'s fortunes."

"Let's hope he's right," said Kati fervently. "When does Mr. Wonderman start work here, do you know?"

"Carol wasn't sure, but very soon, I imagine. One thing I do know, that guy Scott Drummond isn't going to find much to criticize about the way you handle *Rendezvous*." About to depart, Tim paused and regarded her with an anxious look in his mild gray eyes. "Are you feeling okay, Kati? You don't look too good."

Kati heard him as if from far off. Her office seemed to have turned into a vast echo chamber with the hated name reverberating back at her from every wall. Scott Drummond . . . Scott Drummond.

She wanted to fire questions at Tim, to pin him down and make absolutely certain that she hadn't somehow misheard or misunderstood him. But she dared not question Tim for fear of betraying herself. And anyway she needed no confirmation. Of course it was *her* Scott Drummond; everything fit. He had to be the Englishman who'd gone to the States a few years ago, landed himself a big job over there and then was tempted to return home to take on the restructuring of an ailing magazine publishing giant. He'd had eight years in which to become slicker, tougher, more ruthless; eight years in which to lose every last vestige of human kindness and sympathy . . . if he'd still had any left to lose. From a strictly commercial viewpoint Kati couldn't fault the directors of Universal Publications for appointing such a man as Scott Drummond. The company would undoubtedly prosper under his guiding hand . . . at a cost. The cost would be in terms of staff relationships. All thoughts of loyalty to colleagues, of helping one another out and the pleasant feeling of the staffers' all being part of one happy family would have to be jettisoned.

Well, she wanted no part of that sort of prosperity, Kati decided. She'd darn well quit her job before she took orders from Scott.

"I'm fine, Tim," she said with a lift of her chin. "It's just a bit of a headache starting."

He hovered over her solicitously. "Are you *sure* you're okay, Kati? You're looking very pale. Er . . . can I get you anything?"

"No thanks." She grinned weakly and reached for the contents of her in-tray. "I'm as okay as I ever will be, with this much work to get through." As a further hint she picked up the phone, and fortunately, Tim gave up and left her office.

As the door closed behind him Kati dropped the phone and slumped back in her leather-upholstered chair, her whole body sagging. She wondered wretchedly how fate could be so cruel as to bring Scott Drummond into her life again. As if once hadn't been enough. . . .

The intercom buzzed and she reached out blindly and flicked a switch. "What is it, Sandra?"

"It's Lady Dee, Kati, asking if you're free for lunch today."

"Oh. Tell her no for me, will you?" she instructed her secretary. "Say that I'm all tied up."

"Will do." Sandra hesitated, then asked diffidently, "Are you okay? You sound a bit strange, and Tim said you didn't look too good when he came out just now."

What she needed was a short let-up from the unceasing pressures of the job, just time enough to get herself together. "The truth is, Sandra, I'm feeling a bit queasy. . . . It's probably the fish I ate for dinner last night. Just keep people off my back for a while, will you? Lie if you have to."

"Right, Kati. But can I make you a cup of tea or something?"

"No, nothing. Just do as I say and hold my calls." Oh, dear, she thought as she hung up, I snarled at the poor girl when she was only trying to be helpful and sympathetic. I'll have to apologize to her later.

Kati's well-worn chair suddenly seemed hard and uncomfortable. Her spacious office, which she'd had done over to her own taste in fresh clean tones of mushroom and white, with colorful posters and attractive green pot-plants, had become an alien place. She rose and went to the window and gazed aimlessly along Fleet Street to the majestic gray bulk of St. Paul's Cathedral, its dome and towers silhouetted against the clear rinsed blue of the April sky. She closed her eyes and took several deep, steadying breaths. Any of her staff seeing her now would be astonished to find their brisk, efficient editor-in-chief reduced to a state bordering on panic. Today her image was well up to her usual carefully cultivated standard. She always wore rather severe clothes at the office, and today she had on a navy flannel suit teamed with a crisp red blouse. For the past eighteen months, since taking on this job, she'd kept her hair quite short. Once a month she had her lush dark waves expensively cut by a Mayfair stylist, so that she could easily do a shampoo and blow-dry herself and never needed to worry about her hair looking untidy.

Now, Kati felt a sham, an utter fake. Her image of glossy self-confidence was an outer shell that she'd painstakingly built around her, but up until this moment she'd never realized how fragile it was, and how vulnerable she was to sudden shock. Pictures of Scott Drummond kept floating across her brain: Scott in so many different moods and settings . . . from their first meeting soon after her twenty-third birthday to the Scott she had parted from in such bitterness and anger ten months later.

She had first seen him on her fourth day after starting work at her father's firm. She remembered the precise moment—eleven-fifteen in the morning. Fresh out of college, where she'd studied printing and design after her degree in English, she'd been installed at a desk in the roomy outer office of Prestige Print. The challenge she faced was to augment her theoretical knowledge of the printing trade with practical know-how, in preparation for the time when she would eventually take over the firm's management. As an only child, and without a mother since the age of eleven, Kati had grown extremely close to her father. Stephen Young had never talked condescendingly to his daughter, even when she was very small, and as the years went by he'd treated Kati more and more as an equal. On weekends they would go for outings together, driving to the coast in the vintage Bentley he was so proud of, or taking a train to London to look at museums and art galleries. At home they spent a lot of time listening to music together, and poring over books, sometimes reading poetry aloud. There had never been any question that when Kati started work it would be alongside her father, and that ultimately she would succeed him as head of the firm which her great-grandfather had founded in 1895.

On that ever-to-be-remembered morning at eleven-fifteen, Kati had been bent over some complicated figures, struggling with revisions to a bid for printing a new monthly journal. This was the only aspect of the printing trade that she didn't positively enjoy. Numbers had always been something of a mystery to her, a hazard to be constantly battled against, since they formed no meaningful image in her mind. She had just made her fifth effort at adding up a column of figures on the calculator, praying that this time the sum would tally with one of her previous attempts, when her father emerged from his private office and halted beside her desk. There was someone with him, and as Kati glanced up she found herself looking straight into a pair of humorous, smiling eyes that were a rich shade of cobalt blue.

"Meet my daughter, Katherine," Stephen Young said. "Kati, this is Scott Drummond, of Arlington Journals."

His voice was deep, mesmeric and very sexy. "Hello, Katherine. But you're called Kati for short?"

"By my friends."

"Then as of this moment I hope I qualify. Hi, Kati. Glad to know you."

"Hi, Scott," she said off-handedly, though her heart was thudding like a piston engine. "I'm working on the bid for *Farmers and Farming*. You've given us quite a problem keeping the costs down to your limits."

"That's why I'm here this morning. I have a few suggestions to make."

"I'll leave you two to get on with it, then," her father said with a smiling nod, and departed.

Scott found himself a spare chair and drew it up beside her, so close that Kati felt enveloped by his aura of male potency, all her senses tinglingly alert to the strength and virility of his loose-limbed, athletic body. She wasn't totally inexperienced about men, having had several mild romances during her years as a student, but she'd never before been so awakened to her own sensuality. Shocked, she kept her eyes down, staring at Scott's hand on the desk before her . . . at his long, sensitive fingers, and the lean wrist that showed just beneath the cuff of his dark gray suit.

Scott didn't speak, and she finally dared to glance at him inquiringly—to be riveted afresh by those compelling cobalt eyes. He was an incredibly attractive man, she thought dizzily, though not truly handsome. There was a careless lack of symmetry about his features, as if they'd been thrown together in a hurry and had only come out right through some happy accident. His brow was wide beneath a mass of peat-dark hair that had been ruffled by the wind, lending him a slightly rakish air. His prominent cheekbones, slightly crooked nose and emphatic jawline gave a fascinating interplay of planes and angles to his face. His mouth was boldly modeled, very sensuous, and the lopsided smile he suddenly gave her carried so many subtle overtones that she couldn't begin to interpret them. She just knew, with a wonderful feeling of happiness, that this man was going to be important in her life.

"So you're going to help me cut corners?" she said, her mouth dry and cottony.

"Let's call it rationalization. Arlington Journals would like your firm to get this additional order, Kati. We've always been very happy in our working relationship with Prestige Print. However, we're up against costs. If you can't get your bid down by five percent, we'll be forced to look for another printer for this magazine."

It seemed almost unbelievable that she and Scott should calmly be talking print technicalities after such a momentous encounter. Kati had an inner conviction that their meeting was important for him, too. But they had to talk about something, for heaven's sake, and it might as well be printing. Business was what had brought them together, and business would ensure that she'd see more of him. Getting a grip on herself, Kati plunged into a discussion of ways and means.

She was surprised to discover that Scott's knowledge

of her father's firm—the skilled craftsmen employed there and the plant and machinery—was even more detailed than her own. Within minutes he amazed her by suggesting a change in her proposed sequence of operations that would result in an appreciable economy. He followed this up with some schedule revisions on his firm's part which would reduce delays and thus make a further saving. With her abysmal head for figures Kati found it difficult to follow his rapid calculations, but whenever Scott realized that she wasn't keeping up with him he ran through it all again, as if for his own benefit. She felt grateful to him for that; many men, she suspected, would have enjoyed pointing up the fact that they could outdo her.

Time flew by as Kati basked in the warmth of his admiring gaze and listened to the sensual rhythms of his voice. She was astonished when Scott glanced at his watch and announced that it was time for lunch.

"There's a rather nice old-world pub in Wimbledon village that I go to when I'm out this way," he said. "How does that sound, Kati?"

"Great."

The five-minute drive in his car took them past the All-England Tennis Club.

"Are you interested in tennis?" he asked her.

"I love it . . . both watching and playing."

"Will you be taking in any of the championship matches this year?"

"I'd like to, but it's iffy."

"Iffy?"

"*If* Dad will give me the time off, *if* I can get tickets."

"You'd better come with me, Kati. That'll remove both ifs."

"I've just thought of another if," she said, trying to hide her bubbling pleasure.

"Spill it."

"*If* I want to go with you."

Scott laughed. "Whether or not, you'll have to smile

and look willing. I'm the customer, so I name the tune. Right?"

"You play it tough, mister." Name any tune you like, she thought, with excitement prickling her skin, and I'll be more than willing to dance to it. "How come you're so sure of getting Wimbledon tickets?" she went on. "They're like gold nuggets."

"I'll get all I need, don't worry. I've never failed before." This didn't surprise Kati one bit. Scott was that sort of man, destined to succeed in anything he touched. But, she immediately wondered, whom had he taken along to see the tennis on those previous occasions? Oh, no, Kati thought crossly, I've known him for exactly two hours, and already I'm feeling jealous. She tossed jealousy out of her mind, but it came winging straight back as if on a length of elastic.

In the ensuing weeks and months Scott never gave her real cause for jealousy. He seemed just as crazy about her as she was about him, and their romance blossomed and flourished. They saw one another constantly, and quite soon became lovers. Scott was a frequent visitor at the large Edwardian house on Wimbledon Hill, and Kati was thrilled that he and her father got along so well. When Scott announced that he'd been elected to the board of directors of Arlington Journals, they celebrated by becoming officially engaged. He bought her a beautiful ring—a green tourmaline set in a cluster of diamonds—and they fixed a wedding date three months ahead. Life for Kati was blissful, running on smooth, straight rails. She had two wonderful men to love—one with adoring daughterly devotion, the other with intense sensual passion.

Nothing, she had felt with brimming confidence, could possibly go wrong. And yet it did. Within the space of two dreadful weeks she had been robbed of everything she held precious: Her father was dead from a coronary, and Scott had been exposed as a brilliant, ruthless schemer.

Somehow Kati had survived the next few months. When she'd sold up and settled all the debts, she'd been left with no money, no home, and no job. After what had happened she felt a revulsion against the world of print and design in which she'd been brought up, and she looked for employment in a totally different field. She became a dental receptionist. She rented a small studio flat in Highgate, away from all the people she'd known in her growing years. She wanted a new life with no reminders.

It was quite some time before Kati's fighting spirit returned. It was feeble at first, but it had gained strength. She'd show them! Them? Okay, Scott Drummond . . . she'd show him! She didn't learn until much later that Scott had quit Arlington Journals and gone to America.

With her sights set on higher things than a receptionist job, she'd applied for and landed a secretarial post at Universal Publications. At first it had been rather dull, typing one of the half dozen standard answers to readers' comments on a literary periodical; but then, when an assistant editor left suddenly due to her husband's transfer to the west country, Kati got her chance to show some initiative. Her hard work, her single-minded determination and her sheer talent had eventually paid dividends and she'd been promoted up the editorial ladder. There were a few grumblers among those she bypassed, but for the most part she was popular and well-respected at U.P. When the management decided that an aggressive new editor was needed to revitalize the ailing *Rendezvous* and save it from folding, Kati was given the opportunity to prove herself.

She hadn't failed. Under her direction the staff of *Rendezvous* had become a tight-knit team dedicated to the ideal of success. Circulation began to climb. Victor Channon, to mark his appreciation at the end of her first year as editor, took Kati to lunch. It was an honor, though not a pleasure, to receive such attention from the chairman, who had a habit of firing a series of tricky questions and never listening to answers of more than three words.

When rumors first began to circulate among the staff at U.P. that a troubleshooter was likely to be appointed, Kati had voiced approval of the idea, unlike several of her opposite numbers on other magazines who were content to coast along in the same old rut. In her opinion the entire corporation needed a good shake-up. An individual editor, no matter how dedicated, could only do so much. After that it needed someone with far more muscle to instigate the necessary reforms.

But what definitely was *not* needed—by Kati—was that the man appointed should turn out to be the one man in the entire world she had hoped never to meet again. It was too cruel, a vicious twist of fate that she didn't deserve. Anger and pain surged through her, churning her insides. Should she resign right away, and maybe take sick leave if Scott arrived before she'd be able to leave? But why should she be driven from a job she enjoyed, a job she was good at, by Scott Drummond? No, she wasn't about to give in. After all, she was tougher now than when she'd known Scott eight years ago. She'd learned to take the worst that life could hand out. Kati's chin lifted, and once more she looked like a mature woman in charge of her own destiny. If Scott wanted to give her a rough ride, she'd show him that she could stay in the saddle. He'd nearly destroyed her once, and she didn't intend to let that happen again.

Returning to her desk, she buzzed her secretary. Her voice was steady and controlled. "Okay, Sandra, I can take calls again now."

"Oh, great!" The girl sounded mighty relieved. "You're feeling better, then, Kati?"

"Much better. And Sandra . . . I'm sorry if I was snappy just now."

"Don't worry about it. I have a whole string of people wanting you to call back, Kati."

"Okay, let's work through your list. But first, Sandra, call Lady Dee and tell her that if she's still free, I've changed my plans and I'd love to have lunch with her."

It was an act of sheer bravado which Kati regretted the moment she hung up. Lunching with her friend and pretending that nothing was wrong would be an acid test of her ability to survive the bombshell she'd received that morning. As of now, business had to be as usual, with no weakening in her resolve, no return to the feebleness of wanting to quit.

She was Kati Young, editor of *Rendezvous* . . . liked, admired, envied. That was how she was going to keep it.

Chapter Two

*W*henever Kati and Lady Dorothy Faulkner had lunch together, which was normally about once a week, they liked to get away from the U.P. building. Their favorite restaurant was a small Greek taverna in an ancient courtyard just off Fleet Street. The two women were rivals in a sense, since they both edited magazines concerned with fashion—in Dee's case, exclusively fashion—but that didn't stop them from being good friends. Although once in a while they found themselves in conflict when they both wanted to carry similar features in the same month, they'd always been able to resolve the dilemma without ill-will. Kati liked Dee a lot, and she valued her friend's shrewd judgment.

That Tuesday, Kati was thankful to find that the news about the appointment of an executive coordinator hadn't yet reached Dee's ears. She was just back from Athens and bursting with excitement about a new discovery of hers, a young Greek who had recently emerged from a backstreet workshop with a line of the most fabulous evening dresses.

"They're gorgeous, Kati, just gorgeous," Dee enthused over their moussaka, waving her jeweled hands in an extravagant gesture that nearly sent the water carafe flying. "All flowing lines and voluptuous drapes. I'm going to give him a big splash in *Style* the earliest I can organize it."

"Sounds as if that Greek has a big future," Kati observed, "if you're going to back him to that extent. Honestly, Dee, I don't know how you always manage to pick winners the way you do. Don't you ever have doubts about getting it wrong?"

"Not when I rely on my gut instinct." Dee eased her huge spectacles higher up her nose and looked at Kati across the table. "Do *you* have doubts?"

"Frequently."

"In that case, Kati, you manage to conceal them. You give the impression of breezing through your job with sublime certainty. And you're entitled, considering how you've jerked poor tired old *Rendezvous* back to the living and breathing world."

Kati laughed. "My, my, aren't the compliments whizzing around today."

After their lunch they walked back together along Fleet Street to Universal House, Dee topping Kati's five foot six by about three inches. She made a statuesque figure, with the head-turning sort of style and dash that came from supreme self-assurance rather than good looks. In fact, Dee's features viewed singly were far from perfect. She had an oversized mouth, a broad, slightly flattened nose, and her large green eyes were rather bulgy. Yet her face was riveting, glowing with character and good humor. Her title, Lady Dorothy, came in her own right, for she was the daughter of an earl. Dee had been married twice. Her first husband, an amateur racing driver, had been killed on the track; her second, a wealthy financier, she had divorced. Her brother now held the family seat, Avonbury Hall, a mansion in Hampshire that dated back to the fifteenth century. Dee still retained a suite there, and she had often invited Kati for the weekend.

The two women parted in the elevator when Dee stepped out at the fifth floor. Kati had to ride another three floors to the *Rendezvous* suite. As she walked into her outer office she found Robin Wheatley waiting for her. He was leaning against a filing cabinet chatting with Sandra.

"Hello, Robin." Kati glanced at her watch guiltily. "I hope you haven't been waiting too long. I forgot that we had an appointment today."

"It's unlike you to be forgetful," he said, as he followed her through to her office. "Something on your mind, Kati?"

"What's that supposed to mean?" she barked. Had Tim put two and two together this morning about her shocked reaction to the news of Scott Drummond's appointment? Had the word spread around?

"It was just a flip remark." Robin looked hurt by her sharp tone. "I'm sorry, Kati."

She waved him to a chair and glanced at her message pad. There was nothing that couldn't wait. "Give me a couple of minutes, Robin," she said, and went through to her small restroom to wash her hands and freshen her lipstick.

When she returned, Robin surveyed her with appreciative eyes. "You look fantastic, Kati. But then you always do."

She sighed inwardly. It was all very fine for her feminine ego to have a good-looking man like Robin as a devoted admirer. He was likable, sincere and a caring sort of person. Those were the plus factors. Weighing down the minus side were, firstly, that he was a working colleague. Secondly, Robin was rather too conventional and lacking in sparkle to really appeal to her. And thirdly and most importantly, he was married. Kati knew that quite a few people at U.P. believed that there was something going between them. It was what Robin himself wanted, that was very clear, but she'd taken pains to keep their relationship on a friends-only basis.

Robin was thirty-eight, a tallish, chunkily-built man with smooth, sandy hair and a small moustache. He'd been the advertisement manager of *Rendezvous* for the past three years. Privately, Kati couldn't help thinking that Robin had reached his present position by conscientious hard work rather than flair. He could be relied upon to give his best and never let the firm down, but she sometimes wished that he had the imagination to tackle his job in a less plodding way.

"Robin, I asked you to drop by this afternoon to chat about future advertisement prospects. I've decided that we really must add more pages to *Rendezvous*. We're looking a bit thin compared with the competition. But we can't hope to get budget approval for extra pages unless we have the additional ad revenue to support them. I intend to raise this at the next planning meeting, but I wanted a quiet word with you first, rather than have it thrown at your head in public."

Robin looked uneasy, as if she'd put him on the spot. "I don't quite know what to say, Kati."

"Just tell me what you think, that's all. I'm giving you advance warning that if my plans are adopted, the heat will instantly be on your department to sell the extra space. How does that prospect strike you? What are the trends—in advertising generally, and for *Rendezvous* specifically?"

"Not too bad at the moment, all things considered. We'll do our damndest to come up with something if you do decide to enlarge. You can rely on that."

"It goes without saying." She beat a light tattoo on

the desk top with impatient fingers. "I'm asking your opinion, Robin, because you're supposed to be the expert."

He frowned. "It's difficult to give you an off-the-cuff answer," he said worriedly. "I'd need to give the whole issue much more thought before committing myself."

"Okay," she said, managing to keep smiling. "Why don't you go away and start thinking? Come back to me in a couple of days."

Robin was clearly relieved to have won a respite. "Right, Kati, I'll do that. I'll give you a report in depth. That's the best way." He paused, and added with a hopeful smile, "Can I persuade you to let me present it over dinner?"

"Sorry, but I'm all booked up."

"Surely not *every* evening this week? Or how about lunch?"

Kati glanced at her desk diary. "Lunchtimes are solid. Evenings I have . . . let me see—dinner with the woman's page editor of the *Daily Post* about a feature she's doing on the mags; a meeting of a writers' circle at Hampstead; a radio interview in the "Women In The Media" spot; dinner with the boss of a new modeling agency we're thinking of using. Need I go on?"

"You sure do lead a busy life," Robin said admiringly. "How about the weekend, though? Say Saturday evening."

"No, Robin. You ought to spend weekends with your family. It would make a lot more sense if you took Anne out for dinner." She glanced at her diary again. "How about you coming to see me here first thing Monday morning after I've looked at my mail? Nine-thirty. Then you can give me your considered opinion about *Rendezvous*'s advertising prospects."

The news of the appointment of an executive coordinator was all over Universal House by next day. Every time someone mentioned it to Kati, which was often, she dug herself deeper into the crazy position of not admitting that she knew Scott Drummond and that once upon a time she'd even been engaged to marry him.

Scott's appointment was officially announced to the senior staff at a meeting called by Victor Channon in the ornate boardroom. Deceptively benign at first sight, with white hair and chubby pink cheeks, the chairman of U.P. swept them with an eagle eye as he outlined the role of the new man.

"I shall expect a hundred percent cooperation from each and every one of you," he declared when he concluded, and Kati wondered uneasily if his words were directed primarily at her. "Scott Drummond's track record backs up my personal evaluation of his capabilities. He'll do great things for U.P."

His track record, Kati thought bitterly, of being a liar and a cheat, a manipulator of Machiavellian cunning. The great things you so confidently expect, V.C., won't be for the benefit of Universal Publications unless they should happen to be in sync with Scott Drummond's own personal interests.

D-day, Drummond day, was May first. The little joke which rippled around the U.P. building didn't make Kati smile. The date on her desk diary seemed to stand out as if it were heavily ringed in red. Until the dreaded day, she determined to grit her teeth and carry on working. She became a demon to her staff; she let nothing go, not the tiniest detail.

On the morning of D-day minus one a rumor flew around that Scott Drummond had already arrived. The rumor sharpened to certain fact. His name was on everyone's lips, providing Kati with fifty new opportunites to casually let drop that she had known Scott in the days before he went to the United States. But the words were locked in her throat.

How much would Scott have told Victor Channon? she agonized. That he'd known her, that they'd been close, that they were actually planning to get married? All of that, perhaps. One small item he'd be sure to have omitted, she thought grimly, was the reason for their break-up. Or *would* Scott have kept it dark? Maybe he would have judged it something to boast about, just the sort of slick strategy that a tycoon like V.C. would applaud in the hitman he'd appointed.

So perhaps Victor Channon knew the whole horrible story of Scott's relationship with her. In that case, how long before the piece of gossip spread through the grapevine at Universal Publications? Scott Drummond, her colleagues would whisper behind her back, had really pulled a fast one on Kati Young eight years ago, when he'd tricked her father and herself into losing control of the printworks that had been founded by Kati's great-grandfather.

Kati postponed a lunch date with her art director, Bob Edmonds. She couldn't face an hour in the executive restaurant in an atmosphere of speculation about Scott. Instead, she went alone to the self-service cafeteria and pointedly laid a bulging file on the table to fend off any would-be companions. It worked for a while, until the heartily bluff Ray Morgan, technical editor of *Software Futures,* came to join her carrying a heaped plate of fish and chips. Kati smiled at him discouragingly, and made an up-to-the-eyes gesture at the file beside her. But Ray was insensitive to gentle hints. He sat down and reached across her for the salt.

"Had your turn yet, Kati?"

"My turn?"

"The summons to V.C.'s sanctum to meet the new whiz kid. Derek had to cancel his editorial conference at the last minute because he was allocated the spot from twelve-fifteen to twelve-thirty. He came back to the office looking more than somewhat dazed and needing an instant shot of Scotch. It looks like each editor-in-chief in turn is being given an audience. I guess it's reckoned that fifteen minutes' exposure is as much as anyone can stand the first time around." Ray popped a piece of crispy cod into his mouth and chewed it with relish, still talking. "Better be back in your office at two sharp, Kati, to check if your case has come up for trial."

Her appetite gone, Kati closed the file and stood up, leaving half her chicken salad uneaten. "I have to go back now anyway, Ray. See you around."

Sandra was still out at lunch, so Kati had a quarter of an hour alone and undisturbed. It served no purpose except to make her more jittery than ever. Her nerves were stretched to the screaming point when, an hour later, she finally received a summons from Victor Channon's secretary.

"V.C. wants you here at three, Kati. I don't suppose I need warn you what to expect."

"I imagine I'll survive, Carol," Kati said with a forced laugh.

With a last panicky check on her appearance, she left the *Rendezvous* offices and walked to the elevator on shaky legs. Four floors up, she stepped out to a hallway that had double-thick carpeting. The normal intimidating hush at this lofty level seemed to be charged with an extra menace today. When Kati entered the chairman's suite, Carol smiled a greeting and consulted her watch.

"Dead on, Kati. You can go straight in. Best of luck."

"Thanks. I guess I'll need it."

Kati crossed to the inner door, paused fractionally to gather her courage, then knocked and entered.

My God, Scott Drummond thought as Kati walked into the room, she's ten times more beautiful than I remember. His mouth went dry and he felt winded, as if he'd been punched in the solar plexus.

The passage of time, and perhaps the responsibility of her high-level job, had added an astonishing poise and self-confidence to the youthful loveliness that had so attracted him to Kati before. She had lost a few pounds, he judged, and her sensual figure, which even the tailored lines of her charcoal gray suit couldn't conceal, appeared to his discerning eyes to be even more fluidly perfect. The buttoned jacket curved softly over her high, beautiful breasts, and the knee-length hemline of her skirt was a perfect foil for Kati's shapely legs. Her feet, surprisingly small and dainty for a woman of her height, were encased in smart low-heeled pumps.

But it was her face which held Scott's attention, making his pulses thud; her fascinating face with the lovely sculpted bone-structure had always reminded him of the famous statue of Nefertiti. Beneath her delicately curved eyebrows her large eyes were a deep shade of brown, with tiny golden flecks which you had to be very near to see. They were capable of reflecting a thousand nuances of emotion. In the old days he'd always been able to read Kati's thoughts, but he guessed that she was more guarded now. Still, he didn't need any special insight to know that she was far from pleased to see him. The look in those intriguing eyes of hers was cool and watchful; the wide generous mouth that could smile so enchantingly when she was happy was now set in a determined line. Did she still have her dimples? he wondered. Away from her all those years, Scott had asked himself so many times if his memory was tricking him into recalling her as so outstandingly attractive. He'd met many beautiful women, and been intimate with several. They'd been good years, exciting years, highly successful years. And yet the cloud which had hung over his life for those first few months after the break-up with Kati had never quite dispersed. It had lingered remorselessly, somehow hiding the full brightness of the sun from him. There always remained a sense of loss, of incompleteness. Even with another woman in his arms he had sometimes found himself weaving a fantasy about Kati, picturing the form and features that had become so deeply imprinted in his mind and heart.

Knowing that he would be coming face to face with Kati again at U.P., Scott had hoped that seeing her in the flesh would finally lay his ghost to rest. From his preliminary glance at *Rendezvous*'s circulation graph, he'd noted that she'd done wonders with the magazine in her short reign, so it was more than likely that she'd become tough and hardheaded. But now, as he and Victor Channon rose politely from the red leather easy chairs by the window and went forward to greet Kati, he realized with a plunging heart that it had been wishful thinking. A close working relationship with Kati was only going to slash open his old wounds and keep them hurting.

One of the phones gave a discreet buzz. Victor Channon halted mid-stride and turned toward his massive mahogany desk on the far side of the room.

"I was expecting this call," he said. "You two go ahead and introduce yourselves." Picking up the phone, the chairman started barking out a string of instructions about stocks and shares, presumably to his stockbroker.

For a few seconds, Scott and Kati just stood and stared at one another.

"Hello, Kati," he murmured at last. He didn't attempt to shake hands with her. He dared not trust himself to touch her.

"Hello, Scott." Feeling faint, struggling for composure, she inclined her head toward Victor Channon and murmured, "He doesn't seem to realize that we know each other. Haven't you told him anything about us?"

"The need didn't arise," Scott responded, keeping his tone as brisk as he could manage, "so I left it unsaid. What have you told the people here?"

"Nothing."

"Nothing? You mean that *nobody* knows?"

"Not yet," she said, swallowing a lump in her throat.

"Then maybe it's best that we keep it that way."

"Yes, I think so," she said, in hasty agreement. "After all, it's no one else's business, is it?"

"Only yours and mine, Kati."

The intent gaze of his cobalt eyes was so unnerving that she had a sensation of losing herself, and had to fight to keep touch with reality. "It's history," she faltered. "In no way relevant to the current situation."

"Just as you say," Scott returned. "Irrelevant."

He looked marvelous, Kati thought, more attractive than ever. The eight intervening years had matured him a great deal. His teak-dark hair now showed a few traces of gray, mostly at the temples, and his face was etched with fine lines that hadn't existed before, especially around his mouth and eyes. Laugh lines, she thought sourly. Scott must have had a lot to laugh about as he trod on people's backs and levered himself upward in the corporate game.

Victor Channon put down the phone and came to join them, rubbing his plump hands jovially. "Getting to know each other, eh? That's good, that's good! I've been telling Scott that you're one of our brightest editors at U.P., Kati. And I'm sure that you're going to find him an enormous help to you in achieving the even better results we need."

"I'm always ready, Mr. Channon, to have my failings pointed out to me," she said, with a pretence of humility.

"Failings, my dear Kati . . . we're not talking about failings. I want positive thinking. Efficiency, that's our aim from now on. Right, Scott? If we're to survive at U.P., we've got to run a tight ship. Keep everybody's eye on the ball so we can get the optimum yield." The great V.C. was prone to confusing his figures of speech, a fault that no one had ever dared point out to him. Until now.

Scott said with an easy laugh, "That's a mixed bunch of metaphors, Victor."

"Eh, what . . ."

"Tight ships and eyes on the ball and optimum yields."

"Yes, yes, see what you mean." The chairman smiled; he actually smiled. "But you get my drift, Scott?"

"We both get your drift, Victor. Don't we, Kati?" Scott's cobalt eyes burned into her, and she nodded confirmation.

"Good, good! I told Scott about that Cifbids slogan of yours, Kati, and he likes it. I have an idea that he might steal it from you and adopt it as his own."

"I never got around to copyrighting it, Mr. Channon," she replied flippantly, "so I wouldn't sue him for plagiarism." *Does that disappoint you, Scott?* her steely gaze taunted. *I guess you only value what you can obtain by lying and cheating and stealing.*

Unlike her, Scott appeared entirely relaxed as the three of them sat down in the low-slung easy chairs by the window and briefly discussed Kati's particular cog in the U.P. wheel. Scott already had an astonishing grasp of the *Rendezvous* situation. He knew the latest circulation figures and the trend of the sales graph; he could talk about the contents of the magazine, the ratio of advertising to editorial matter and the quality of the artwork and printing.

Why should I be surprised, though? Kati mused sourly, thinking back on their very first meeting when he'd astounded her with his comprehensive knowledge of her father's printing business. Figures and their correlation had always been child's play to Scott, and he had a photographic memory when it came to balance sheets and other data. He could doubtless be equally precise about every other of the thirty-odd periodicals published by U.P. If this afternoon's interview was a foretaste of the way Scott intended to operate, the days and weeks and months ahead were going to be even harder to take than she'd envisioned in her worst imaginings.

Suddenly the interview was over; her scanty allowance of time was up. The two men came with her to the door and ushered her out with courtesy, but all the same Kati felt summarily dismissed.

It was a tough job to keep her mind on work for the rest of the afternoon, and to stop herself from snapping impatiently at every inoffensive staffer she encountered. Weakly, she quit her office a good half hour earlier than usual and set off through the cloistered gardens of London's legal district to her underground station on the Thames Embankment.

The first train to come in showed its destination as Wimbledon. Wimbledon . . . where her relationship with Scott had started. Oh, God, how was she going to cope? she thought, feeling a rush of shameful tears stinging behind her eyelids.

Chapter Three

Kati swore softly to herself when she heard the doorbell chime. It couldn't have come at a worse moment; she was down on her knees cleaning the grime off the inside of her oven. She'd tackled this long-neglected chore this evening in a mood of aggression, hoping to get rid of some of her pent-up tension after the wretched day she'd had at work.

For an instant she thought of pretending she wasn't at home, but the caller would have heard her radio. With a sigh Kati stood up and peeled off her rubber gloves before heading for the door. Whoever it was, she hoped to get rid of them quickly.

She opened the door and gave a gasp of dismay. It was Scott.

"Hello, Kati." His glance swept her up and down and he smiled wryly. "I seem to have caught you at a bad moment."

She stared back at him with an angry frown. "What do you want, Scott?"

"That's not very welcoming." Uninvited, he came strolling in, walking with the slight sway of his shoulders that she remembered so well. At one time she'd found it endearing; now it seemed to stem from arrogance. "Quite a place you have here," he said, glancing in through the open door of her living room. "You must be doing better than I realized, Kati."

"No doubt you know what my salary is, down to the last penny," she said scathingly. "So maybe you think that I've been fudging my expense account?"

Damn him, she thought, for having instantly pounced on the one thing she felt a bit guilty about. The rental of this smart mews cottage in Chelsea cost her more than she could really afford. It was her one luxury, apart from a fairly good wardrobe, which she considered a requirement of the job. Her car was small and an old model at that, and she'd always resisted the temptation of taking expensive vacations. After having spent her struggling years in drab, uncomfortable studio flats, as soon as she was given the editorship of *Rendezvous,* she'd looked around for somewhere to live that she really liked, somewhere it would be a pleasure to get home to after work. And once the ink on her lease was dry, she'd set about furnishing the mews cottage in a style that reflected her personality.

"You don't have to be so touchy," Scott said, looking amused.

"And you don't have to make snide cracks."

"It wasn't a snide crack, Kati. As a matter of fact, I haven't started looking at salaries yet. But whatever you're making, I'm sure you deserve every penny of it."

"I do," she agreed coldly, refusing to be mollified by this compliment. "How did you find out where I live, Scott?"

"Easy. I checked it out with personnel."

"Stupid question!" Kati jerked her shoulders angrily.

"I guess you figure you have the right to go poking and prying into the staff records."

"I do have that right, Kati. You'd better get used to the idea." The corners of his mouth quirked. "I won't bother to take issue with you on the poking and prying bit."

"Huh," she said scornfully. "So now that you've intruded on my private time, what do you want? You still haven't told me."

Kati felt terrible. Clad in a none-too-clean coverall jacket over old jeans and a crumpled shirt top, she knew that her hair must be all mussed-up and most likely there were smudges on her face. Yet, in a contrary way, she was glad that she looked a mess. Let Scott see her like this. Let him know that she didn't care a tuppenny damn what he thought of her. She wanted, absurdly, to burst into tears, and that added a fresh impetus to her fury. How spineless even to *want* to cry because of Scott Drummond!

Watching her, seeing the spark of anger in her brown eyes, the flush of high color in her cheeks, Scott thought how excitingly sexy she looked. This afternoon, he'd been startled to see a poised, confident, beautiful woman come walking into Victor Channon's office. Now, caught in the sort of situation that would daunt most women, she could face him with the fighting spirit of a tigress. He longed to touch her, to hold her, to caress her satiny flesh and breathe in the fragrance of her glossy dark hair. He had to conquer the reckless urge to step forward and sweep her into his arms in a passionate kiss.

Instead, he said mildly, "The reason I came, Kati, was to ask you to have dinner with me."

"You . . . what?" She was stunned. Then, rallying, she burst out, "You have some nerve."

Scott lifted his thick eyebrows. "Have you eaten already?"

"No, but . . ." Oh, no, she thought, she should have said yes. But why should she bother to lie? Scott could get the unpalatable truth. "I'm not about to have dinner with you, Scott, because I don't choose to associate with you except at the office, where I unfortunately have no option. Do you hear me?"

"I hear you, Kati, but I don't understand you. Circumstances have thrown us together again so, like it or not, we need to talk."

"I don't agree," she snapped. "You and I have nothing to talk about."

"No? I'd say it was pretty important for us to hammer out a *modus vivendi* . . . a way of getting along together."

"Thanks for the translation," she said ironically. "But I repeat—we have nothing to talk about. You just get on with your job, and I'll get on with mine."

Scott met her eyes in a long, searching gaze. "Kati, why didn't you say anything to anyone at U.P. about having known me before?"

Thrown by his question, she found herself stammering, "Like I said this afternoon, it . . . it's nobody else's business. What happened between us is history . . . just water under the bridge."

"Those are just meaningless phrases," he said impatiently.

"Okay, then. You tell me why *you* said nothing to Victor Channon."

"Because I thought it was up to you. You know what they say about the woman's prerogative."

Kati gave him a withering look. "I should leave the gallantry bit to other men, Scott. It doesn't suit you."

He ignored her sarcasm. "My suggestion of our having dinner together this evening makes sense, Kati. A neutral setting would make it easier for us to discuss the situation calmly and rationally."

"Forget it," she retorted. "I don't intend to go anywhere with you this evening."

"That's okay by me. We'll talk here, instead."

"No, we won't. I want you to leave, Scott, right now."

"I'm not leaving, Kati . . . not yet. Not until we've talked."

She glared at him furiously. "I suppose I can't throw you out."

"You suppose right. So be sensible and listen to reason. I'm sorry to have dropped by and caught you unprepared like this. I realize that no woman likes that, but . . ."

"If you imagine that I care two straws about how you think I look," she stormed, "you're under a serious delusion."

Scott continued just as if she hadn't spoken. ". . . but if I had called you first, you'd have turned me down cold. Right?"

"Dead right."

"That's why I dropped by without giving you a buzz first. Listen, why don't you go and get changed, and we'll try one of the local restaurants? There's a seafood place quite near here in the King's Road which I'm told is first rate, or if you fancy Indian, there's a place a bit further along."

Kati looked at him. "You've been in England since when, Scott . . . yesterday?"

He nodded. "I flew in yesterday morning. Why?"

"One day here, after an absence of nearly eight years, and you've already sorted out the best eating places in Chelsea."

Scott seemed to take it as a compliment, the exact opposite of what she'd intended. "It's not so clever," he said modestly. "I took a cab here—I'm not fixed up with a car yet—and I asked the driver to suggest a couple of likely restaurants nearby."

"Well, you were wasting your breath," she said in a clipped tone.

Scott frowned at her, looking exasperated. "We're

going to meet up with each other at the office quite a lot, Kati . . . mostly when there are other people around. How do you propose to act toward me?"

"Does it worry you?"

"Yes, and it ought to worry *you*," he threw back grimly. "We're both in high-level positions, so . . ."

"I don't equate my position with your lofty status, Scott."

His mouth tightened. "Considering that we're both in managerial jobs, it's up to us to put on a show of unity, even if it's faked. You know that makes sense, Kati. There's nothing that delights people lower down the pecking order more than to see two executives sniping at one another all the time."

"I wouldn't have expected you to care *what* other people think of you, Scott. Don't you just trample them underfoot if they get in the way of your goals?"

He took a deep breath and said in a carefully even tone, "Every word you say, Kati, just underlines the fact that we need to sort out a reasonable working relationship."

Kati balled her fists while she struggled for poise. Scott was right, darn him. Why did he manage to make her attitude look petty and childish? It only needed a moment's calm thought to realize that they would have to adopt a show of harmony in public, if there was to be any hope of concealing their past relationship.

"Okay, then, Scott," she said, through tight lips. "I'll have dinner with you, just so that we can thrash out a policy for working together."

"That's great." His sudden smile caught Kati off balance. Against her will she felt its radiant warmth thawing out some of her hostility. That smile made it hard for her to keep in mind that Scott was a tough, ruthless negotiator, a man without any human conscience.

"I'll have to change first," she said. "Why don't you go on ahead, and I'll join you at the restaurant?"

"No, I'm happy to wait for you. There's no rush. Take as long as you need."

Did he think that she was intending to spend a lot of time and effort in beautifying herself for his benefit? Or maybe he feared that she might try to skip out of the date if he left her. Kati said coldly, with an indifferent shrug of her slender shoulders, "Just as you like." She gestured to a small table in an alcove of the living room. "Help yourself to a drink while you're waiting."

"Thanks, I could do with one."

Scott did need a drink—badly. When Kati had disappeared upstairs, he was shocked to find that his hands were trembling. He'd not realized how pent-up he'd become, how crucial it had been for him to win Kati over. There'd been merit in his argument, of course; open splits at top level were notoriously bad for company morale. But that was only a small part of it. He needed to get on good terms with Kati again for strictly personal reasons; the realization had hit him the moment she'd walked into Victor Channon's office. Those tenuous strands of memory, of nostalgic yearning, that had kept his mind linked with Kati all these years had suddenly twined together into a strong cord that tugged at him.

He was a damn fool, he knew that. Any man pursuing a relationship with a woman who thought of him as poison needed his head examined. The needs of the job required him to make peaceful overtures to Kati Young, but it was the pull of his emotions that had brought him to her home this evening. He'd never been a man to dodge hard facts, and he wasn't about to begin now. Okay, so his physical desire for Kati was as keen as it had ever been . . . accepted, agreed. Precisely how much he wanted from her was something he'd not yet begun to think out. He'd just felt an urgent need to see Kati tonight, to talk to her, and she'd reluctantly consented to have dinner with him. So where do we go from here? he wondered.

Scott poured himself a vodka and tonic from the tray on the corner table, and wandered restlessly around her living room. It had been done over with real imagination and flair. There was nothing affected or overfussy about Kati. He liked the white paint and pale mushroom walls, which beautifully set off the nicely chosen items of furniture. A few of her things he recognized. On the walls were some of the delicate flower paintings that she'd had in her bedroom at Wimbledon, and also an ornate Venetian mirror with a gilded frame that had dominated the mantel of the family living room. There was the antique bureau with a glass-fronted top that contained china and porcelain collected by her parents in the early days of their marriage, and Kati had also kept her father's favorite wing armchair. The masculinity of the heavy piece with its well-worn leather upholstery and brass studs didn't entirely fit the rest of the furnishings, but it was expressive of Kati's intense devotion to her father. Scott liked the deep comfort of the plum-colored L-shaped sofa, and the touch of luxury given by the Chinese carpet, with pile a half-inch thick, which toned in beautifully with the cream-and-turquoise striped curtains. Long white bookshelves beneath the window carried the books that Kati always loved to have around her, and standing on the top shelf was a vase of daffodils and various potted plants. It was the sort of home she would have created for the two of them, he thought with a pang, if things hadn't gone so disastrously wrong.

A spurt of his old anger returned, the painful anger which had remained dormant for so long. Damn her, she'd had no right to judge him the way she did. The Kati of eight years ago had possessed every quality he could ever have wanted in a woman, except for one. At the final showdown she'd displayed an unforgivable lack of trust.

And yet, he thought, softening again, was it fair to heap too much blame on her? In a way, the fault had been that she'd trusted too much.

Up in her bedroom Kati took off her coverall, the jeans and shirt, then went thoughtfully to the closet and flicked through her many outfits. She paused at a gray crepe dress with a faint, smudgy design in white, a garment she'd had doubts about buying as soon as she'd tried it on again at home. It made her look frumpish, Dee had said, and that had killed it. Maybe it was just the thing to wear this evening, Kati thought. She took the dress out and tossed it across the bed while she went to the bathroom to wash up.

Returning, she looked at the wretched gray dress musingly. In a twisted sort of way, wouldn't it seem like an open admission that she was consciously fending Scott off? If she truly cared nothing for his opinion of her, she would dress to please herself. For a few moments she teetered indecisively, then finally discarded the idea of wearing the gray dress. Now she hesitated between a blue one with dolman sleeves, and a silk knit dress in a soft shade of apricot that had a matching jacket. Finally, she chose the apricot outfit. It did suit her, particularly when she pinned her hair into a French knot and applied deeper eyeshadow and glossier lipstick than she usually wore. She stood back from the long mirror, surveying the result. Kati Young, a woman who had carved out a successful career for herself in the sophisticated world of the media. She looked the part. Definitely.

Kati's self-confidence threatened to crumble as she realized she had done exactly what she'd wanted to avoid. She'd taken a long time over changing for her dinner date. It would give Scott entirely the wrong impression. She cursed herself for a fool as she snatched up her purse and made for the door.

Scott's second surprise was greater, if possible, than his first had been. This time he voiced his thoughts aloud.

"Kati, you look wonderful. It's incredible. You're not eight years older, you're eight years more beautiful."

"Please, Scott," she protested, frowning at him. But what woman wouldn't be gratified by a remark like that, whatever the circumstances, whoever the man? His overt admiration restored her ebbing confidence. "Let's go, if we're going."

It would only have been a short walk to the restaurant, but a fine rain misted the air. Four taxis shot by, all taken. Then, miraculously, Scott secured one that was free; it emerged from a side street as if summoned up by sheer willpower on his part. Typical, Kati thought. Small problems had always seemed to melt away when he was around. Scott Drummond was equated with success . . . in work, in life. And, it was safe to surmise, success in his relationships with women. Any woman who hadn't good cause to know the ruthlessness that lay behind his easy charm and confident manner would find Scott hard to resist. Just as she herself had in her innocence, eight years ago.

Fruits de Mer, an "in" place since its opening a few months before, was crowded. It wasn't clear to Kati whether Scott had dropped by to make a reservation on his way to her cottage—in which case he had a nerve assuming she'd accept his invitation—or whether the fact that they were immediately escorted to a good table was just another of those small miracles he seemed to perform so effortlessly. Best, she decided, to let it pass without comment.

"Have you been here before?" Scott asked, as they sat down.

"Yes, once."

He glanced around approvingly. "It's comfortable. Is the food as good as the cab driver claimed?"

"It was excellent when I came," she said, wishing that her escort that evening—a television designer she'd dated a few times—had been a quarter as attractive as the man with her now. "The place has a very good reputation."

"That's a relief. At these popular spots you often get poor food thrown at you by surly waiters." The menus were presented to them, and Scott scanned his. "What d'you fancy, Kati?"

She fancied nothing at all. Her stomach felt knotted with tension. "Oh, something light. *Sole Bonne Femme*, I think. With creamed spinach."

"An appetizer?"

"I don't think I . . . well, maybe honeydew melon."

He gave their orders, choosing salmon for himself. "How about wine, Kati?"

She shrugged. "I'll leave that to you."

"So you haven't become a militant feminist?"

"Which wine I'm going to drink hardly rates as a feminist issue."

"You wouldn't defer to a man so easily in other areas?"

"Where is this leading us, Scott?" she demanded irritably.

"It's conversation, Kati. We need to spend some time talking together in a relaxed atmosphere if we ever hope to bury the hatchet."

She sucked in a quick breath. "I have no intention of burying the hatchet. You insist that there are things we have to discuss. So let's discuss them."

From across the table Scott gave her a long look. "What happened between us, Kati, was eight years ago. Eight years is a long time . . . much too long to harbor feelings of bitterness."

"If it were fifty years," she stated, "it wouldn't alter the way I feel about you."

His mouth went taut. "I find it difficult to believe that you've changed so much. You always did have a very lively mind, and a crisp way with words that I really admired. But you had a softer side to your nature, too. You could be so sweet and tender. We had some wonderful times together, Kati."

She didn't want to remember those wonderful times. Steeling herself, she stared back at him and drummed her fingertips impatiently on the table. Scott shook his head sorrowfully, then beckoned the waiter. After he'd ordered and they were alone again, he addressed her in a changed, neutral voice that conveyed no more than a polite interest in her. "Tell me what you've been doing these past years."

"My record with U.P. is all on file for you to scrutinze," she replied belligerently.

"What about before you joined U.P.—after you left Wimbledon?"

"If you really want to know, I became a dental surgeon's receptionist."

Scott pulled a wry face. "That seems a terrible waste of your special talents. It was a big mistake for you to walk out of Prestige Print the way you did. You'd have had an assured future there . . . quite apart from me, I mean."

"As an employee of the firm my father owned? The firm that I was due to inherit? No thank you."

"Out of pride?"

"What's wrong with pride?"

"Everything—if it blinds you to what's in your own best interest."

"You think? But then, you're an opportunist. Pride is something basic in a person's makeup, Scott, not a casual emotion that can be discarded whenever it gets in the way."

Their appetizers arrived. Kati spooned her melon

lethargically. Scott tackled his mushroom quiche with relish. Kati was glad when the wine was served. She needed something to calm her jittery nerves.

"So, you were a dental surgeon's receptionist," Scott prompted. "Then what?"

"Nothing else. After about six months I started with U.P. as a secretary."

"Seven and a half years ago. And now you're the editor-in-chief of a popular glossy monthly. That's impressive progress, Kati."

"Compared with yours, it isn't all that impressive."

"Don't forget I had a few years start on you."

"I haven't forgotten," Kati retorted. "I haven't forgotten anything. Doubtless, your scintillating record of success at Arlington Journals helped to land you the big TV job in America. Arlington must have been broken-hearted to lose a go-getter who aimed straight for his target, and no messing around with inconvenient scruples. You really hauled in a fat prize for Arlington, didn't you? But you can't pretend they weren't suitably grateful to you for handing them Prestige Print on a plate. A directorship wasn't a bad reward, especially for something you got a kick out of doing anyway."

Scott listened to her diatribe without any sign of emotion. When she had finished, he took an unhurried sip of wine and set the glass down on the table. "It's good to be home again," he said affably, changing the subject. "It was great working in the United States, and I learned a lot. But after a while, however exciting the life you're leading, you feel your roots tugging you back."

"Do you intend to stay with U.P.?" she asked, somehow making it a criticism.

"I learned, a long while ago," he said, with a significant pause, "not to make plans too far in advance. Still, I'll probably stick a while with U.P. It's a terrific opportunity I've been offered, the sort of challenge I enjoy."

"Victor Channon had better watch it."

Scott raised his eyebrows interrogatively.

"Meaning, if you stick around you won't be satisfied with anything less than the top job," she spelled out.

He shook his head, smiling at her in reproof. "How d'you like the wine?"

"It's very good. And very expensive, I don't doubt."

"Only the best for the best, Kati."

"That line of talk," she said frostily, "you can cut right out."

Scott seemed totally unruffled by her snappiness. "Shall I tell you about where I'm living?"

"Is it relevant?"

"That depends." The vivid blue eyes were dancing with deviltry, and his keen, penetrating look wrenched at Kati's heart. The years slipped away, and he was again the Scott who could twist her around his little finger with just a laugh or a kiss.

"Depends on what?" she found herself asking before she could stop herself, and bit down on her lower lip in vexation. How dangerously easy it was to become entrapped by Scott, whenever she lowered her guard for an instant.

"On how we manage to resolve our differences, of course. I've been lent a rather fabulous houseboat by an American friend of mine who's in the oil business. He's normally based in London, but he's just been sent to the Middle East on a six-month stint. It couldn't have worked out better for me. He needs a caretaker, and I need a place to live until I can find a permanent home. For the time being, it's everything I could want."

"And where is this fabulous houseboat?" she asked.

"It's moored off the Chelsea Embankment," he said delightedly. "I guess you know where I mean. There's quite a little colony of houseboats there. Very bohemian. That's why Jesse likes it so much. He's quite a guy."

While Scott cheerfully rattled on, Kati was staring at him with a feeling of chill. "Chelsea Embankment?" she echoed faintly. "But that . . . that's only . . ."

"I know. We're hardly more than a five-minute walk apart. Amazing coincidence, isn't it? Who'd have guessed that you and I would end up like this, closer neighbors than we've ever been before?"

Kati made an effort to get hold of herself. "Coincidence or not, you and I are still as far apart as we have been these past eight years," she said flatly. "Working together, living close by, makes not one jot of difference."

Scott smiled back at her amiably, as if he didn't believe that she really meant it. Kati felt a sense of helplessness as her pulses started to race under the effect of his extraordinary magnetic charm. Even hating Scott as she did, she still found him the most attractive man she'd ever set eyes on.

Their main course was served and he chatted with the waiter, saying how good his salmon steak looked.

"It's fresh today, sir. We have it flown down specially from Scotland."

"That's the sort of enterprise I've been used to in the States," Scott said approvingly. "How long has this restaurant been open?"

"About a year, sir."

Scott glanced at Kati with a warm look as he said, "That makes another good reason to have come to Chelsea."

The man departed, and Kati applied herself to the food before her, tender flakes of fish in a delicious wine and egg sauce that was flavored with herbs. After a few mouthfuls, she looked across at Scott and said, "Right, let's get down to basics."

"Isn't that what we've been doing? How is your sole, Kati?"

"Never mind about my sole. We should be working

out our attitude to one another at the office. Can I assume that, like me, you'd prefer to let it be thought that we never even met before today?"

"That's the best way, I think. It would make for a lot of gossip and speculation if it ever emerged that you and I had been engaged once upon a time." He grinned ruefully. "Besides, no man likes to admit that he's been chucked by a woman."

"My, my," she mocked. "Is Scott Drummond confessing to the sin of pride, after giving me a stern lecture on the subject?"

"I said that pride is out of place if and when it clashes with one's best interest."

"And *your* best interest is served by projecting an image of infallibility? The all-powerful Scott Drummond, who manipulates people. Never the other way around."

He seemed unperturbed by her jibe. "Anyone—man or woman—would prefer to do the string pulling rather than be the puppet. Don't pretend that you're above maneuvering things the way you want them to go, Kati. You'd never have reached your present level if you were squeamish about manipulating people."

"I might use people on occasion," she said hotly, "but never to their detriment."

"And you're under the delusion that I do?"

Her fork clattered on the plate. "Of all the colossal nerve to say that to me."

Scott's blue eyes drilled into her. "We've come full circle, haven't we? Eight years ago, Kati, you suffered through your own prideful choice. You had a wonderful future lined up, but you threw it away. Without question you were the person best qualified to run Prestige Print for Arlington after your father's death; ... nobody would have disputed that. With Arlington's backing you'd have been in charge of a thriving business with permanently full order books, and sufficient capital behind you to keep up with modern technology."

"All for the price of becoming your wife. No thanks."

"Marrying me was an entirely separate issue, Kati."

"Okay, then—for the price of having you as my boss. Again, no thanks."

Scott paused, considering. It was a great opportunity to spell out a few home truths to Kati. He had no wish to hurt her, but it was high time she saw things in a less prejudiced light—for her own sake. As for himself, he needed to get his priorities straight. The job had to come first, way ahead of any vague stirrings in his mind about getting together with Kati again.

"Whatever your personal reasons for turning against me and breaking our engagement," he said in a carefully level tone, "you shouldn't have let it affect your career, Kati. If you weren't capable of coming to terms with the situation and somehow finding a way of working under me in reasonable harmony, it meant that you wouldn't have been a fit person to handle the job of running Prestige Print after all. And the same thing applies right now, just as much. If the way we do our jobs at Universal Publications is going to be adversely affected by our private relationship, then it would be up to either one of us to admit it. And resign if necessary."

She gasped in outrage. "Do I hear you right? Are you suggesting I should resign?"

Scott shook his head. "The only thing I'm suggesting, Kati, is that you should examine your thoughts and motivations very carefully. I hope that you'll come up with a more positive attitude."

Chapter Four

The rain had stopped by the time they emerged from the restaurant, but the wet streets gleamed with reflections of the bright Chelsea lights. A pale crescent moon floated serenely overhead in a cloud-flecked sky.

"It's a beautiful evening," Scott said. "Shall we walk back to your place?"

Kati's independence asserted itself. "You don't have to see me home."

"Don't be silly, of course I'm going to see you home. It's almost on my direct route to the boat, anyway."

Kati sighed: Scott always seemed to win. But the thought didn't sear her as it would have done earlier. She had mellowed a lot during the meal, aided by the excellent wine. She now felt that she'd more or less adjusted to an unwanted situation that had been thrust upon them both. It wasn't peace between them, and never would be, but it made sense for there to be a truce of sorts. Otherwise, her job editing *Rendezvous* would become quite impossible.

Astonishingly, against her will, she'd realized that she was enjoying herself over dinner. She had discovered an appetite, after all, and she had allowed Scott to tease her into joining him in a slice of rich, cream-oozing chocolate torte that used to be their favorite dessert in the old days and was something she hadn't tasted in years. Scott, she remembered wistfully, had always been so stimulating, not just as a lover, but as a companion and friend. He'd entertained her this evening with amusing stories about the American TV scene in which he'd been working. Watching his mobile features as he talked, and coaxed into laughing with him, she couldn't help but speculate about the women in his life since herself. There had been several women whose names had cropped up more than once in the conversation—one was a TV publicist; another, a top model, and a third who was a stunt woman used in dangerous film work. But none of them seemed to have rated as extra special as far as Kati could judge. And Scott had returned to Britain *alone*. Wondering why he wasn't married by now, she'd marveled that American women had allowed such an eligible bachelor to escape them. Or *had* Scott been married, and already divorced? There were so many questions she wanted to ask him.

When they came to a corner, Scott halted and looked with a puzzled expression at a new apartment building. "Wasn't there a movie theater here?"

"Yes, I believe there was," Kati said casually. "It had gone before I moved to Chelsea, though."

"We came to it once, remember? They were rerunning *Cabaret*, which I'd missed the first time around and you said was a terrific film. Which it was." Scott turned to stroll on. "That was a good evening, wasn't it? After the film, we decided to take a walk along the river. It was June, I think, or maybe July, and it had been a beautiful day. It was still very warm and the sky was a soft pinky-gray fading to purple, with the lights of the Albert Bridge shimmering on the water. I remember that we finished up eating ham and eggs at a little bistro somewhere that way. I wonder if the bistro's still there."

"Yes, it is. I was there a few weeks back." Oh, blast, Kati thought, I didn't have to admit that. She had happened to be passing the place one day, and on an impulse she had dropped in for a cup of coffee. Then she'd immediately wished she hadn't, hating the flood of memories evoked by the cozy intimacy of that quaint, shabby little cafe.

Scott seemed to be smiling to himself, looking smug. At the next corner he lightly took her elbow as they crossed the street. It was a simple gesture of courtesy that any escort might make, one to which she could hardly object. But so far Scott had taken care not to touch her, and Kati knew that it hadn't been a casual action on his part. The effect on her was riveting. Even through the thickness of her velvet jacket she could sense the warmth of his hand and feel the pressure of each individual finger, causing ripples of sensual excitement to spread through her. And after they crossed the street his hand lingered there. They had walked on for some yards before Kati came out of her daze. Not too pointedly, she drew her arm away.

When they reached the mews off Old Church Street where Kati's cottage was, she couldn't help feeling regretful. It was time to thank Scott for the dinner, say good-night, and go swiftly inside. Instead, she found herself saying, "You can come in for coffee, if you want to."

"That would be nice." She couldn't decide whether or not Scott had been expecting the invitation.

Indoors, she hung her jacket on a peg and leaned around the living room door to switch on lights. "If you like, you can have something stronger," she told him, waving a hand at the drinks tray.

"Coffee will be fine. You always used to make great

coffee, I remember. Let's see if you still have the magic touch."

Unable to think of a suitable riposte to that, Kati just went straight to the kitchen where she set water to boil and put out cups and saucers. Scott followed her and stood in the doorway with his shoulder propped against the door frame. The sight of him like that, looking so casually at home, brought back such a flood of poignant memories that Kati's hands shook with nerves and she spilled some of the coffee grounds onto the countertop as she was filling the filter.

"I don't like to be watched," she said crisply.

"No? You never used to mind."

"That was then," she snapped. "This is now. Please go and wait in the living room."

Scott gave her a smiling shrug and left the kitchen. In the living room he glanced around him, once more admiring the flair and taste with which Kati had furnished the room. His eyes alighted on a piece that he hadn't noticed before—a small inlaid rosewood sewing table that had been her mother's. With a sudden rush of memory, he fingered the button of his shirtcuff. Giving a quick tug, he pulled it off and slipped it into a pocket. When Kati walked in with the tray a few minutes later, he held up his wrist with a look of helplessness.

"I've lost a button."

"When did that happen?" she queried. It was definitely since dinner; over their meal she had spent a lot of time watching his hands rather than meet his eyes.

"I've just noticed it," he said. "What a curse."

"The laundry will attend to it."

He made a face. "I haven't had time to make any arrangements about that sort of thing yet. Can you recommend a good laundry?"

Reluctantly, Kati named the one she used herself, and wondered despairingly what was happening to her. Scott seemed to be forging fresh links with her all the time, and she was just letting him get away with it. On this, his very first day, he had persuaded her to have dinner with him. They had reminisced about the old days and returned to her cottage late in the evening for a cup of coffee. She'd never have believed it possible, yet it had happened.

Okay, she could put a stop to this foolishness right now. She'd just give him his coffee and then send him packing. And after that, any contact between them would be restricted to the office. Easy. No problem.

As if she hadn't even heard her own good advice, Kati put down the tray and went to her workbox, opening the lid and rummaging for her tin of odd buttons. "I should find one or two shirt buttons in here from my father's time," she said. "I can't promise you an exact match."

"That won't matter." Scott slipped off his jacket and came to her, holding out the other arm to show her the button to be matched. "Sort out something as near as you can, Kati."

Selecting a suitable button, she snapped off a length of white thread from the reel with her teeth; then she threaded a needle, licking the tip of her finger to make a knot. Telling Scott to sit down on the sofa, she sat beside him and started work.

What a fool I am, what a total damn fool, her mind chanted. I've walked slap into this cozy domestic situation—the woman humbly ministering to the male and the male complacently accepting such womanly subservience as his due. I ought to drop this needle right now and tell him to get on with it himself.

His wrist was smooth and lightly tanned, the short dark hairs glinting in the lamplight, encircled by the broad leather strap of his watch. With a deep sense of shock that made her pause in her task, Kati realized that the watch he was wearing—although the strap had been replaced—was the one she had given him as a birthday present.

"You're right," he said quietly, as she glanced up and met the direct gaze of his eyes. "It is the watch you gave me."

"I'm astonished that you've kept it all this time."

"It's cost me in repair bills. But I happen to like it."

She stared at him for a moment, caught up in emotions she didn't dare to analyze, then adopted a brisk tone. "Keep still while I finish this job."

Scott said nothing and held his arm steady, but Kati felt stupidly clumsy. She even managed to prick her finger, drawing a bead of blood. She could feel the tension building up between them. She was intensely aware of Scott's nearness, of the vibrant warmth of his skin when she unavoidably brushed it. She could feel his breath gently ruffling her hair and caught the aroma that was uniquely Scott, a subtle amalgam of fresh air and cologne and maleness that teased her senses and sent her mind winging back to the old days with bittersweet memories.

Scott, giving a quick bubble of laughter, broke into her thoughts. "The last time you sewed on a button for me, Kati, it was in a rather more intimate place than my shirt cuff. Remember? The waist fastening of my jeans had come adrift."

She flushed. "You seem to have a remarkable memory for trivia."

"Are you saying that you've forgotten, Kati?"

"I don't clutter up my mind with bits and pieces from the past."

Scott laughed again. "I thought you might remember that particular incident . . . and how it ended."

Her flush deepened and she tried to avert her face so that Scott wouldn't notice. That incident, like so many other details of their relationship, was clear and sharp in her mind. It had been a winter Saturday, cold and beautiful, with frost bejeweling the trees and bushes, the afternoon misty and the sun a great smoky-orange ball as it sank in the west. After a long walk across

Wimbledon Common they'd returned home for tea. Her father had been out all day, playing in a golf tournament somewhere in Kent, and wouldn't be back until late that night. While Kati made tea, Scott built up the fire, piling on logs from the metal basket beside the mottled marble fireplace, and they sat together on the hearthrug toasting muffins on long spiked forks, buttering them liberally and spooning on strawberry jam.

"Oh, lord, the button's gone on my jeans," Scott had suddenly exclaimed, with a rueful grimace downward.

"Let me look."

She'd inspected the damage, then gone to fetch sewing things from her mother's workbox. To give better access, Scott ran down the zipper a few inches, but it didn't really make the job any easier to accomplish.

"Keep still, can't you," she grumbled.

"Easier said than done," he laughed. "Watch where you're aiming that needle, woman, for pity's sake."

Somehow the metal button had been sewn into place, though Kati had made rather a botch of it. Scott's obedient stillness had vanished the moment she broke off the thread, and he grabbed hold of her. The next moment they were wrestling together on the hearthrug, laughing and giggling. Finally, Scott sat astride her and pinned her wrists to the floor; with a shiver she remembered the desire that glittered in his cobalt eyes.

"I love you, Kati."

"And I hate you, you're such a bully."

Lightly spoken words, all part of the game of love. She could never have guessed on that lovely afternoon that within months her pretended hatred would have become real.

"I see that you do remember," Scott said, just above a whisper.

Kati didn't answer. The job finished, she snapped off the thread. Then automatically, before she thought about what she was doing, she began to rebutton his shirt cuff with the easy familiarity of their long-ago relationship. Subtly, against her will, Scott was exerting his potent spell and making her feel soft and tender toward him.

"There, all done," she said crisply, dropping his wrist. "Now, drink up your coffee and get going. It's late."

Scott's lips curved in a one-sided smile. "Okay, I can take a hint." He retrieved his jacket and shrugged into it. As he picked up the cup of coffee she poured for him, he met her gaze levelly. "I enjoyed our having dinner together this evening, Kati. How about you?"

"It was a very good meal," she hedged.

"And the company?"

"I wasn't aware that this evening was supposed to be a social occasion," she said coolly. "We've reached a kind of understanding, okay, but it's pretty fragile as far as I'm concerned. So don't press your luck. Maybe we can just about get along at the office without too much friction, but I have no desire to see you again outside of work."

"Pity. The way it seems to me, Kati, you and I still have a lot to offer one another."

"Forget it. And I mean that, Scott. I mean it from my soul."

Kati deeply regretted the impulse that had made her invite him in for coffee. It would have been far better to have parted from him right after dinner, when there had been a sort of harmony between them. Now, too many poignant memories had been revived, too many old wounds reopened. She waited impatiently for Scott to finish his coffee, making it clear that she wanted him gone. Maddeningly, Scott took his time, keeping up a flow of chatty remarks.

Even when Scott finally rose to leave, he didn't hurry. "I see that you still like Renoir," he observed, nodding at a framed reproduction of *Les Parapluies*. "Do you remember when we went to see that exhibition of French Impressionists at the Royal Academy?"

Kati didn't bother to answer, but led the way out to the hall and opened the front door for him. As Scott went to pass her, he paused and gave her a long, intent look.

"You're so lovely, it takes my breath away," he said softly. Before she realized his intention, he cupped her face in his two hands and put his lips against hers. It wasn't a passionate kiss, but it held a richness of meaning, reawakening her to the thrilling feel of him.

For a few earth-rocking moments she was powerless to move, then anger surged through her and she jerked away from him with a violent wrench. "Cut that out, Scott. I won't stand for it, d'you hear?"

He gave a faint smile, a slight shrug. Could he see that she was trembling? she wondered. Did he realize that she was scared by the electrifying response of her senses to the press of his body against hers? In the dizzying moments before shock and anger had hit, it had seemed so good, so right, so golden and beautiful.

"Good night, Kati." Scott's voice had a ring of tenderness. Then he was gone, striding off along the cobbled pavement of the mews. Kati closed the door behind him and stood unmoving for long seconds, washed by waves of heat and chill. Scott had contrived to leave her tonight almost in the role of a lover, instead of as the reluctantly invited guest to her home that he had truly been. While her mind raged at him, her treacherous body was reacting to him as though to a departed lover, warmed by his touch, sensually alerted, and yearning for him to hold her again.

To try to drown out her clamoring thoughts, Kati switched on the stereo. A cassette already in the deck began to play. The noisy beat of the music filled the room, engulfing her, but she didn't take in what she was hearing . . . until Liza Minelli began to sing a poignant love song from *Cabaret*.

Kati stumbled in her rush to switch it off. For an instant she thought that Scott must have sorted this tape out while she'd been making the coffee and left it set up for her as a ploy in his game plan. Then she recalled that she'd been playing the cassette of hits from *Cabaret* a few evenings before, and had forgotten to remove it afterward. She pressed eject, dragged out the cassette and flung it into the wastebasket.

Every such insidious reminder of Scott had to be erased from her life. Books! He'd given her several during their ten months together, for no special reason other than that he'd wanted to please her. Somehow or other she'd hung on to them, despite the fact that she'd had to jettison many of her personal belongings for space reasons when she'd been compelled to sell her father's old house at Wimbledon. Now, while her rage was still at white heat, Kati knelt before the long bookshelves under the window and ran a finger along the rows of titles. She sorted out five books that had been gifts from Scott. Still on her knees, she riffled through a slim anthology of love poetry. Half of the poems she knew by heart from constant rereading; some of them brought tears to her eyes, some a smile to her lips. But always, reading them, she was emotionally moved, hearing the poet's voice as if it were Scott himself speaking to her.

The book fell open at the flyleaf. Across it, eight years ago, Scott had written boldly, *To my love, with my love, for ever and ever.*

One by one, with tender care, Kati replaced the five books on the shelves, and retrieved the cassette from the trash basket.

The office door opened and Dee's head appeared around it. "Okay to come in, Kati?"

"Sure, Dee. Want some coffee?"

"No, thanks, I had a cup just now with my art director. As I was passing your floor I dropped by to ask if you're free for lunch today."

"Sorry, no can do. I'm lunching with Jeanette." Jeanette Hart was the fashion editor of *Rendezvous*.

"What are you two up to?" Dee queried. "Trying to get a jump on me?"

"Get a jump on Lady Dorothy Faulkner? That'll be the day. Actually, I have to break it to poor Jeanette that her next quarterly budget is being cut."

"Orders from on high?" Dee asked sympathetically.

"No, just the simple economic facts of life. We've been overspending on fashion."

Dee laughed. "So what? Cast your bread upon the waters, is my motto. It always pays dividends." She perched on a corner of Kati's desk, absently twitching a fold of her red and black skirt into a more graceful line. "Fortunately, our new executive coordinator agrees with me."

Kati clenched her hands together on the desk. "Are you talking about Scott Drummond?"

"He's really something, isn't he, Kati? I reckon it's about the best thing Victor Channon ever did for U.P., appointing that guy. This whole organization needs waking up—with two notable exceptions, naturally."

"He seems to have impressed you a lot," Kati said through tight lips.

"Not so with you?"

Kati shrugged, wishing she could get off this subject. "Well, it's too soon to form a reasoned judgment," she said evasively. "Hasn't it struck you that he's a tad too sure of himself?"

"Personally, I always go for self-assured men— especially if they're as dishy as Scott Drummond. If a man's going to get anywhere, he has to look sure of himself—and that goes for women, too. Which is what makes you and me such shining examples in this place."

"Bighead."

"You don't take an overly small size in hats yourself."

Kati gave her a weak grin. "I have a ton of work to do, Dee. Bob Edmonds is yelling for approval of some illustrations, and I haven't even looked at them yet."

Dee stood up and moved to the door with serene elegance. "I'll take your sledgehammer hint." She paused and glanced back at Kati. "You'll come around to my opinion of that Drummond guy, see if you don't. Didn't you say just the other day that I'm always able to pick winners?"

That evening Kati set out in her small blue Ford for a dinner date with her friends Fay and Harry Pemberton. She chose the route through Richmond Park, even though it would take a few minutes longer, because it was such a lovely evening. As she'd expected, the park looked beautiful. A light breeze stirred the long grasses in silky waves, and the setting sun was turning a distant lake to gold. Birds flitted everywhere, and here and there clusters of wild deer were cropping contentedly. Through the trees Kati caught a glimpse of the columned frontage of White Lodge, built as a royal residence and now occupied by the Royal Ballet School. The sight of it brought a sudden pang, and Kati cursed herself for having come this way.

Here was yet another memory of Scott. They had visited White Lodge on a day when some of its most gracious rooms were open to the public. Afterward, they had strolled together for an hour or so, exploring new corners of the great park, two happy lovers. They had finished up, she remembered, in the pretty garden of an ancient pub in Richmond town. It hadn't rated, then, as an extraspecial day—she'd experienced such happiness every day, and she'd imagined that her life would be the same for evermore. Some fool!

The Pembertons had a small modern bungalow,

quite near the River Thames, that had been skillfully converted so that no obstacles remained to Fay's wheelchair. As Kati turned in at the gate and drew up on the short driveway, the Pembertons gave her their usual eager welcome by coming to the door even before she was out of the car.

From Fay's face no one would ever suspect that she was disabled. Always well groomed, with soft clear skin and lovely hair that had turned prematurely white, Fay looked out at the world with bright, intelligent eyes. They were eyes that asked for no pity, but readily gave out warmth and compassion for other people. Her husband, Harry, upright and alert, was lean almost to the point of gauntness. At one time the works manager at Prestige Print and Kati's father's long-time friend, Harry had stayed on in his job after the takeover by Arlington Journals until his retirement some five years ago.

"Hello Fay . . . Harry." Kati bent and kissed the older woman's cheek. "How beautiful your garden is looking. Those red tulips are a real show."

"Yes, Kati dear, we're pleased with our tulips this year."

As usual, before going inside, the three of them did a tour of the small garden, using the smooth-surfaced paths specially laid to give Fay wheelchair-access to every corner. In a couple of places the beds of soil had been raised to a level that made it possible for Fay to cultivate them unaided; elsewhere she did what she could with long-handled tools, and Harry did the rest. Their garden always looked charming. At the moment it was especially colorful with spring bulbs and rockery plants. Forsythia made a vivid splash of yellow, and some early-flowering prunus trees were smothered with pink and white blossoms. There was a marvelous fresh scent of new growth.

Indoors, they had drinks, then sat down to one of Fay's superlative meals. Harry, his wife's willing helper in every respect in the household chores, would have tackled the cooking too. But that was one area that Fay kept exclusively to herself. Harry understood how much it meant to her to fight the disability that had struck her down, and he never tried to interfere in the preparation of meals beyond making sure that she had every possible aid to her restricted capabilities. In fact, the Pemberton kitchen had become something of an experimental laboratory for new equipment designed to help the disabled.

Kati forked up a tiny shrimp puff that Fay had made as an appetizer. "Mmm! Dreamy. Why can't I make pastry like this? When I have guests I always buy store pastry, I'm afraid. But it just doesn't compare to homemade."

"It's different for you," Fay said. "You're a very busy lady."

"And you're not? Tell me, Fay, how many committees do you serve on now? What's the latest tally?"

"But that's all volunteer work. I don't have the heat on me . . . press deadlines, staff difficulties, bosses breathing down my neck."

"What you do have driving you, Fay, is the supremely high standard you set yourself. Aren't I right, Harry?"

He smiled fondly. "Fay couldn't be any other way, Kati. I keep telling her that she takes on too much, but she won't listen."

His wife sniffed. "You'd have me vegetate, I suppose?"

"The thought of you vegetating, darling, is beyond the power of my imagination," he said, with a wink at Kati.

Fay's story was inspiring. She had formerly been a healthy, active woman who enjoyed playing tennis and swimming. One icy winter night, she had been driving home from a sports club committee meeting and her car skidded out of control when she'd tried to avoid a wandering dog. After long months in hospital and several spinal operations, Fay was finally given the verdict that she wouldn't ever walk again.

Kati, since quitting Prestige Print and leaving Wimbledon, had kept in touch with the Pembertons only at a Christmas cards level. It was some months after Fay's accident that she happened to hear of it through a chance meeting with a mutual acquaintance. She started visiting Fay in the hospital. At first this was out of compassion, but Kati had been overcome with admiration for Fay's unquenchable courage, her total lack of self-pity, her single-minded determination to get back to leading as normal a life as possible. When Fay was discharged from the hospital Kati had continued to visit her at home, and her admiration for her friend had deepened. Fay had looked upon herself as a guinea pig. The problems that she personally encountered had shown her how much needed to be done to help handicapped people, and gradually Fay had become a leading light in the locality for her propaganda work. She battled with the municipal authorities about creating wheelchair access to various public buildings, and she took issue with shops and stores that didn't provide adequately for disabled customers.

And now, through *Rendezvous,* the name Fay Pemberton was known nationwide. Soon after Kati took over the editorship she had run a feature about Fay's brave fight. This had attracted a lot of interest from readers, and letters came pouring in. A follow-up article had been the start of a regular series. Now, every month, *Rendezvous* carried yet another inspirational story about someone who had fought to overcome a disability, as well as giving factual information about new products and facilities that were beneficial to the handicapped. There was a red star awarded each month for progressive thinking from either a public or private organization; a black star for the most thoughtless act. There was also a problem corner which was edited by Fay.

The meal continued with a mouth-wateringly tender roast of beef, with broccoli fresh from the garden, and *mange-tout* peas frozen from the previous summer's crop. As they ate, Fay held forth with her usual enthusiasm about a new lightweight folding wheelchair designed for air travel.

"I have one to try out," she said. "I'll show you later, Kati. It's really wonderful, only weighing six pounds, and it folds up so small it can be carried as cabin luggage. Such a help."

"So where are you and Harry flying off to this summer, to try it out?" Kati asked.

Fay and Harry glanced at one another and shared a smile. "Shall I tell her?" Fay queried.

"Why not?"

"Well, Kati, we haven't settled it yet, but we're thinking of going to Kenya on safari."

Kati looked at her in amazement. "On safari?"

"I've always wanted to go to Africa, and I'd love to see wild game in their natural habitat."

"If anyone can do it, you can. That's a really terrific idea, Fay. And it will make a wonderful feature for *Rendezvous*."

Interested as Kati was in the conversation, her mind kept straying. The Pembertons had known Scott Drummond, and in fact Harry had worked under him briefly before Scott had quit Arlington Journals to go to the United States. Sooner or later it would reach their ears that Scott was back in England and working for U.P. Wouldn't it seem very odd to Fay and Harry if she had never mentioned the fact? Besides, she rather wanted to tell them; they were the only people she *could* tell. Fay and Harry would understand her dilemma, and they'd sympathize with her.

All the same, Kati found it difficult to bring up the

subject. Eventually, after they'd finished the lemon meringue pie and were having a second cup of coffee, she blurted out, "By the way, you'll be surprised to know that Scott Drummond has joined U.P."

The Pembertons seemed not to catch on at once. Then Harry said cautiously, "You mean . . . *your* Scott Drummond?"

"Yes," Kati said. "Him. He's been made what they call the executive coordinator."

The Pembertons were clearly at a loss for something to say. After a long moment, Harry asked, "How did this come about, Kati?"

She lifted her shoulders in a shrug. "It seems he made a big impression on our chairman when they happened to meet in the States. Victor Channon dangled a big job in front of Scott, and it was too good an offer for a go-getter like him to refuse. His mission is to jerk U.P. back into the black. You can imagine how I felt when I heard of Scott's appointment, sick right through, down to the soles of my feet. It's going to be sheer hell—and not only for me. Scott will just love cracking the whip and making people jump through hoops."

Fay and Harry looked embarrassed at the bitter way she was talking. "When does he start?" Harry inquired.

"He already has. He arrived yesterday, a day early. The Scott Drummonds of this world don't let grass grow under their feet."

"Does that mean that you two have met up again?" Fay asked.

Kati nodded. "Victor Channon sent for me to be introduced to him."

"How did it go?" Fay gave an uneasy laugh. "Mr. Channon must have been surprised to find that you two knew each other already."

"Well . . . that bit of information didn't emerge."

"I don't follow you," Harry said. "Do you mean, you and Scott pretended not to know each other?"

Kati shrugged defensively. "Since it turned out that neither of us had happened to mention anything about the past to anyone at U.P., we think it's best to leave it like that."

Fay jumped on her words. "Are you saying that you and Scott have talked this through?"

"Yes, we have. It was lucky, really, that the moment I got to Victor Channon's office, he was called to the phone. So Scott and I had a few moments to talk in private. But we've talked since, as well." Kati tried to give an impression of indifference as she added, "Actually, we had dinner together last night. We thought it best to discuss the whole situation and decide what to do."

There was a puzzled silence. Then Fay asked, "So what did you decide?"

"To leave things just as they are. That is, let people at U.P. think that we've only just met."

Harry rubbed his chin reflectively. "Is that really a good idea, Kati? Won't it look very odd if it comes out later?"

"There's no reason why it ever should." Kati glanced at Fay. "I think you are the only person in contact with U.P. who knows about Scott and me."

"I won't give the game away, Kati, if that's how you want to play it." Fay had contact with several of the *Rendezvous* staff in connection with her problem corner, and once in a while she came to the office, driving herself in her specially adapted car. "Whatever you want is okay with Harry and me, you know that. We're just questioning the wisdom of trying to keep your relationship with Scott Drummond secret. It's not as if you just happened to know each other in the past. You were engaged to be married."

"That's the whole point," Kati flashed out. "If we

admit to anything at all, the whole horrible story would probably come out. Neither of us wants that. No doubt Scott wouldn't object to its being known that he cheated Dad. He'd figure that it just showed what a smart guy he is. But he shuns the idea of anyone's knowing that I rejected him. That would really dent his macho-male image."

"Did Scott actually say something like that?" Fay asked. "Is that why he wants to keep your relationship in the dark?"

Kati would have liked to give a straight yes, to say that Scott's motive stemmed purely from self-interest. But her sense of justice prevented her. "He said something about it being up to me . . . the woman's prerogative and all that."

"Well, you can't fault Scott for that attitude," Harry observed thoughtfully as he pushed his coffee cup toward his wife for a refill. "It seems to me that he did the decent thing."

"And it seems to me, Harry, that you're siding with Scott. You, of all people, who knows the sordid truth."

Harry shook his head at her in gentle rebuke. "It's not a question of taking sides, Kati. I'd back you all the way, you know that, if only because your father was the best friend I ever had."

"Listen," she said desperately, "I've got to hold Scott at arm's length, or . . ."

"Or what, Kati?" asked Fay, watching her with troubled eyes.

Kati felt a rush of color rise to her face. Or what? She had discovered the answer to that question the previous evening. If she allowed Scott anything more than an armed truce, if she pretended friendliness, the pretense would be in danger of turning into reality. She'd never for a moment have believed, until it happened, that she would agree to have dinner with Scott—and then actually find herself enjoying the meal. It was incredible, and it showed her the insidious danger of associating with him at a personal level. During a restless night, and at her desk today, she had kept recalling in little cameo flashes of memory some of the happy occasions she'd shared with Scott. It was so fatally easy to let her mind focus on the happy times, only to find pain waiting to pounce when she remembered his treachery.

Or what? Fay and Harry were awaiting an answer to the question. But she had no answer she could give them. Instead, she faced them aggressively. "Are you saying that I ought to let bygones be bygones where Scott's concerned? Just forgive and forget? Is that how *you* would act toward him . . . if you happened to meet him in the street, for instance?"

"I wouldn't be unfriendly," Harry said. "There'd be no cause. You're forgetting, Kati, that I worked closely with Scott Drummond for a short while after you quit Prestige Print. I have to say, in all fairness, that he did a darned good job."

"You'll be telling me next," Kati burst out, "that you were sorry when he left Arlington Journals to go to America."

"In a way I was," Harry said mildly. He gave Kati a thoughtful look. "I know that you felt very bitter about the takeover by Arlington Journals, Kati, but I can only say that Arlington turned out to be very fair employers. When Fay had her accident, they were extremely good to me. They let me have lots of time off to visit her in the hospital, and afterward, too, when she came home, to help get her adjusted."

"Oh, hooray! Never mind what Arlington Journals did to your best friend, my father."

"I have to call them as I see them, Kati," he said quietly.

"So do I," she retorted. "So we'd better leave it there and talk about something else. Okay?"

Chapter Five

"Kati, I want to see you."

The sound of Scott's voice on the phone unnerved her. It was exactly as she remembered it from the time when they used to find various reasons to call each other during the day because the evening ahead seemed too long to wait. Rich and deeply husky, brisk and incisive, yet with the hint of a lazy drawl.

"I, er . . . what do you mean, Scott?"

"I want to see you." He sounded faintly impatient. "Isn't that plain enough?"

"But where?"

"Here, in my office. Shall we say ten minutes? Unless you have something vital on hand?"

"I'll be there," she said coolly.

This was it, the summons she'd been expecting and dreading. But now that it was halfway through Friday afternoon she'd thought she was off the hook until after the weekend. Keep calm, she instructed herself, as she quickly checked her hair and makeup. He can't eat you. Then, telling Sandra where she'd be if she were needed urgently, she set forth.

Scott's office, speedily prepared for him, was up with the other top executives of U.P., not far from Victor Channon's suite. A secretary, whom Kati vaguely recognized, slick and efficient-looking, and wearing huge dark-framed glasses, glanced up inquiringly.

"I'm Kati Young . . . *Rendezvous*. Mr. Drummond wants to see me."

"Oh, yes, Miss Young. You can go right in."

As Kati went through the doorway, Scott looked up from his large steel and leather desk. He gave every appearance, she thought, of having been established there for some while instead of just a couple of days. There was no hasty, put-together look about his office. The furniture was functional, without frills. The main window was behind Scott, putting his visitors in the full glare of light.

Scott rose to his feet to greet her. He had never been short on courtesy. "Hello, Kati. Have a seat." He was in shirtsleeves, and the jacket of his dark-gray suit was slung over another chair. He wasn't smiling, and Kati guessed from the look on his face that he had something unpleasant to impart. "This is just a preliminary meeting, to let you know how I'm thinking." Scott sat down himself and leaned back in the swivel chair, looking totally relaxed.

I can play it cool too, Kati thought, and deliberately made herself comfortable, linking her hands loosely on her lap. She awaited Scott's next words in silence.

"I'm afraid that things don't look too rosy for *Rendezvous*," he said.

"Things look a whole lot better than they did when I took over eighteen months ago," she retorted, glad that her voice held up without wavering.

"I'll grant you that. But unfortunately better isn't

good enough. I shouldn't need to give you a lesson on the economics of running a magazine, Kati. Okay, so a nice steady rise in circulation is great . . . exactly what everyone wants. But it has to be matched with an equally steady rise in advertisement revenue if the accounts are to balance. Your circulation has risen by seventeen point one five percent since you took over," he stated, and she noticed that he didn't even flicker a glance at the papers on his desk for verification of the figure, "while the advertisement revenue, after allowing for inflation, is only eight point five percent up. Since each copy of a magazine costs more to print and distribute than its cover price, the more copies we sell, the more money we lose—unless we can attract more revenue from advertisements."

"That's not my department," Kati objected.

"Everything to do with *Rendezvous* is your department," Scott tossed back sharply. "You can't shrug off responsibility like that."

"So what do you suggest I do?" she inquired coldly. "I imagine that you don't expect the editor to go out and hawk space herself?"

"Not directly."

"Not directly? This sounds interesting, Scott." She stressed the mockery in her voice. "Please tell me more. Is it some new technique you've dreamed up?"

He smiled, but there was no warmth in the smile, and his cobalt eyes pierced through her. "So I do need to go back to first principles with you, Kati. Okay . . . let's define the job of an editor-in-chief. First, identify your readership. What is the readership of *Rendezvous*?"

"Social groups A and B," she replied promptly. "Mostly aged between twenty and forty-five. Forward-looking, independent-minded women who, although they may not be militantly feminist, still don't accept male domination. The majority are married; but, even so, they expect their husbands to take their careers seriously."

Scott's lips twitched. "You regard yourself as a role model, I imagine?"

Kati was momentarily taken aback. She'd never consciously regarded herself in that light, though it was true that she used her feelings as a sounding board, and only carried topics in the magazine that had a certain interest for her.

"Okay, that's fair enough," she said. "I do more or less fit the mold."

"Except that you're not married."

"Right, I'm not married. Is that a criticism?"

Scott ignored that. Leaning forward, he rested his folded arms on the desk in a posture that she'd seen many times in the past, and looked across at her. "If the magazine is to be made viable, potential advertisers wanting to reach career-oriented women in classes A and B have to be convinced that *Rendezvous* is the right medium for them."

"The facts and figures speak for themselves. Our latest readership survey proves . . ."

"We're into an area that goes beyond mere readership surveys," he interrupted, and there was a frayed edge of impatience in his voice, as if he were disappointed in her. "Advertisers, and the men and women in the agency business, are *people*, Kati, not just computers who tote up tabulated columns of figures. They've got to *feel* that a particular advertising medium is right for them. I'm questioning if you take that angle sufficiently into account."

Seeing the drift of his argument, Kati bristled and launched into the attack. "*Rendezvous* is not—I repeat, not—an advertisement sheet padded out with a few articles to give it authenticity. And never will be as long as I'm editor. I hope you aren't about to suggest that we should reward our advertisers by giving their products some extra, unpaid-for advertising in the guise of editorial write-ups. No way. That sort of thing is sheer dishonesty to the readers, who expect their magazine to be objective and unbiased. I suppose, though, that I'm wasting my breath trying to talk ethics to someone like you."

Scott shot to his feet, for the first time visibly losing his cool. He swung away from her, keeping his back turned as he stared out of the window.

"You really got a kick out of saying that, didn't you, Kati? Maybe it's a sign of what I'm trying to say—that you're too darned ready to indulge your own partialities and prejudices—whether good or bad." He wheeled around to face her again. "Just to refute your accusation, I'll tell you a story that harks back to my days at Arlington Journals. We published a monthly called *Hi-Tech in Industry*. You'll remember it, because it was printed by your father's firm. One of the big multinationals dangled the promise of an advertising contract that amounted to six color pages in *H.T.I.* per issue. They had the nerve to think it would give them the right to dictate editorial policy, that we would favor their products against the competition." He smiled in grim satisfaction. "It pleased me no end to confront the advertising director of that firm and tell him precisely what he could do with his contract."

"How noble," Kati mocked, in an effort to conceal her surprise. "Do you expect me to clap hands because for once in your brilliant career you allowed yourself to be guided by ethical principles, even though it lost you a contract?"

Scott didn't answer at once. His face showed exasperation, but his eyes glinted approval, as if he'd expected her to hit back. After a few moments, Kati found herself asking, against her will, "So what happened? Did *Hi-Tech in Industry* suffer for it?"

The grim set of his mouth broke and his lips curved in a grin. "As it happens, we didn't lose out. Arlington got that contract—an even bigger one, actually."

Kati met his gaze challengingly. "In that case, you've

proved my point—that advertising copy and editorial matter are separate entities, and should be kept that way."

"Wrong," he said, shaking his head at her. "There's a subtle interrelationship that has to be acknowledged. In the final analysis, of course, editorial integrity must be paramount. But, short of that, there are all sorts of legitimate ways to encourage a healthy flow of advertising."

He was right, Kati knew. She had foolishly let herself take up a position that couldn't be maintained. Fortunately, Scott didn't press the point any further.

"I want you to think about what I've said, Kati. We all have a lot of thinking to do, if U.P. is to be turned around into profitability. I'll be talking to Robin Wheatley about *Rendezvous*'s advertising, and we can hammer out ways of getting more space sold."

Looking at Scott, noting the determined set of his jaw, Kati wondered how Robin would fare against such a forceful, dynamic man. Scott had the muscle to match his ruthless determination, and Robin would have to knuckle under—just as she had to.

"Do you have any specific criticisms of *Rendezvous?*" she asked, seeming to adopt a more cooperative stance.

Scott reached for a copy of the current issue that lay on his desk, and flipped through the pages. "It's a nice-looking magazine, well presented, and the artwork is imaginative. You seem to have collected a good team of writers who aren't afraid of being provocative."

"I'm waiting for the buts."

He balanced the magazine on the palm of his hand. "It's too thin. Weight for weight, compared with your competitors, it doesn't suggest good value for money."

"I was there ahead of you," Kati said. "What's needed is a bigger production budget."

"Which means . . ."

"I know, more advertisements," she said. "I've already talked to Robin, and he's exploring ways to push up the revenue."

"And what does he say about the prospects?"

Kati hesitated, then said cautiously, "Well . . . it's a difficult period for advertising at this point."

"When isn't? Advertisement space has to be *sold*. Orders don't fall into your hands like ripe fruit."

Kati gave him a challenging look. "Have you any other comments to make?"

"I'm puzzled by some of the features you carry." Scott flipped again, then stopped and laid the magazine flat on his desk. Kati saw that it was open at the handicapped spread. "This is a prime example. It's *campaigning* journalism, Kati, which doesn't seem to fit too happily in a glossy up-scale monthly." He shot her a shrewd glance. "Is there a personal angle to this?"

"What if there is?" she said defensively. "I happen to think that it's a very important subject."

"I wouldn't dispute that. What I want to know is how you came to involve *Rendezvous*."

With a sense of reluctance, since it meant referring to their shared past, Kati told him how she had written the original article after hearing about Fay Pemberton's accident and being so impressed by her brave fight against disability. "You'll remember Fay," she added, "because you met a couple of times. Her husband is Harry Pemberton, who was the works manager at Prestige Print."

"Yes, I remember her. We played a game of tennis with her and Harry one time, didn't we? I liked Fay." Scott looked genuinely concerned. "I'm very sorry to hear about her accident. How is she getting on? Is there really no hope of any improvement in her condition?"

"None at all. But Fay has become reconciled to the fact, without any sign of bitterness. And that's what makes her such a wonderful example to other people. The original feature about her created a lot of interest among our readers, so I ran a follow-up about someone else who had conquered her disability, and from that we developed the regular monthly feature." She looked at Scott earnestly. "I wish I could make you understand what I'm aiming to do in running this sort of thing in *Rendezvous* . . . why I think it's so important. Our readers are every bit as caring and sympathetic as anyone else, but when people have interesting careers and busy, fulfilling lives, it's only too easy to overlook the plight of people whose lives are sadly restricted by a disability—even more restricted than need be because of the attitude of the general public who tend to think in 'them and us' terms. It's the sort of women who read *Rendezvous*—intelligent, forward-looking women— who can help change public opinion. And to capture their interest we need to present them with straight facts in the bright, informed way they're accustomed to getting in *Rendezvous*. I'm aiming to create a climate that gives handicapped people their rightful place in society along with the rest of us."

"That's very laudable, very worthwhile," Scott said, "but I still maintain that this sort of campaigning journalism isn't really the job of a glossy monthly. However, you've started it now, and I'm not asking you to drop it. Any good cause like that needs someone with your vitality and enthusiasm to give it teeth. Just so long as you keep it firmly in mind, Kati, that this two-page spread every month doesn't help us pull in as much as a quarter page of advertising."

"That's a crude, commercial outlook," she muttered.

Scott raised his thick eyebrows. "Commerce is the name of the game—or hadn't you heard? The aim of *Rendezvous* is to make a profit for Universal Publications. If, in the process, it can also fight a good cause, that's fine. But remember, if *Rendezvous* doesn't start showing a profit soon, it will have to fold. And then you won't have a platform at all, for any cause."

He had argued her into a corner, Kati knew it. And, worse, he knew it. She stood up. "You've made your point. May I go now?"

Scott rose too, and gave her a straight look from beneath his dark brows. "We'll talk again next week. Before you leave, though, how about our fixing to see each other over the weekend?"

It was as if he'd knocked the breath from her body. "My God, you have a nerve. After summoning me to your office and bawling me out as if I were a junior clerk, now you're calmly asking me for a date."

"I have the right to send for you whenever I like," Scott reminded her in a humoring tone. "And as for bawling you out, what we've just had is a frank exchange of views. You'd better be prepared for a lot tougher handling than that, because it's my job to get some action around here. I don't intend to pull my punches whoever happens to be at the receiving end. You'll have to learn, Kati, to separate your professional life from your private life."

Another breath-robbing remark. "That's really rich, coming from you."

"Meaning?"

"Oh, work it out for yourself."

He met her eyes in a steady, questioning look. "So how about the weekend? Dinner tomorrow evening?"

"No."

"Sunday, then. We could make a day of it on the river. I want to take the *Pagan* away from her moorings, to see how she handles."

"I said no, Scott."

"Does that mean you're going to be busy the entire weekend?"

"Correct." She was immediately sorry that she'd grasped at the easy way out, because it wasn't the flat rejection that she'd intended to give Scott. Walking to the door, she added defiantly, "Not that it makes any difference. Even if I had nothing planned for the weekend, I still wouldn't go out with you."

Saturday, and absolutely nothing on her agenda. It was an unusual occurrence, but after the stresses of the week it seemed a golden opportunity to Kati to be lazy and let the day drift by. She was scheduled to drive to Somerset on Sunday to visit the author of a new book on diet that was going to attract a lot of media attention. Kati hoped to get the serialization rights for *Rendezvous*. The writer seemed to be a difficult lady with an outsize ego, so, reluctantly, Kati had decided to pander to her vanity and make the journey to see the woman personally.

But Saturday turned out to be anything but restful. Kati's mind wouldn't let her rest; memories of the previous day's encounter with Scott kept intruding. It was bitterly unfair that he had turned up in her life again, and it was even more unfair that his fatal power to attract her was in no way lessened.

In the morning Kati did household chores and shopped for food. After a salad for lunch, she started on the load of work in her briefcase, which she always brought home with her in hopes that she'd get some of it done. By six o'clock she was wishing rather desperately that she had something arranged for the evening. She fixed herself a Campari and soda, then switched on the television. Soon she found herself doing what she abhorred in others—random channel hopping. In the end, too restless to remain indoors, she slid into her white cotton trenchcoat and went out into the mild May evening.

Chelsea's King's Road, especially on Saturday night, was always a stimulating place to be. Some of the young people strolling around in boisterous groups were outrageous in their bizarre outfits; all the same, their clothes were a useful guide to tomorrow's fashion trends. For once, though, Kati couldn't summon up any interest in people-watching.

Eventually, irritated by the bustle and laughing chitchat around her when her own mood was so downbeat, she turned away from the crowds and wandered toward the River Thames. The elegant period houses of the elite in Cheyne Walk glowed in the evening sunshine, and the newly-leafing plane trees made a lacework tracery against a serene sky. The sight of the Albert Bridge, with its looped suspension chains, made her pause. Was that why her footsteps had been unconsciously drawn this way . . . the knowledge that Scott's houseboat was moored nearby?

A crazy thought; but it was true, she realized as she walked on and came to the houseboat colony. Most of the boats were somewhat dilapidated, no longer intended for sailing on the open waters of the Thames. But a few were much smarter. Kati slowed her steps, searching for the name *Pagan*. She took care not to be too obvious about it, and was ready to hightail it if she caught a glimpse of Scott.

Pagan was at the end of the row, a white and navy motor cruiser with sleek lines. Kati edged forward, but not too close in case Scott should happen to spot her through one of the wide windows of the cabin.

"Looking for someone, love?" The cheery voice came from a fat man on one of the boats, who was lounging at ease in a deckchair, a magazine in one hand and a can of beer in the other.

"No thanks, I was just . . ."

A car drew up right behind her, and another voice called, "I expect the lady is looking for me, Wally. Hi there, Kati."

Shocked, she spun around to see Scott grinning at her from the wound-down window of a silver blue car. Her face flaming, she raged against her bad luck. Why did he have to show up at just the wrong moment?

"Hello, Scott," she managed shakenly. "I was just out for a stroll, and I . . ."

"You thought you'd look me up. That's nice."

"Nice nothing. I had no intention of looking you up."

His smile was sorrowful. "I don't take kindly to that, Kati. Here you are, going right past my door—or should I say gangplank?—and you weren't planning to check if I was home."

"How egotistical can you get?" she said ironically, struggling to regain her poise. "Coming to see you, Scott, isn't the only reason a person might have for taking a stroll along the Chelsea Embankment on a fine spring evening."

"Still, you were showing quite an interest in the *Pagan*."

"Only because I caught sight of the name and it rang a bell," she lied. "I remembered you mentioning it that night we had dinner together."

"I'm glad you did remember, Kati. Just give me a minute to park, and then come aboard for a drink. How do you like my car, by the way? I just collected it. Drives like a charm."

Ignoring the car, she said, "Thanks, but I won't go aboard. I have to get back."

"In a hurry? It didn't look that way just now. You were definitely loitering, Kati."

"Didn't you hear me?" she snapped. "I said no."

All the same, Scott noted, she wasn't walking away. Would it be stupid to press her? She had clearly spelled out how she wanted their relationship to be in the future, so why not go along with that? But the situation between himself and Kati nagged at him, and he knew that he'd never be easy in his mind if he let things ride when they were caught up in such a tangled web of emotion. In all those eight years apart he had never been able to forget Kati, often finding himself yearning for her with an intensity that dismayed him. And now that they'd met up again, he knew that he wanted Kati very badly. *Wanted* her. Not to marry her. That wasn't even distantly on his horizon. A long-term affair? Could be, if things panned out that way. Just for sex, then; plain, uncomplicated sex? Scott shook his head in bemusement. He just wanted Kati, longed to be near her. Needed her.

"Kati, please," he said, stepping out of the car and touching her arm. "I'd like to show you the boat."

"Why?"

He gave her a shrugging grin. "You could make a feature out of it. *Living in Luxury on the Water.*"

"Could be. I'll send one of my feature writers and a photographer."

Scott kept a clamp on his patience. "Give me a half-hour of your time. That won't hurt you. One drink, and a look around the boat." Damn it, he was actually pleading with her. While Kati hesitated, his heart was racing and thudding against his ribs.

Kati's heart was racing, too. "Okay," she said finally, letting out her held-in breath. "Just for a half-hour."

The way Scott smiled at her, looking genuinely pleased—not triumphant—was undermining. "That's great, Kati," he said. "I'll park the car and be back in a couple of shakes. Promise you won't run off."

Kati watched him swing the car across the stream of traffic and turn into a small side street. She sighed to herself; it was done now, and there was no sense in having regrets. After all, it couldn't do any harm to go aboard the *Pagan* for a short time, any more than there had been any real harm in dining with Scott the other night. No way did she intend to become involved with him again. Suppose, she argued to herself, the circumstances had been different and they'd never had any previous connection. Suppose it was just that Scott had been newly appointed to the executive job and she had recently met him as one of the editors under his control. In that case, if they'd happened to meet up like this by his boat and he'd asked her to have a drink on board with him, wouldn't she have accepted without hesitation? Refusing his invitation, as she'd started to do, only served to underscore the strength of her feelings about him; it would suggest to Scott that she was still vulnerable where he was concerned. Which was the very last thing she wanted.

Scott came back across the street, dodging between the fast-moving traffic. Reaching Kati, he took her elbow to help her across the gangplank. The *Pagan* was rocking gently in the swell of a passing police launch. Scott unlocked a door, and they passed through into a spacious saloon that was tastefully done out in cream and blue, with teak trim. There was generous headroom, and the wide, curtained windows all around gave a splendid view of the river and its desultory evening traffic. The floor was carpeted in royal blue, and a paler shade of blue leather covered the long cushioned banquettes that lined the side walls. On the right stood a table, fixed to the floor. On the left was the steel-framed helmsman's seat behind the wheel, with an elaborate panel of navigational equipment. Kati noted that not only was the *Pagan*'s interior luxurious, but spotless too, a fact she commented upon as she slipped off her trenchcoat.

Scott grinned. "I can't take the credit, Kati. Along with use of the boat, I inherited Jesse's cleaning lady. She comes aboard and keeps everything shipshape." He went to a cupboard and opened it to reveal shelves of assorted bottles, neatly protected from falling by brass rails. "Shall we splice the mainbrace?"

"Very nautical! I wonder you don't wear a brass-buttoned blazer and a shiny peaked cap to add the finishing touches."

"There's sailor-type gear in one of the lockers. I guess Jesse found that it impressed the women."

"You'd better try it out, then."

"On *you*, Kati?"

She shot him a withering look, and went over to the helmsman's seat. "It all looks very lavish. There's even a phone, I see."

"That's a radio phone. Very handy. It can be used even when the boat's underway. What's your poison, Kati?"

"What do you have?"

"You name it."

"White wine, then. Dryish."

Scott found a bottle of chablis in a small refrigerator, and poured two glasses of wine. "Here's to us, Kati."

She wouldn't drink to that, so she offered a different toast. "To the long life of *Rendezvous*."

Scott's mouth twitched in amusement. He gestured for her to sit on one of the banquettes, and came to sit beside her. He laid his arm casually along the back of the seat, without quite touching her.

"What happened to your date this evening, Kati?"

"My date?"

"You told me that you'd be busy for the entire weekend. Not a minute to spare, the way you made it sound. And then I come across you strolling along the Chelsea Embankment as if time hadn't been invented."

"So I lied," Kati said carelessly, tearing her eyes away from his disturbing dark gaze. She steeled herself for Scott's next remark, ready to cap it with a slapping-down retort. But, typically, Scott went off at a tangent.

"Do you know what surprises me, Kati? That you aren't married by now. You must have had plenty of offers."

She rested her glass carefully on a ledge. "Not so many, as it happens. I don't encourage men to propose."

"Because you're more interested in your career?"

"That's not so far out."

"For someone with your capabilities, I wouldn't have thought that a career and marriage would be mutually exclusive."

She turned her head and gave him a long look. "You seem to be forgetting that I had a lot of catching up to do. I had to restart my career from square one."

Scott's color deepened, but he met her gaze steadily. "We've already been through all that, Kati. It was your own choice to go back to square one, not a matter of necessity. All the same, you've made brilliant headway in the past eight years. Do you really want to climb much farther up the corporate ladder?"

"Why not? Because I'm a woman? Aren't women supposed to have ambition?"

"Whew! I seem to have touched a nerve."

"Don't patronize me, Scott," she said dangerously.

"Sorry." He shifted on the seat, and his arm brushed against her. "I mean it—I really am sorry, Kati. It was the sort of sexist jibe that women are entitled to resent. I take it back."

"Apology accepted, as long as you don't do it again." And then, to divert the conversation from herself, she added, "You never married either, Scott . . . or did you?"

"No. I never met anyone else I wanted to marry."

"Oh, don't give me that," she said impatiently, and glanced away from him.

Scott sipped his wine in silence, watching Kati as she gazed out at the river scene. Even now, even when she was in a hostile mood, her face was beautiful to look at. It was such a mobile face, full of character; but no longer could he tell what Kati was thinking, as in the old days. Just as he'd guessed, with maturity she had learned to conceal her thoughts and feelings.

Scott found himself regretting these past years away from her; he felt jealous of the men she'd known, the men she'd dated. Even though she had steered clear of marriage, she must have had a few involvements in that time, just as he had done. It was true, though, that he'd never met anyone since Kati whom he'd even remotely wanted to marry. Yet, eight years ago, marriage to Kati had seemed to offer everything a man could possibly want from life. What if they *had* married way back then? Would it have worked out? Would they still be together now? These days Scott couldn't envisage himself as a married man. Marriage didn't feature in his thinking at all.

He and Kati had both changed a lot; they'd become different people. But what still remained, without any question, was the sensual magnetism that had first attracted him to her . . . and her to him. Scott was acutely conscious of it in himself, now, this very minute. His body was restless, tense, impatient. He longed to hold her, to kiss those wonderfully soft lips. He longed for the freedom to roam his hands over her enticing curves and feel the voluptuous warmth of her naked flesh against his own. Scott released a long, soft groan of sexual frustration, and hoped that she hadn't heard.

"More wine?" he asked.

"No, I'm fine."

Kati had given up asking herself what in God's name she was doing aboard Scott's houseboat, alone with him. She was there, period. And right now it was where she wanted to be. Although ostensibly gazing out across the river, she was watching Scott from behind the shield of her dark lashes. He had taken off his jacket and wore only pale khaki slacks and a brown and white striped shirt. Glancing down covertly, she saw that he was holding the wineglass resting against his right thigh. She felt a sudden reckless urge to run her fingers down its firm, muscled length, to feel again the well-remembered shape of him and experience the thrilling, pulsing warmth of his flesh. Scared that she might betray herself, she moved a few inches away along the banquette, pretending that she was shifting to a more comfortable position.

The raucous sounds of a party aboard a steamer heading downstream seemed to highlight the silence in the *Pagan*'s saloon. Kati was aware that Scott had turned to face her; she could even feel his breath against her cheek.

"Kati, I . . ."

The sensible thing would be to stand up, to ask him brightly to show her the rest of the boat. But she remained motionless, rigidly tense. As the sounds of the party drifted away, she could hear the heavy drumbeat of her heart.

"Kati . . ." Scott said again, his voice a husky murmur.

Silence, her nerve ends prickling. Then came Scott's first touch, his fingers tangling lightly into the hair at her nape. Kati closed her eyes, startled and shocked by the sudden overwhelming need to have him take her into the clasp of his arms.

It was like a sequence in slow motion, each passing moment prolonged and fraught with danger. Yet she didn't try to stop what was happening, she didn't really want to; there was a beautiful inevitability about it. Putting his wineglass aside, Scott brought his other hand up to touch her cheek, letting his fingertips trail across the petal-soft skin reverently.

"Scott . . ." His name floated to him softly. There was no rejection in her voice; even, dared he hope, a note of invitation?

His hands slid to her shoulders, and he drew her closer with the gentlest pressure while looking deeply into her eyes. Kati caught the sweet familiar male scent of him, and felt a warm radiance of feeling flooding through her bloodstream.

His lips touched hers cautiously, testingly, drew back a moment, then locked on her mouth once more in a long, shared melding of lovely sensations. His arms encircled her, drawing her to him, holding her close. She felt his heartbeat thudding against her ribcage, felt the pulsing passion barely held in check. Kati didn't try to analyze her feelings but just enjoyed the wonderful moment. Her hands slid around him and she laid her palms against his back to savor the feel of his hard-muscled flesh beneath the silky texture of his shirt.

"Oh, Kati, where have the years gone?" Scott whispered wonderingly, when they finally broke the kiss. "The magic is still there between us. Don't you feel it too?"

Yes, I feel it too. She wouldn't let herself speak the words aloud, but her answer was spoken with her eyes, with her softening, yielding body.

Scott feathered kisses all around her mouth, then slid his lips lingeringly across her cheek, inhaling the delicate fragrance of her skin. With a low groan he buried his face in the hollow of her neck. Kati brought up one hand to caress the springy dark hair, plunging her fingers into it luxuriantly. If only they could remain like this forever, just the two of them shut off from time and place, from reality. Her mind winged back and with vivid clarity she pictured the big living room of her father's house at Wimbledon; she and Scott on the sofa before a blazing fire, locked in one another's arms. It had always been so wonderfully good between them. Life had seemed so perfect in those days, with the prospect of happiness for ever and ever.

As Scott continued to hold her, cradling her tenderly, the then and the now became inseparably confused in Kati's mind. She seemed to slip right inside the skin of her younger self—to feel again what she had felt, to want again what she had wanted.

Unconsciously, she let her head fall back in sensuous delight and Scott's lips moved over her throat, caressing its creamy softness. Then his lips came up to find hers again, more insistently now, while his hands roamed her back, sliding down to hold and caress the soft curve of her hips. His mouth coaxed, requested, demanded, and Kati responded willingly. Her lips parted to receive the exciting, sensuous probe of his warm tongue in a deeply passionate kiss that seemed to have no ending.

Scott drew back at last, but only to murmur hoarsely, "Kati, you're fantastic. I want you, I want you so much."

Slowly, she opened her eyes, seeing him in soft focus as if through a mist, while her whirling brain steadied. She felt . . . what did she feel? Not regret, at just this moment, though that might come later. It was as if the Kati of the present had been observing coolly the Kati of the past, and the new Kati must put a stop to this madness.

"No, Scott," she said in a crisp tone.

"No? But why, Kati? For heaven's sake, why?"

She shook her head, pressing him back gently but very firmly.

"I don't understand," he said, his eyes stabbing into her. "You can't just shrug me off. Not now, not after this."

"It shouldn't have happened, Scott."

"Why not? We want each other, don't we? It's still there, that old feeling, as strong as ever."

"Yes," she admitted with reluctant candor, "it's still there. But . . ."

"I knew that you felt it too," he cut in. "Right from the moment we met again, in Victor Channon's office."

Kati fought against the emotional pressure he was applying. "It's only physical, Scott, nothing more," she said determinedly. "I guess, when you think about it, it's not so surprising that we still find each other attractive. Our 'chemistry,' as they say, was right before, and there's no real reason why that should have changed."

"It hasn't, no question. So . . ."

"But nothing else can ever be the same," she insisted. "The feelings of love and tenderness and trust, they've all gone."

Scott's eyes held hers in a searching look, while the silence throbbed between them. At length he muttered, "Okay, maybe we can't recapture what we had. But what we do have still . . . it's something very special, Kati."

"But not enough."

"No? Ask yourself this question . . . how many men have you known these past eight years with whom you've felt the same fantastic chemistry?"

"None," she admitted truthfully. "All the same . . ."

"So why go on demanding the moon and the stars?" he interrupted.

"I used to have the moon and the stars," she said with a sad sigh. "At least, I thought I did. I'd never settle for anything less."

Scott seemed about to make an impetuous retort, but checked himself. He reached for his wineglass again, and twirled it in his fingers thoughtfully. His next words, when they came, seemed carefully weighed. "Is that an invariable rule of yours, Kati? Or does it apply only to me?"

"What's that supposed to mean?"

"Have you settled for something less than perfection with other men?"

"What gives you the right to ask me that?" she demanded angrily, rising to her feet.

"No right . . . except self-interest."

"That won't buy you an answer."

Scott stood too and caught hold of her arm, but she flung him off violently, as if his touch contaminated her. And it did; even now, even though she was angry with him, she had still reacted to the sensuous pressure of his fingers.

"You put me through hell once, Kati," he said bitterly. "I'll not go through that again, on account of you." He took a quick, sharp breath. "There's something I want to ask you. Exactly what is the situation between you and Robin Wheatley?"

"Robin?" she jerked out. "What sort of question is that?"

"Don't act the innocent with me, Kati. You have to know that it's going the rounds at U.P. that there's something between you two."

"And you believed it? That's great. Don't you know that in a set-up like U.P. there are always rumors going the rounds?"

"Why shouldn't I believe it?"

"Because it's just idle gossip."

"Would Wheatley agree with that assessment? I got a somewhat different impression."

"Have you been talking to Robin?"

"Naturally I have. It's my job to talk to staff."

"I meant about . . . him and me?"

"So there *is* something?"

Rage took hold of her, and she seemed to be seeing Scott through a red mist. "I don't either confirm or deny it," she stormed, "because it isn't any of your business, Scott. Even in my harshest thoughts about you, I never imagined that you'd stoop to using your position in the company to nose into my private life. But I guess I shouldn't be surprised at your underhanded tactics. I've seen you in action before, haven't I? I've seen how low you're ready to go."

"Have you finished?" he demanded. "Or have you just run out of breath?"

"I've said all I need to say." Kati reached for her trenchcoat and dragged it on. "Except good night."

Scott came out of the saloon with her, but he made no attempt to stop her from leaving. She could feel his eyes drilling into her back as she crossed the gangplank on unsteady legs. Ashore, she strode away quickly into the gathering dusk.

Chapter Six

Tuesday morning. Sandra, who had been taking dictation from Kati, hesitated on the way back to her own office. "Er . . . I hope you think what I'm wearing is okay," she said, glancing down at her overalls outfit in yellow and black. "I mean, is it Cifbids enough?"

"Not to worry, Sandra, you look fine." Kati grinned. "The males around here might find it a bit disturbing, though."

The door opened and Robin Wheatley looked around it. "I guessed that Sandra was here with you, Kati. Okay to come in?"

"Sure, Robin. You can give us your considered opinion. I was just telling Sandra that she would look very sexy to a man in that gear. Was I right?"

He studied the girl gravely, making her blush. "Sure thing she looks sexy. If I wasn't already spoken for, she'd have to fight me off."

"There, Sandra, that ought to make you happy," Kati said with a laugh.

The girl departed, looking pleased. Robin came and perched on Kati's desk.

"I'll tell you something, Kati. That girl's not in the same league as you when it comes to looking sexy."

Letting that go without comment, Kati asked briskly, "What brings you here, Robin? Good news, I hope."

"Well, not bad. I've just had a call from Zamba Cosmetics. The bossman there was so delighted with the feature you ran last month on the new season's makeup that he told his ad agency to book six color pages in *Rendezvous*."

"Great, as long as it's not meant as a bribe. We have Zamba's lipgloss applicator under test at the moment. That report, Robin, will be printed exactly as it comes, good or bad."

"I know the score, Kati. They're not expecting any favors." Without much hope in his voice, he went on, "No chance you're free for lunch, I guess?"

About to refuse, Kati pondered. She had planned to spend lunchtime at her desk with a cup of yogurt and an apple, but maybe going out to eat with Robin would be a good idea. If their being together was noted, and it reached Scott's ears, that would suit her just fine. She'd still not completely simmered down after the incident aboard the *Pagan* on Saturday. Every time she reran the scene in her mind, her anger flared again.

"Okay, Robin, I'd like that."

He was obviously expecting a refusal, and looked faintly stunned but delighted. "Great. There's a really nice new bistro that just opened at Covent Garden."

"Oh, I don't want to go that far. How about the place across the street? It's quick service there."

They left the building together, crossed Fleet Street and entered the restaurant which was often used by U.P. executives who wanted a change from the staff restaurant. It could even be that Scott himself would lunch there, Kati thought, glancing around with sudden anxiety. Defiant though she felt, she didn't want a confrontation in public.

Scott wasn't there, she was relieved to see, at least not yet. Giving a wave to Lance Penney, the editor of *Auto Weekly,* and his chief car tester, and spotting Ruth Dudley who ran the fiction mag, *Love Parade,* sitting with a guy from accounts at a table in the far corner, Kati followed the head waiter to a table for two in the center of the restaurant.

"A cocktail?" Robin suggested, when they were seated.

"Not for me. A tomato juice would be fine. I have to keep a clear head for this afternoon."

"Why, what's on?"

"Nothing special. I never drink at lunchtime if I can avoid it. But don't let me stop you, Robin."

He ordered her tomato juice, and a beer for himself. They studied menus, and Kati chose veal escalope with a green salad. Then she sat back and gazed around her, relaxing for the first time that day.

"This is nice," she said, without thinking.

"Very nice," Robin agreed warmly. "We should do it more often."

Kati smiled in a vague sort of way and avoided his eyes; she didn't want to give Robin any further encouragement than she had already, just by accepting his invitation. She felt a bit guilty that she was using him like this for her own ends, in the hope that it would get back to Scott. There was really no reason why the editor and the advertisement manager of a magazine having lunch together should cause comment in the normal way. It was just that everyone at U.P. knew that Robin fancied her.

It was sad, she thought, that Robin was unhappily married. From a woman's point of view, he had a lot going for him. He was amiable, even-tempered and considerate, aside from being good looking. And yet, even if he weren't married, Kati knew that she could never feel more for Robin than warm friendship. He just wasn't her type. The sort of man who attracted her was . . . Kati felt herself flushing as she realized that there was only one man in the entire world who had the power to attract her now. She sipped at her tomato juice and struggled to regain her poise.

"I'm afraid, Robin," she began in a crisp tone of voice, "that the report you did for me on our advertisement prospects didn't offer a lot of encouragement."

He pulled a long face. "Do we have to talk business now?"

"Why not? It's a good opportunity. Besides, I want to give you a friendly warning. You'll really have to pull something out of the hat, Robin. I don't know how—but somehow. Scott Drummond is going to demand a whole lot more from your department than even your most optimistic figures."

"Don't I know it!" Robin said gloomily. "He's had me in the hot seat twice already. But he's asking the impossible, Kati, and I told him so."

"What did he say to that?"

"What didn't he say! That guy's a workaholic," Robin declared. "When I pointed out there are only so many hours in a day, he said I'd better find ways of cramming more into each hour. He seems to think that I should live, breathe and eat space-selling for *Rendezvous*."

Kati nodded, feeling sorry for him. Robin wasn't the sort of man to stand up to a driving force like Scott. But he hadn't a chance if he closed his eyes to unpalatable facts.

"The trouble is," she explained, "what we're having to face is the question of our very survival. It's hellishly unfair when the circulation is climbing the way it is, but unless we can begin to show an upward turn on the overall balance sheet the directors may decide to cut their losses and close *Rendezvous* down, along with a few other magazines that are borderline cases. The way it looks to me, U.P. is about to be slimmed down into a more profitable operation."

Robin moodily swallowed the rest of his beer, and when the waitress brought their orders he asked for a refill. "I heard a rumor this morning, Kati, that *Yachtowner* is for the chop."

"Really? I hadn't thought of that as a possible casualty, though I can't say I'm surprised. It's been losing ground for quite some time, and there's a lot of competition in the yachting field."

"And *Quarterly Builder* is to be amalgamated into *Construction Trade Journal*."

"Oh, dear!" Kati laid down her fork, her appetite suddenly gone. If these rumors were true (and why not? she thought grimly, since they made sense judged on a strictly economic basis), then Scott was losing no time in showing his muscle. He was acting with the ruthlessness she'd expect of him. And that meant that *Rendezvous* was really up against it. As she'd just warned Robin, they were facing the question of its very survival.

But almost at once her spirits rallied. So Scott was turning on the heat, was he? Well, she could fight, too. *Rendezvous* might not be turning a profit yet, but it was no longer ailing, as it had been when she'd taken over as editor eighteen months ago. It was now a darned fine magazine with a terrific future. She wouldn't accept defeat without a struggle. If necessary, she'd carry the fight right up to board level. She'd demand meetings with the directors to put her case. And she would win.

Cheered, she picked up her fork again and applied herself to her food. Robin looked at her in surprise.

"What's tickling you, Kati? You're grinning from ear to ear."

"Am I?" She shrugged. "It's no use letting things get us down, is it, Robin?"

"You're right. Eat, drink, and be merry, eh?"

"That's not what I meant. I have absolutely no intention of dying tomorrow."

"Good for you." Robin stretched his hand across the table and covered hers. "You know the thing I really admire about you? That is, apart from your great personality and your lovely sexy body? It's the gutsy way you live your life. I wish you'd let me share some of it with you, Kati, darling. I wouldn't ask you for too much. I don't expect you to fall madly in love with me, the way I am with you, but we could be great together. I'm certain of it."

Kati wanted to drag her hand away from his. She hated the feel of his fingers pressing hers. But she knew, without looking, that interested eyes from across the room were observing the scene. Okay, she'd come for a cozy lunch with Robin in hopes that it would get back to Scott. Why not let there be something to add meat to the bare bones of their being seen together?

So, for the moment, she allowed her hand to remain and pasted a smile on her face. "Robin," she said, with quiet deliberation, "you're way out of line. There isn't going to be anything between us—not ever. How many more times do I have to tell you? Even if I wanted to have an affair with you—which I don't—I'm not the sort of woman who goes around breaking up marriages."

"But you wouldn't be," Robin insisted. "My marriage has already broken up—or as good as. It's just habit that's kept Anne and me together, nothing else. Our life together is just a facade; there's nothing left between us. All she's interested in is the children. Even when I'm home, Anne hardly seems to notice I'm there."

"Perhaps," Kati suggested, firmly withdrawing her hand now, "the answer would be to spend more time at home, not less."

"In *my* job? Are you serious? Half the deals I make

are clinched over drinks or dinner or whatever in the evening."

She nodded. "I know how it is, Robin, I have the same problem. One's free time is always at the mercy of the job. This week, for instance, I spent Sunday driving to Somerset to see an author about the serialization of her book, and tomorrow evening I have another TV show to do."

"What's this one?"

"Oh, I'm appearing on the Paul Ross talk show. Fay Pemberton—you know, my friend who helps out with the disabled feature—was approached by Paul Ross's office and she suggested my name. It's a nuisance in a way—I don't like facing the cameras—but I'm glad to do what I can in such a good cause. On top of which, it will be a useful plug for *Rendezvous*."

"You'll put on a wonderful performance, Kati. I remember the last thing you did, on that fashion panel with Lady Dee. I thought you were the dishiest woman of the lot. I'll be watching tomorrow."

"If you're home," she reminded him dryly.

"I'll make a point of being home."

"Then you should switch the television off, and talk to your wife, instead."

Robin shook his head at her in exasperation. "I'll get through to you one of these days, Kati. You see if I don't."

Lance Penney and his colleague were just leaving. She gave them a friendly "Hi!" as they passed the table. "I think we'd better be going, too, Robin. I have a very full schedule this afternoon."

The following evening, a minor editorial crisis made Kati later leaving the office than she'd intended. Then her taxi got stuck in a traffic jam around Trafalgar Square, and she began to think that she'd have done better taking the underground instead. She finally arrived at the TV studios in West London with hardly enough time for a quick briefing with Paul Ross. Apart from Fay, he had one other guest that evening, a genial giant of a man with gray hair and alert eyes. They were eyes which, Kati had once read in a financial gossip column, could quell a recalcitrant board member with one swift glance. Like Fay, Sir Roland Maynard was confined to a wheelchair. He'd been badly smashed up four years before when the company aircraft in which he'd been flying to a conference in Brussels had crash landed.

Kati was dealt with speedily in makeup. "You don't need a lot of attention, with skin like this," the girl told her. "You have a super English Rose complexion."

"Thanks. Nice of you to say so."

"I don't feel nice, I feel bloody jealous. Hey, I think *Rendezvous* is just great. I never miss a copy."

Kati laughed. "You'll have me purring in a minute."

Sir Roland was the first to be interviewed, followed by Fay. While waiting off the set, Kati kept up her spirits by chatting to a sound technician whom she'd met on a previous TV appearance.

"How're those twin boys of yours?" she inquired. "They were just starting school last time I saw you."

He grinned at her, his face oddly youthful behind a drooping moustache. "They're brilliant, of course, like their dad."

"Bighead," she said. "Oh, lord, I'm on. Here goes."

Taking several quick deep breaths, she walked demurely down the steps of the studio set while Paul Ross did his intro. "Now I want you to meet a lady who is a perfect example of the intelligent, ambitious, elegant women of today who make up the readership of the fine magazine she edits. Ladies and gentlemen . . . Kati Young."

The studio audience applauded as he met her at the foot of the stairs, took her hand and led her across to where the others were sitting. Paul Ross was very tall and rake thin. He had no looks to speak of, and his speech was marred by a slight stutter. It was his warm personality and a reputation for sincerity that kept him at the top of the league of talk show hosts.

"Kati, nice to have you with us this evening. You know Fay, of course, but not Sir Roland, I believe?"

"No, we haven't met before."

"I'm sure that you'll find you have a lot in common, since you're both so heavily involved in the disabled issue . . . you from the outside, as it were, and he from personal experience. Now, do tell us how you first got involved, Kati."

Prepared for this question, she told her story as concisely as possible. She explained how impressed she'd been at the terrific fight her friend Fay put up after a car accident had paralyzed her legs . . . a fight against odds that would have beaten most people, Kati suggested. She added sincerely, "I'm sure of one thing. I myself would never have coped with a disability the way Fay has."

Amazingly, Kati's nervousness vanished once she started speaking. She could sense the rapport of the studio audience. Even though she was talking about a tragic happening she wove in a comic incident—with Fay's full blessing, she knew—about how a new electric-powered wheelchair had once gone out of control and landed Fay precipitately in the middle of a wedding party posing for photos at the church porch. "Anyway," Kati continued after the laughter had died down, "I asked Fay if I could write up her story for *Rendezvous*, and she agreed. That first article led to a regular monthly feature."

Paul Ross nodded. "If you'll forgive me for saying so, Kati, *Rendezvous* seems an odd choice of mouthpiece for this sort of propaganda. I think of *Rendezvous* as a magazine for very liberated ladies, ahead of the crowd in their thinking. Bright, intelligent career women who are very sure of themselves. Women like you, Kati. Women of the nineteen-eighties."

"And what makes you think, Paul," she said sharply, but with a friendly smile to take away the cutting edge, "that many handicapped women aren't liberated ladies, ahead of the crowd in their thinking? How about Fay? How would you classify her?"

"Touché," he said. "Okay, but even so, women like Fay must represent a very tiny proportion of your readership, which amounts to . . . what?"

"Within a blink of half a million," Kati supplied. "But you're quite right, Paul, the vast majority of our readers are lucky enough *not* to be handicapped. Having full use of their faculties, they're mostly busy, active women with demanding careers and crowded personal lives. *Rendezvous* is introducing them to the idea that there are other, less fortunate women who have physical handicaps that limit them, but who are every bit as capable of leading useful, fulfilling lives. Provided—and this is the bottom line—provided that their limitations are recognized and catered to in our modern society. It's the 'them and us' mentality that we're fighting."

"Bravo!" said a deep voice from one side, and the monitor screen switched to a close-up of Sir Roland. "I must confess that, as a widower, I'm not familiar with your magazine, Kati. But from now on I shall follow its progress with great interest. Such a worthy publicity campaign deserves lots of support."

"Don't forget the name, folks," Fay interjected, looking around with a bright smile for both the studio and viewing audiences. "It's *Rendezvous*. And it's on the newsstands monthly."

"Thanks for the commercial, Fay," Kati said with a grin.

The four of them chatted for another fifteen minutes

about recent provisions made for handicapped people, and stressed the work still remaining to be done. They could only touch the fringes of the problem, of course, but every viewer whose sympathy could be caught was one more member of the public converted.

Kati deliberately mentioned the safari vacation that Fay and Harry were planning, and Paul seized on that.

"An African safari? The mind boggles at the thought. How are you going to get up on an elephant's back, Fay?"

"With great difficulty," she said with a laugh. "They'll need a block and tackle to haul me up, I shouldn't wonder."

At last Paul was winding up the show. As the three guests smiled at the audience, Kati saw the credits begin to roll on the monitor. Then it was over.

"Drinks, everyone?" Paul invited, after congratulating them.

"Phew!" Fay let out a long sigh. "I sure could do with a stiff drink. I'm jelly inside."

"Yet you look so cool and collected," Sir Roland said admiringly. "Both of you do."

"Don't let that fool you," Fay said in a dry tone. "It's just a front to hide our nervousness. Isn't that right, Kati?"

"Dead right."

"Huh!" said both men together, and Paul added, "That doesn't play too well with me, Fay. I'd call you both formidable ladies . . . in the nicest possible way."

Kati indeed felt like a bag of quivering nerves. That was the way a public appearance always affected her the moment it was over. But a drink, in the friendly atmosphere of the TV hospitality room, soon calmed her down.

With an uncharacteristic air of diffidence, Sir Roland said, "Is it too much to hope that you two ladies are free this evening? I was wondering if you'd do me the honor of dining with me. I'd love to continue our interesting conversation. It was a revelation to me, hearing what you had to say. So how about it?"

Kati and Fay glanced at one another. "I'm clear," Kati told him, and Fay said, "I'd just have to call my husband to explain why I'll be late arriving home."

Fay had driven herself to the studio, and her car was parked right outside. Sir Roland suggested that she leave it there for the time being, and that they should ride to the restaurant with him in his chauffeured Rolls Royce.

"I feel like royalty," Fay said with a giggle, as they glided through the crowded West End streets. "It's the first time I've ridden in a Rolls."

The restaurant was just off Grosvenor Square, close to the American Embassy. The chauffeur, aided by the liveried doorman, unloaded two folding wheelchairs before assisting Fay and Sir Roland out of the car. Right beside the three steps up to the entrance doors was a gently-sloping ramp which was easy to negotiate on wheels.

"Now you know why I chose this restaurant," Sir Roland commented with a smile. "I had to bully the management into fitting the ramp, but now I'm told that it's viewed with favor by their customers."

"So you too, Sir Roland, do your bit for the cause," Kati said, as soon as they were settled at a table.

He inclined his head. "I try to, Kati, though I'm afraid that my business interests don't leave me as much time as I'd like. Still, I contribute to the funds of various organizations. That's something, I suppose."

"Believe me, it's a lot," Fay said fervently. "Every organization I know of could do a lot more if only they had more cash."

"You must give me a note of the various groups you're involved with, Fay," he said, "so that I can send them a little something."

A waiter brought them large, elaborate menus. They spent a pleasant few minutes studying them, Sir Roland strongly recommending the lobster. He suggested a vintage wine to mark the occasion. When it arrived, he raised his glass in a toast.

"To all the fine work you two are doing. More power to you."

Fay raised her eyebrows expressively at the excellence of the wine. "To think that I was going home to a humble beef casserole and a glass of apple cider," she said, laughing.

"I hope your husband didn't mind your change of plan," Sir Roland said.

"Not a bit. Harry is a dear. Right, Kati?"

"Absolutely. He's a real honey."

Sir Roland put his glass down and looked at them seriously. "I'm ashamed to admit this, but until I became physically handicapped myself, I scarcely spared a thought for the problems that disabled people were up against. That's why I admire you so much, Kati. For you, it wasn't necessary to encounter the problems first-hand to appreciate them. If only there were more able-bodied people like you around, who are aware of how much needs to be done in the way of public understanding."

"That's what we're aiming for at *Rendezvous*. And there's evidence of a growing interest and sympathy among our readers. They're nice people, most of them, and they just need to have a few real-life situations written up to bring the facts home to them." A thought came to Kati, and she voiced it immediately. "Sir Roland, you'd make an ideal subject for a feature."

"I beg to differ," he said, with a deprecating smile. "There could be absolutely nothing interesting to your readers about me. The sort of victories that I win are all to do with corporate politics, which to the lay person is just about the dullest subject on earth."

"I'm thinking of your victory over disability, Sir Roland. To suffer what you suffered, and emerge from it wielding even more power and influence than you did before . . . it would be an inspiring story."

Sir Roland glanced at Fay with a rueful grin. "Kati has a persuasive tongue, hasn't she? But I'm afraid I must refuse. I know that I've acquired a reputation for being a tough egg, but in fact I'm a retiring sort of person in my private life. It would embarrass me dreadfully to be featured in print. To tell the truth, I regretted letting myself be conned by Paul Ross into appearing on his show. But having met you two ladies as a result, I'm really glad that I did."

"So why not let us con you into a write-up in *Rendezvous?*" Kati pressed. "Maybe you'd turn out to be glad about that."

He laughed. "If you ever need a job, Kati, you know where to apply. But quite honestly, you'll have to count me out as a profile subject. I'd like to help your campaign, but not this way."

Kati gave a rueful smile of resignation. "Pity. Still, you can't win them all. It would have been quite a scoop for . . ." Her voice faltered as her glance strayed to the restaurant's entrance and she saw a couple entering. The man, tall and immaculate in a dark suit, was Scott Drummond. With him was a beautifully elegant woman only a couple of inches shorter, wearing a halter-necked white gown in a clinging fabric, her hair an artfully careless tumble of pure spun gold. They made a very striking pair, she thought, and was immediately pierced by a sickening shaft of jealousy.

Scott swept the room with a rapid glance, and his gaze homed in on her. Ten yards apart, their eyes met and locked, and even at that distance Kati saw a glitter of cobalt.

Sir Roland was speaking; he seemed not to have noticed her sudden silence. She dragged her glance away from Scott and tried to pay attention. If their host was unaware of her disquiet, Fay wasn't. Kati hoped that her friend hadn't spotted Scott. It was more than eight years since Fay had last seen him; in any case they'd only met a couple of times. A fevered glance out of the corner of her eyes showed Kati that Scott and the woman were being escorted to a table on the far side of the room.

Later in the evening, when Kati and Fay headed for the powder room, she steeled herself not even to glance in Scott's direction as they passed near his table. When they were safely inside, Fay, redoing her lips at the mirror, said quietly, "So you're keeping up a sort of vendetta against Scott Drummond."

"How do you mean?" Kati managed to make her voice steady, but her heartbeat had lurched.

"That's Scott in the restaurant, isn't it, with the glamorous woman in the white dress? I don't think I'd have recognized him if I hadn't seen the way you reacted when he walked in."

"Our association now is confined strictly to work," Kati said through tight lips.

"Even to the extent of cutting him dead away from the office? It's none of my business, Kati, but . . ."

"That's right, Fay . . . it's none of your business. Ready? Then let's get going."

The Rolls drove back to the TV studio and dropped Fay right beside her own car, then continued on to Chelsea to deliver Kati to her mews cottage. Before getting out, Kati thanked Sir Roland for the dinner and the ride home.

"Don't thank me, my dear, it has to be the other way around. I've had a most instructive and enjoyable evening. Keep up the good work you're doing with your magazine, won't you?"

That's all very fine and dandy, Sir Roland, she thought as she went inside. But you don't know what it's costing me to stay in the editor-in-chief's chair at *Rendezvous*.

Later, she was making some coffee when the phone

rang. Her heart stopped. Could it be Scott? And if so, what would he have to say?

But it turned out to be Fay. "Kati, I'm just home. I wanted to say I'm sorry if I poked my nose in this evening. I mean—about Scott Drummond. Am I forgiven?"

"Forgiven?" Kati echoed with a light laugh, and lied, "I'd forgotten all about it, Fay. Er . . . did Harry see the Paul Ross show?"

"Yes, and he videotaped it, so I could see myself on screen. I'll replay the tape when I feel strong enough to stand the strain. 'Night, Kati."

Kati felt restless and lonely. Her mind drifted to the luxury houseboat, hardly more than a stone's throw away. Had Scott returned there by now with that glamorous, sexy woman? She closed her eyes against the thought, but the pain wouldn't go away.

Chapter Seven

It was a big disappointment to Kati when Dee called on Thursday evening to say that she wouldn't be able to come to her birthday party the following evening. This year Kati was thirty-two, and she couldn't escape the gloomy feeling that her youth was behind her now. Having someone like Dee around, who was living, breathing proof that glamor didn't need to take a back seat even when a woman was closer to forty than thirty, would have been nice for her morale.

"I tried to catch you before you left the office, but I was in such a rush," Dee told her. "The thing is, I'm leaving for Rome right now, so I'm afraid it means I can't make it tomorrow night. Sorry, sweetie."

"Oh, dear," Kati wailed. "My birthday won't be the same without you. So what's happening in Rome that has you dashing off at a moment's notice?"

"Nothing for you to get excited about, Kati."

"Which means that you aren't going to tell me for fear that I'll try to cash in on the act for *Rendezvous*?"

Dee laughed. "That's about the size of it. Much as I love you, Kati, there are times when I don't altogether trust you. So I'll just say that I've had a tipoff that my journey will be worthwhile, and I'll leave you to wonder."

"Meanie. When do you expect to be back, Dee?"

"Probably about Tuesday, so the weekend at Avonbury Hall is still on. You will come, won't you?"

"Sure. I'm looking forward to it."

"Good. Look, Kati, I just managed to slip a birthday card in the mail to you, plus a little silky boudoir number that I thought you might put to effective use one of these nights."

"Huh! So long as you don't expect a detailed report on its effectiveness. Thanks a lot, Dee. Have a wonderful time in Rome."

"What else? Bye-ee!"

Kati had to jump out of bed to open the door for the postman the next morning, because there were a couple of packages that he couldn't push through the letterbox, plus a thick handful of birthday cards. Excited as a child, she returned upstairs and climbed back in bed again to open them.

Dee's little silky boudoir number turned out to be a gorgeous georgette nightie in a soft peach shade, with lace insets. Her card was a beautiful reproduction of a Degas ballerina painting, good enough to be framed. The other package was from Fay and Harry Pemberton, a silk scarf with a leopard spot design. Unfortunately, they weren't going to be able to come to her party either, because Fay was due to chair the annual meeting of one of her disabled societies.

Kati recognized Robin's handwriting on one of the envelopes. The card was highly flowery and romantic, the sort of thing a man would send to the love of his life. The verse inside was an outpouring of passion. She frowned; Robin was becoming quite a problem.

After getting up, Kati arranged her birthday cards

along the top of the bookshelves under her living room window. She included Robin's card, then moved it to a less prominent position behind a potted cyclamen. On second thought she took the card away and hid it in the drawer of the bureau. Too bad if Robin's feelings were hurt, but she really couldn't allow other people to see a card like that from him.

The party was timed for six-thirty so as to be convenient for people who were coming straight from the office. Aside from a couple of her neighbors, the guests were mainly from U.P., the majority of them staffers on *Rendezvous*. On this occasion the catering was simplicity itself. A local wine store would be delivering the drinks plus a supply of glasses, and the food was all coming from *Rendezvous*'s experimental kitchen.

The idea had originated from Lena Godwin, who was the food editor. "Don't you think it's about time we did another feature on party food, Kati? So why not schedule our trial run to coincide with your birthday? Then we just need to transport the stuff to your place."

"Sounds like a great idea, Lena."

"It means that you won't need to do a thing," Lena continued. "We'll just bring everything—food and tableware. I always prefer having an actual event to plan for. It stops us from going over the top with some of our crazier ideas."

Kati quit the office around four o'clock that day to be home for the delivery of the drinks. She'd already rearranged the furniture in her living room the previous evening, so all she had to do was flick a duster around and arrange a couple of vases with the armful of tulips and narcissi she'd bought on her way home. The drinks arrived at the promised time, so she was able to take a leisurely, relaxing bath. She was still in her robe when, just before six, Lena and her assistant turned up in a car packed with goodies. Kati was waved away when she started to help.

"Off you go and pretty yourself up to be the belle of the ball," Lena ordered her. "Just leave all this to Debbie and me."

At the office Kati always dressed in a formal, authoritative style. This evening was different. This was her chance to show her colleagues that she could look really feminine, too. She had bought a sleek-fitting black taffeta dress with a flaring skirt, pretty puffed sleeves and a lace yoke especially for the occasion. Up in her bedroom, to the accompaniment of sounds from below as the two women laid out the food, Kati slipped into her new dress, then sat before the mirror to do her hair. Drawing the thick waves backward and upward, she fixed them there with a couple of fancy combs, and arranged the front in a cluster of loose curls on her forehead. Then she applied blush to her high cheekbones, a rosy lip gloss and a pearly green eyeshadow. When she finally went downstairs, Debbie gave a low whistle.

"Gosh, Kati, you look terrific. I wish I could shed a few pounds and have a figure like yours."

Kati grinned at her. "And I wish that I could shed a few years and have an age like yours."

"Would you really like to go back, Kati?" asked Lena, who was Kati's age, plus some.

"I guess not." She shuddered at the thought of reliving those painful years. It had been a tough struggle, getting her life together again after the debacle with Scott, and regaining a sense of purpose.

Now, at last, she had won. She had made headway in her career and established herself in a high ranking, fulfilling job. She had gained the respect and affection of her colleagues, and she had lots of friends. Why, then, wasn't she happy?

The question stole up on Kati, catching her unaware. Of course I'm happy, she chided herself indignantly. But she knew deep in her heart that it wasn't true.

Lena and Debbie had brought a long, folding buffet

table with them. Kati walked its length, admiring the sumptuous array of food. There were pizzas and quiches, pâtés and cheeses, barbequed spareribs and spicy chicken drumsticks. Salads came in all shapes and sizes—watercress and orange, radishes cut into roses, endive with crispy bacon, sliced tomato and chives, cucumber with mint, crisp lettuce with avocado and walnuts. And the desserts were even more mouth-watering. There was a rich cream gateau, raspberry cheesecake, eclairs and meringues, and fresh fruit salad laced with green chartreuse.

Kati picked up a prawn tart, adjusting the arrangement on the platter, and popped it into her mouth.

"Mmm! Delicious. You've brought enough to feed an army, Lena."

"You'll be surprised. There won't be much left by the end of the evening."

The doorbell chimed. The arrivals were Tim Bradford, the feature-writer, and his girlfriend Carol, who was Victor Channon's secretary. They had brought a fern in a pretty terracotta bowl as a present for Kati.

"This is lovely, thanks a lot," she told them. "I'm glad you've arrived early, Tim, because I'd like you to act as barman for me. How about fixing us drinks all round, okay?"

From then on the guests turned up thick and fast. First, the Graingers from next door, then the two men—Rolf, a photographer and Guy, an advertising copywriter—who shared a cottage along the mews. Bob Edmonds, her art director, had brought along his wife, and a whole bunch arrived together in two taxi loads. By around seven o'clock over thirty people were crowded into Kati's living room. With everyone laughing and chatting, there was quite a din.

Kati kept Tim pouring drinks, and detailed Robin to help him. She calculated that this would keep Robin too busy to hang around her all the time. Even so, he seized every chance to corner her. She wished that he had brought his wife along; most of the others had a partner with them, whether wife, husband, boyfriend or girlfriend. But she might have known that Robin would come solo. He tried to present her with an expensive gift—an Italian leather handbag—but she had to refuse it. She could have accepted a small item, but this must have cost far too much.

"Give it to Anne instead, Robin."

"It wouldn't suit her. And anyway, she'd think I'd gone crazy. I want you to have it, Kati."

"Well, I'm afraid you're out of luck," she said, rewrapping the handbag and making him return it to his briefcase.

"You haven't even put my birthday card up," he reproached her.

"Did you really expect me to do that with a card like that?"

"Well, maybe not," he said, brightening, clearly missing her point. "I guess you're right, Kati. We wouldn't want other people to know about us, would we?"

"There's nothing for people *to* know," she said sharply, "and that's how it's going to stay. I meant, Robin, that you shouldn't have sent me a card like that at all. And now, please see who needs a fresh drink. Don't leave all the work to Tim."

Grumbling, he moved away from her. Kati put another tape into the stereo and people started to dance, gyrating slowly in the restricted space. While talking to Bob Edmonds and his wife, she heard the chime of the doorbell, and called across the room, "Answer it, someone, please."

A minute later there was a sudden hush. Kati glanced up and saw Scott advancing toward her, bearing a bouquet of long-stemmed yellow roses. The heady perfume of the blooms seemed to fill the air and tangle around her senses, making her feel lightheaded and panicky.

As if on a given signal, before Scott reached her, the buzz of conversation was resumed and dancing started again. But there was an artificial note to it now, and Kati knew that everyone in the room was covertly watching. She steeled herself to greet Scott in a casual, friendly way, arranging a smile on her face.

"Hi, Scott. Glad you could make it."

"Hello, Kati." He held out the roses. Accepting them, Kati buried her nose in the fragrant petals in an attempt to hide her deepening color.

"Quite a crowd you have here," he remarked conversationally.

"Yes. They're mostly people from U.P., as you can see."

Scott glanced about him, greeting the people he knew, then let his eyes scan the room with every appearance of seeing it for the first time. "I like your home, Kati. It's very attractive. Did you realize that I live within a few hundred yards of here? I have a houseboat moored on the Chelsea Embankment. I'm borrowing it from a friend who's out of the country on business."

"How convenient for you."

Interest in them was waning, Kati could tell. Her guests were beginning to relax and act naturally again, laughing and talking easily. Keeping the smile pasted on her face, Kati asked in a low voice, "Why have you come, Scott?"

"For the same reason the others are here. Because it's your birthday."

"They were invited," she pointed out cuttingly.

"Do I need an invitation to visit you?"

She dodged answering that. "Anyway," she went on, fishing for confirmation of what she had guessed—and hoped, "how did you know it was my birthday? Who told you?"

A brief flash from his eyes stabbed her through. "As if I'd have forgotten the date of your birthday,

Kati. I didn't realize that you'd organized a party, though."

So he'd remembered, and he'd come hoping to catch her alone. Kati had to make a conscious effort to conceal her pleasure at the thought.

"Hello, er . . . Scott." Robin had sidled over to them. He looked determined but faintly apprehensive.

As Scott became aware of who he was, a frown creased his forehead. "Oh, hello. I didn't imagine that you'd be here, Wheatley. You must introduce me to your wife."

"My wife hasn't come," Robin mumbled.

"No? Pity. I always think it's a good idea for staff to bring their wives, husbands or whoever along to social occasions. It helps give them a sense of belonging to the firm."

Kati felt that she couldn't cope with the fencing between the two men. "I must go and put these roses in water. Aren't they lovely, Robin? Fix Scott up with a drink, will you?"

She retreated to the kitchen, but she wasn't going to be granted a few moments alone in which to get herself together. Tim was there, fetching more ice from the fridge.

"It's going great, Kati," he said. "We were all a bit thrown when Scott Drummond walked in. You should have warned us that he was coming. Still, he seems to be friendly, not the tough nut he is at work. He brought you those roses, didn't he? Nice of him."

When she emerged from the kitchen, bearing the vase of roses, which she set down on top of the bureau, she saw that Scott had moved away from Robin and was standing over by the buffet talking to Lena. When he spotted Kati, he beckoned her to join them.

"Lena has been explaining the source of the food. I complimented her on a superb array."

"Yes, it's fantastic," Kati agreed warmly. "I'm very grateful to her for coming up with the idea."

Lena smiled acknowledgment. "You'd better grab what you want, Mr. Drummond, while there's still some choice left. If you'll excuse me, I see that we need another batch of vol-au-vents. I have some warming in the oven."

"Have you eaten yet, Kati?" asked Scott, as Lena departed. "Or have you been too busy playing hostess? That's the usual fate of the partygiver."

"No, I haven't eaten. But I don't want anything yet."

"You must eat," he said firmly, and picked up two plates from the stack, balancing them in one hand. He moved along the table, piling food on both plates. In the end, Kati protested, "Ease up, for heaven's sake. I'll never get through half that."

"You used to have a hearty appetite," Scott stated. "You aren't going anorexic, I hope."

"Do I look as if I am?"

He glanced her up and down, slowly and deliberately. "I'd be a liar if I said so."

Kati flushed, cursing herself for handing him a cue for a comment on her figure. Her next-door neighbors, the Graingers, were standing close by, and she seized the chance to bring them into the conversation. "You won't have met Scott Drummond," she said. "He's my boss at U.P."

They both shook hands with him, and Chloe Grainger gave Scott a close look. "Somehow your face looks familiar."

Oh, God, Kati thought, her stomach clenching, Chloe must have noticed Scott when he came to the mews cottage the other evening. She could do without having that visit talked about.

Fortunately, Josh Grainger saved the day by saying, "That's because you saw his picture on the financial page of the newspaper, Chloe. I pointed it out to you because the item concerned Kati's firm. Remember?"

"Oh, yes, of course. You've come from the United

States, haven't you? But judging from your accent you're not an American, Scott."

"No. I worked in New York for several years, but I hail from this side of the water."

The Graingers had visited New York a number of times and they got talking with Scott about the city, trading "Do-you-knows?" Kati stayed on the sidelines, wondering how long Scott proposed to hang around. Would she have a job getting rid of him?

It was a problem that didn't arise. To her relief—she tried not to acknowledge the feeling of disappointment that went with it—when the first exodus began, Scott also came to bid her good-night.

"It's been a great party, Kati."

"Thank you."

His eyes held hers captive for a moment. "See you."

"Sure."

Her heartbeat was fast and unsteady as she watched him leave. Robin, who had stayed well clear since that first encounter with Scott, came up behind her.

"That man's a real bastard," he said feelingly.

"What deserved that much venom?" Kati inquired, turning her head to look at him.

"Need you ask? You heard him sneering about Anne not being here with me."

"Well, he had a point."

Robin threw her an accusing look. "Defending him now, are you? Drummond's jealous of me, that's the point. He fancies you himself, Kati—what man wouldn't?—and he's damned annoyed that you're not interested."

"Scott has nothing to be jealous about regarding you, Robin."

"No, I guess he hasn't at that," Robin agreed sorrowfully. "But it's not from want of trying on my part. We could be so good together, Kati, if only you'd let yourself admit it. I warn you, I don't intend to give up trying."

"I'm sorry to hear that, Robin, because you'll be wasting your time."

"It's my own time to waste."

She should, perhaps, have countered by reminding Robin that his spare time belonged to his wife and family. But she couldn't face another argument right now, so she just shrugged and moved away from him. She went over to chat with her photographer neighbor, Rolf Leyland, from whom she'd occasionally commissioned photographs for *Rendezvous*.

"Who exactly was the macho guy whose entry caused such a stir, Kati?" he asked, fastidiously brushing a few pastry crumbs from the front of his shirt.

"He's the newly appointed executive coordinator at U.P.," she told him. "A word from him, and any one of us could be out of a job."

Rolf arched his eyebrows expressively. "I thought he looked . . . masterful. You'd better keep on his good side, my love."

She turned abruptly, causing Rolf to take a backward step. "To hell with that. I do a darned good job on *Rendezvous*, and Scott Drummond had better recognize the fact."

"My, my, you're acting as masterful as he looks, Kati. You two must strike sparks off each other at the office."

She grinned at him weakly. "Sorry, I didn't mean to let fly at you, Rolf. Put it down to nerves."

"Poor Kati." He laid his lips to her forehead in a fond but dispassionate kiss. "Don't let it get to you, love. None of us can choose the people we find ourselves attracted to."

"Is this a game of riddles?" she asked evenly.

"I'm just trying to say . . . well, it's a shame to cut off your nose to spite your face. *Ciao*, darling. Lovely party. See you around."

With a sense of shock she realized that Rolf knew about her and Scott—if not everything (he couldn't possibly know everything), then far too much. Maybe Rolf just had extrasensitive antennae, but how long could things go on without other less perceptive people guessing something of the truth?

Almost all of the food had been eaten, and what little was left Kati persuaded Bob Edmonds and his wife to take home with them, since there were three young children in the Edmonds family. She cleared away the worst of the mess, piling it in the kitchen for her cleaning lady, Mrs. Barker, who was coming in specially the next morning. On Monday Kati would take a taxi to work and transport all the dishes and tableware that had been borrowed.

Finding a bottle of wine that wasn't quite empty, she poured herself a final glass. If she were going to get any sleep tonight, she needed to relax and slow down before going to bed, so she went around switching off lights until just the glow of a single silk-shaded table lamp remained. She sorted out a cassette of soothing mood music and inserted it in the tape player then stretched out on the sofa and deliberately tried to empty her mind.

But her mind refused to empty. She was haunted by thoughts and memories of Scott.

The sound of the door chimes nearly made Kati jump out of her skin. What now? Had someone left something behind? Sighing, she stood up and made her way to the front door, switching on the outside carriage lantern. Scott stood there, propped against the wall by a raised arm.

Kati gasped in surprise. "Oh, it's you," she exclaimed.

"Were you expecting someone else?" he inquired in a silky tone.

She shook her head angrily. "Go away, Scott. You can't come in."

"Kati, I came by earlier without realizing that you were throwing a party this evening. Then, when I heard all the noise coming from your living room, I couldn't resist ringing the bell. That's how it was. But I'd hoped to catch you alone, so we could talk. . . . I was going to suggest that we go somewhere for dinner, the way we did before."

Kati inhaled a deep breath and said forcefully, "Can't you grasp the fact that I want nothing more to do with you than I'm forced to? Go away and leave me alone."

"No, Kati, I can't do that." He met her eyes in a long look that sent little eddies of excitement racing through her veins. "Not until I've had a chance to talk to you."

Kati glanced uneasily up and down the mews. Nobody was around, but lights showed in the upstairs bow window of the Graingers' bedroom. Suppose they heard voices and looked out to investigate?

"You'd better come in," she said grudgingly. "But only for a minute, mind. When you've said what you came to say . . . out!"

She pressed back against the door as Scott passed her. Even though he didn't actually touch her, his nearness was enough to make her skin prickle and she felt suddenly breathless.

"It was most embarrassing having you turn up here in front of my friends," she managed in a catchy voice as she closed the door. "Heaven knows what they're thinking now."

"Does it really matter what people choose to think?" In the living room Scott turned to face her. The glow from the single lamp illuminated his face slantwise and cast fascinating shadows. His eyes were dark, mesmerizing pools. "We've agreed that it's best to conceal what we were to each other in the past, Kati, but that doesn't mean we can't be seen to have an interest in one another now."

"I have no interest in you," she said doggedly, fighting for an even breath flow.

"Don't fool yourself, Kati. Whatever your precise attitude is, you're not disinterested."

"Okay, I'll rephrase it; I dislike you intensely."

The flicker of emotion in his face was instantly gone. "Try again," he said. "The other night, aboard the *Pagan,* you admitted to feelings that could hardly be called dislike."

"I'm not proud of that."

"But you don't repudiate them?"

She shrugged her shoulders. "When something once existed between two people as strongly as it did between us—the right mix of chemistry—it can't be rendered inoperative by sheer willpower. My intellect tells me that you aren't to be trusted, but . . ."

"But your body is giving you a very different message?"

"So what?" she challenged. "Women throughout history have been attracted to men who are blackguards and not to be trusted. But, luckily for me, my mind controls my body, not the other way around."

The corner of his mouth lifted in a smile. "Why allow either side of your nature to have overriding control of your life, Kati? Dislike me if you're hellbent on it, but permit yourself to enjoy me, too."

"It's a matter of self-respect," she protested.

"Stubborn pride, you mean. So we're back to that."

"Call it what you like—same difference."

Scott shook his head regretfully. "What it amounts to, Kati, is cutting off your nose to spite your face."

That shook her, the selfsame phrase that Rolf had used not long before—and in the same connection. She looked at Scott, her mind a confusion of spinning thoughts, of shadowy memories she could not suppress.

Watching her as she half turned away from him, Scott felt his body tightening, and desire stabbed in his groin. He knew now, he'd known from their first meeting in Victor Channon's office, that his leaving Britain and going to America had not in truth stemmed from ambition as he had fooled himself at the time. He'd been running away, running away from an intolerable situation. Kati had turned against him, denounced him, and looked upon him with hatred flaring in her lovely brown eyes. And there had been no way he could see to change her attitude toward him. So it was a sense of defeat—and anger, too—that had driven him to America. Returning home eight years later, discovering that in taking on the job at Universal Publications he would inevitably meet up with Kati again, he'd thought that sufficient time had passed for his old feelings to have died. But he'd been wrong, unnervingly wrong.

In one respect, he was like Kati. His intellect told him to leave her alone; it would be crazy to get involved with her again on a personal level. But his feelings urged him differently, constantly prodding him to act against all reason and common sense. He, Scott Drummond, a man who would fight with everything he had in a corporate situation, no matter what the odds stacked against him, was finding it impossible to fight his own emotions. He still wanted Kati, *needed* her desperately. Right now he felt that he'd go out of his mind if he couldn't again possess that beautiful body he had once known so intimately.

But Kati, he knew of old, was not a woman to be enticed with soft words. Neither would she be browbeaten into submission. He had to tread a careful path, appealing to her through her reason, step by step, until she agreed that they had something to offer one another even now, despite everything.

"Okay," he said at length, and added quietly, without rancor, "So you dislike me. I have to swallow that. But it's not entirely a one-sided situation, Kati, as you seem to imagine."

She gave him a puzzled, uncertain look. "You mean . . . *you* dislike *me?*" She couldn't help the note of faint incredulity in her voice.

"Dislike is too strong a word," he returned. "I could never dislike you, Kati. But you make me very angry. For an intelligent woman you can sometimes be incredibly stupid."

Robbed of breath, she faltered, "My God, you have a nerve, coming here and throwing out insults. So you think I'm stupid, huh? Then I'd like to know why you bother about me—why you keep wanting to see me."

"A good question. I've asked it myself, more than once."

"And?"

"I said the other day that you should be able to separate your professional life from your private life, Kati. Equally, you should be able to separate your thinking mind from your feeling mind. Our intellect and logic, based on past experience, tells us that we're not right for one another on a long-term basis, certainly not as partners for life. But our body chemistry tells us that on a purely physical level we still have a lot to offer each other. So doesn't it make sense to separate the two aspects of our makeup?"

She glared at him scathingly. "So what are you advising me? To be thoroughly promiscuous and jump into bed with every man I happen to find physically attractive?"

"Sounds like we're getting into large numbers. Are there so many men—apart from Robin Wheatley—you find so attractive that you want to have sex with them?"

On the point of denying that she was attracted to Robin, Kati checked herself. Instead, she said offhandedly, "What if there are? It's none of your concern, Scott."

"I don't accept that. My feelings for you are pretty darned exclusive at the moment. Uncomfortably so. I wish to God they weren't, Kati, but they are. Still, if I thought that I was just one of a large number of men to whom you feel attracted, then I guess I wouldn't be interested any more."

"In that case," she said defiantly, "it might be a kindness to inform you right now that I'm a liberated lady and don't see any big deal about going to bed with a man if I fancy him."

Scott's cobalt eyes locked to hers. "*Are* you saying that, Kati?"

Unable to meet the challenge in his glance, she looked away, shaking her head. "No."

"Anyway, I wouldn't have believed you if you'd said yes. But you couldn't lie to me about that, could you? It would go against the grain to have me think you were promiscuous."

For the first time since his arrival, Scott reached out a hand to touch her. Tense and on edge, Kati wrenched herself back from him with such force that she hit her thigh on the corner of a small table, sending it flying and almost losing her balance. Instantly, he was beside her, holding her steady.

"Are you okay, Kati?" he asked, concerned.

"I'll live," she responded with a shaky laugh.

Scott didn't relinquish his hold, and she didn't try to push away from him. They seemed to be frozen to stillness in those fragmented moments of time. It was as if her heart, and his too, had stopped beating. With a sense of dread, of inevitability—and, also, a sense of joy—she knew that he was going to kiss her.

A strange kind of numbness invaded her brain, and yet she felt acutely sensitive and alive. She could see everything in sharp focus—Scott's tanned face drawing closer, with those fascinating planes and angles and the tiny mole on his left cheek; the wonderfully sculpted mouth; the intensely blue eyes holding hers in thrall. The subtle male scent of him enveloped her, and her senses floated headily at the sweet reminder of past joy and the promise of joy to come.

His lips made a feather-light, whispering touch against hers, the contact deepening slowly and thrillingly into a kiss of all the old remembered passion. Scott ran the tip of his tongue sensuously along the line of her teeth, and Kati opened her mouth willingly to his intimate probing. Without conscious volition her hands crept up to encircle his neck, caressing the springy, curling hair at his nape while her body molded fluidly to his firm, masculine contours. There was such a feeling of rightness in their being together, sweeping away all the intervening years as if the two of them had never been apart. When at last they broke the kiss, Scott still held her against him, his hands on the curve of her waist. His voice was a husky murmur. "This is so good, Kati . . . so right."

Yes, yes, yes, she thought, but wouldn't let herself admit it. Yet she couldn't stop her eager cooperation as he began to kiss her again, delighting in the sensation as his lips trailed the soft skin of her throat, nuzzling into the hollows of her neck. Her fingers tangled into his hair, cradling his head, holding it there, wanting the bliss to go on. They were embarked on a voyage that could only have one ending.

Soon Scott's fingers found the zipper of her dress. It slithered downward with a hushed purring until he could slide the fabric over her shoulders and let the garment fall, rustling, around her feet. Scott's glance traveled over her slowly and appreciatively, and he met her eyes again with a tender smile. Then he drew her to him again, holding her close. Her tingling nipples, covered only with her thin satin bra, were conscious of the texture of Scott's jacket. He slid his hands downward over her back, pausing to sample and savor, before inserting his fingers beneath the waistband of her panties and caressing the soft, yielding flesh of her buttocks.

"You're so lovely," he whispered, "so incredibly desirable. There's never been anyone else who's made me feel the way you do."

Letting go of her briefly, he slipped off his jacket and tossed it carelessly aside. His action brought Kati a sudden sense of urgency; his clothes were a needless barrier between them. She longed to see again the superb body she had once known so intimately, to run her hands across the firm contours of his chest and feel his supple skin heated and moist with passion. Her fingers fumbled with the buttons of his shirt, and she tugged it impatiently from the waistband of his trousers. Scott's own impatience took over and he peeled off the shirt, jerking the still-buttoned cuffs over his hands. Then he dragged off shoes and socks, unbelted his trousers and let them fall, stepping out of them and sliding down the one brief garment that still remained. He reached for her again, but for a moment Kati held him back. Looking at him now, standing nude before her, she realized that she had carried this picture of him in her heart for all the years between. The sight of him naked had always made her catch her breath in awe and started her pulses racing. He was so magnificent, so beautiful. Scott was like a God in the harmony of sinew and muscle, the broad shoulders and chest that tapered to a narrow waist; the satiny ripple of skin over his ribs, the slim hips and the long, powerful legs.

Scott quickly removed her bra and panties and stood gazing at her with a kind of reverence. Kati felt the color rising in her cheeks, but she didn't flinch. There was an honesty in his expression that moved her; she felt honored by his admiration as she always had—and she felt a deep sense of thankfulness that after all this time, when Scott must have seen so many other women naked like this, her body could still please his eyes.

"Kati," he murmured throatily, "I've thought of this so often, dreamed of it. I can hardly believe that it's become real at last."

"Oh, Scott."

"Stay still just like that," he begged. "Don't move. I want to go on looking at you . . . I want to touch you."

His hands drifted over her, stroking, feeling, caressing her, making Kati shiver with sensuous delight. He wove feather-light patterns across her rounded thighs that seemed to leave a trail of scorching sensation. He shaped the curve of her hips and counted the ridges of her spine, one by one, then ran his fingertips lightly over the satiny smoothness of her shoulders and down her arms to the sensitive spots at her inner elbow. He held her slender wrists, massaging the tender pulse points with his thumbs, and made tiny circles in her palms that shot sparks of fire along her veins. When his hands came up again, it was to pay homage to her breasts, weighing their soft roundness in his cupped palms. His head bent and he touched each rosy nipple with his lips.

"This is the beauty I remembered," he said in a wondering voice. "Except that you're even more beautiful now, Kati. You're the loveliest woman I have ever known."

"Scott, I . . ."

As if knowing that she would have no words to express her feelings at this declaration, he promptly covered her mouth with his in tiny, nibbling kisses. Then, lifting her in his arms, he carried her to the sofa and laid her down gently. At first he knelt on the carpet beside her as he recommenced his exploration of her body, but after a while, at Kati's urging, he stretched his full length alongside her, flesh to flesh.

Their first union was swift and frantic, born of a hungry need for each other—exciting, tumultuous and explosive. Afterward they made love more slowly, savoringly, caressing each other with a longing to reestablish the intimacy they'd once shared, the artless bold freedom that was the sweet privilege of lovers.

But their passion could not be held in check for long. It kept showing itself in wild, flaring surges, when Scott would grip her more tightly, his fingers clenched into the softness of her flesh, while his lips ravaged her mouth and his tongue thrust in to taste her essence and search every secret crevice. Kati felt his whole body trembling, and she trembled with him. When his fingers circled the rosy peaks of her breasts, arousing her to a fevered pitch, she reacted with unconscious abandonment as she used her hands to coax him to the ultimate ecstasy that her body craved. It was Scott's strength of will, much more than hers, which spun out these blissful minutes of soaring desire.

"Beautiful, beautiful Kati. Do I please you, darling Kati?"

"Oh, yes . . . yes!"

Kati felt the throbbing, pulsing heat of him against her skin as again he fought for mastery over his desire. She herself felt half wild with longing for another fusion of their bodies. When at last Scott let it happen, she gasped in relief and delight. It felt so wonderful, so right, and finally she cried out in breathless joy as she was swept upward to a mounting, breaking wave of rapture.

Scott shuddered too, and huskily murmured her name against the curve of her throat. Then they were still, their passion-moist bodies entwined and linked, held captive in echoing shivers of the glory they had achieved together. Scott kissed her tenderly, and she clung to him. Slowly, as the peace of fulfilment came to them, they drifted together toward sleep.

Chapter Eight

Kati awoke to the faint predawn chill on her skin. Scott still slept. When he gave a smothered murmur and shifted his position so as to bring her closer to him, she remained without moving. After their time of passion, his body was quiescent, his breathing soft and even. The lamp, still burning, showed her his face. Sleeping, he looked sweetly youthful, a little vulnerable, more like the younger Scott she had known before.

She regretted nothing of this night; when Scott had returned after her party it became inevitable. The flames of desire they kindled in each other could only be quenched by making love. Love? No, she wouldn't honor it with that name. They weren't in love with each other now as they had been in the old days—if Scott had ever truly loved her. Having sex, that was how she had to think of it. But the scornful term took nothing away from the ecstatic experience. Tiny quivers of delight still danced within her, and she felt a sense of deep fulfilment.

In this strange, ambivalent mood, Kati contemplated the future. During the next few weeks or even months, would there be a place for Scott in her life? It went against her deepest sense of rightness to enter into a casual affair, knowing in advance that it could not possibly lead to anything permanent. But there was nothing casual about her relationship with Scott. Perhaps her sense of emotional involvement with him now was no more than an echo of the all-embracing love she had once felt for him. Perhaps this one night together would put an end to her body's need of him, which had flamed anew the instant they came face to face again, but which, she knew now, had never truly died away. Perhaps Scott would lose interest in her after this. It might well be that what had motivated him was not so much real desire for her as the excitement of a challenge. The ugly thought brought a sudden sense of depression down upon her, and she stirred restlessly.

Scott wakened at once. He opened his eyes and blinked at her sleepily, then suddenly became alert.

"Beautiful Kati. Did I ever tell you that you're one very sexy lady?"

"And you're a . . ." She broke off as she became aware of Scott's reawakening desire. She knew that, whatever tomorrow and the time beyond tomorrow might hold for them, she didn't want Scott to stay through to the morning.

"You must get going," she said briskly.

Scott crooked his arm and glanced at his watch. "Hey, I'm not leaving yet. It's not much past three-thirty."

"Please," she said. "I want you to."

"Just like that? Don't I get to stay for breakfast?"

"No, Scott."

Lazily, his fingers circled her breast, and she felt her body respond with a surge of excitement. She pushed his hand away.

"Kati," he remonstrated. "We have some talking to do."

"You're always saying that. I don't see what we have to talk about, except at work. Let me up, please."

Not moving, he regarded her through half-closed, heavy-lidded eyes. "It's lucky I know you, Kati, or I might start to believe that you really are as hardboiled as you're trying to make out."

She began to panic. She knew how easily Scott would be able to persuade her to change her mind and let him stay. With his warm weight pressing her into the sofa cushions, feeling the ripple of his chest and shoulder muscles and his hand gently stroking her hair, her current determination would dissolve in a wave of luxurious contentment. When Scott touched his lips to her face, trailing them around the curving line of her jaw with tiny kisses, she wanted only to curl her arms about him once more, to tangle her fingers into the teak-dark hair which was tousled from their earlier passion. She twisted her face away, irritated—with Scott for persisting, and with herself for wanting his persistence.

"Leave me alone," she said, pushing him away from her.

Scott resisted momentarily. Then he gave way with a sigh, releasing his hold and raising himself on his two arms so that his torso was poised above her. His eyes glittered in the lamplight.

"Okay, then, we'll play the game your way, Kati. But next time . . ."

"You're taking a lot for granted," she interrupted.

He smiled lopsidedly, confidently, but his words were submissive. "Don't get me wrong, darling, I'm taking nothing for granted. If, after tonight, you decide that you don't want me any more, it will be my own fault. I'll have failed to please you, and left you unsatisfied. And I don't think that's true, is it?"

Not to agree would be dishonest. Pressing a hand to his chest as a warning to keep his distance, she said softly, "You were wonderful, Scott."

"And you, Kati." He laughed. "We're quite a pair, aren't we?"

In a swift movement he rose and reached for his clothes. Kati remained on the sofa, curled up, hugging a cushion. Scott dressed in her full view, casually, pulling on his briefs and trousers, then his shirt, buttoning it unhurriedly, tucking it into the waistband and zipping up. She watched him for a few moments covertly, through half-closed eyes. Then, impatient with pretense, she observed him openly, her heart beating fast at the sight of his lithe, muscular leanness.

When Kati sat up with the intention of reaching for her clothes, Scott stopped her. Sitting on the edge of the sofa he lightly trailed his fingertips down the length of her arm.

"This was how I held you in my memory at your most beautiful," he said softly. "In the afterglow of lovemaking."

A faint flush came to Kati's cheeks at his compliment, and Scott felt an even stronger impulse to take her into his arms again. He would have liked to stay with her all through the weekend in a glorious feast of lovemaking, forgetting everything else and disregarding the days, just sleeping when they needed to, and eating whatever was at hand. He felt confident that he could coax Kati into willing agreement without much difficulty. But he smothered the urge. Instead, he just held her briefly against him and touched his lips to the silky softness of her hair.

"I'll call you early," he said, with a quick grin. "Around nine? No, I'll make it ten, to give you a chance to sleep late. The only pity is that I won't be sharing the sleep with you." Another gossamer kiss on her cheek and he was striding toward the door. As Kati watched him leave she cradled herself in her arms, feeling suddenly cold and bereft.

Scott was discreet. The street door closed with only a faint click, and she didn't even hear his footsteps on the cobbles of the mews. With a sigh, she made her way upstairs to her bedroom, and slid in between the cool sheets.

The mood of ambivalence still hung over Kati when, too restless to stay in bed, she rose at seven-thirty. Her whole body sang with delight, but her mind pondered gloomily. Normally she was an incisive person, accustomed to seeing her way ahead. The idea of living for today and letting tomorrow take care of itself was anathema to her.

And yet, in her away-from-the-office relationship with Scott, doubt and uncertainty were the bottom line. No commitment, no promises . . . which was okay by her, because right now she was so confused that she didn't know *what* she wanted regarding Scott. She just wasn't capable of making the choice of whether to allow what they'd started to continue until their passion had burned itself out, or whether to call a halt at this point. What she desperately needed was time to think, space to stand back from the problem and get an objective look at it. The knowledge that in a couple of hours Scott would be calling to make plans for the weekend brought a spurt of panic. It felt as if he were crowding her, allowing her no chance for rational thinking.

The best thing, obviously, would be to simply say no to whatever Scott suggested when he called. Yet she doubted her ability to carry that through. She could claim, of course, some important prior engagement that had slipped her mind and that she'd be busy all weekend. But would Scott believe that? No way, after he'd exposed the same excuse last weekend as a lie.

Kati could guess that Scott would keep on badgering her—and that in the end she'd weakly give way. Then she'd be inches deeper into involvement with him, entangled in something it was impossible for her to control.

While she made toast and coffee for her breakfast she kept on arguing with herself. "I'm Kati Young, successful career woman, and I belong to nobody but myself. Okay, if it suits me I'll respond a little to a man, and take a little in return. But I won't give up my independence or my total freedom of choice."

It was easy to say privately, to herself. But what happened when Scott came to see her, when his virile, charismatic presence seemed to fill her home? What happened when he took her into his arms and kissed her? Would she find the will to resist?

A feeling of panic washed over her once more. Her only hope was to get away somewhere, she decided, out of Scott's reach. The moment the idea struck her, she went to the phone and dialed a familiar number. "Fay . . . it's me, Kati. Hi, how are you? I hope I didn't wake you."

"What, after eight o'clock! I'm always up by seven. Harry and I were just doing the breakfast dishes."

"Thanks a lot for the birthday present," Kati said.

"Was the design okay? I could change it if it's not."

"It's fine, I really love it. Fay, I've just had a thought. . . . As it happens I have a free weekend, and . . ."

"And you're going to pay us that weekend visit you've been promising for so long. That's wonderful. Listen, it's going to be a lovely day, so get here just as soon as you can. We'll have a picnic lunch by the river, and I'll get Harry to call The Star and Garter hotel and book a table for dinner this evening. How's that?"

"You'll be spoiling me," Kati objected, feeling guilty because she didn't deserve this enthusiastic welcome from Fay when in reality her main reason for coming was to avoid Scott.

"Well, if we do spoil you," Fay said with a soft chuckle, "it'll only be because we want to make sure you'll come again."

"How did your meeting go last night?" Kati asked her.

"Splendidly. I'll tell you about it when I see you. And you can tell us all about your birthday party. We'll expect you in time for coffee, if not before."

Kati still felt mean as she threw some clothes into a small suitcase, then checked around that everything was secure before she left. She scribbled a note for Mrs. Barker, who was due soon to clear up after the party, and carried her case out to her car.

Chloe Grainger stuck her head out of next door's bedroom window. She was still wearing a negligee. "Off for the weekend, Kati?"

"That's right. I'm going to stay with friends."

"Lucky you. Josh and I can't make up our minds whether to drive to the coast or have a lazy day at home." She yawned. "I'm still not properly awake yet. That was a fantastic party, Kati."

"Thanks. It went pretty well."

"Nice crowd you work with," Chloe went on. "It must be great being on a magazine, where it's all happening." She herself worked in a lawyer's office and was always grumbling that her job was the pits for dullness. "I liked the look of that new boss of yours. Some guy." She jerked her head to indicate her husband, who was still presumably in bed. "Josh will have some competition if I ever bump into Scott Drummond when I'm on my own. Have fun, Kati."

The weekend with the Pembertons couldn't be called a real success. Kati, knowing that it was entirely her fault, kept trying to get herself together and be a pleasant guest, but she felt too distraught. Fay obviously sensed that something was wrong, but after a couple of probing questions she mercifully left well enough alone.

Kati's mind returned to Scott constantly, and she kept wondering what he was doing now, at this very moment. What had he thought when he'd found her not at home? Presumably he'd have tried to make contact with her later in the morning, but when he couldn't, what then? Thwarted in his plans, he might have fixed some other date—perhaps with that sexy blonde he'd been with the other night at the restaurant. Or some other woman, identity unknown. Oh, to hell with him, she thought, angry with herself. She turned to Harry with some flip remark about a news item on TV. But she was brittle, and she knew it showed.

She stayed at the Pembertons' bungalow at Richmond for Sunday night, too, only arriving home Monday morning in time to summon a taxi to transport the loaned tableware used at her party. At work there were meetings scheduled all morning with various staff members. She was discussing forward plans with Tim and another feature writer, Una Meredith, when her phone rang. It came as a shock to hear Scott on the line.

"Kati, my office, please. Now!" He sounded grim.

"I can't for the moment. I'm tied up."

"I said *now*. Your secretary can rearrange your schedule."

She felt rebellious. But, as Scott had reminded her caustically the other day, he had the right to demand her presence at work any time he chose, as much right as Victor Channon himself. She apologized to her two feature writers, adopting a rueful smile. "Sorry, you guys, I have to leave you. Boss's orders."

"Was that Scott Drummond?" asked Una.

Kati nodded. "Uh huh. Sandra will buzz you later to fix a time for us to continue this."

"That guy is certainly chucking his weight around," said Tim thoughtfully, as they all three rose and headed for the door. Amazingly, Kati found herself defending Scott. "He's taken on a tough assignment, so he can't waste time pussyfooting around."

Up on the executive floor Scott's secretary waved Kati straight in, eyeing her curiously as she went past.

"Shut the door, Kati," said Scott in a level, dangerous tone. He didn't invite her to sit, but came around the desk to confront her, just two feet away. His chiseled face was set in a mask of tightly held control, but his blue eyes scorched her with cold fire. "Where the hell were you all weekend?"

Kati wished that she was sitting down. Her legs felt suddenly boneless. But to take a chair now would be a telltale sign of weakness.

"You want to know what I was doing on my own time?" she asked, injecting sarcasm into her voice.

"I want to know why the devil you stood me up."

"You seem to be implying that we'd made a definite date."

"Damn right we did. I was to call you at ten on Saturday morning."

"I remember you saying that you'd call me," Kati retorted. "I don't remember promising to be home at that time." What was happening? she thought despairingly. She'd never wanted to quarrel with Scott like this. It was his arrogant attitude that needled her. That, plus the regrettable fact that she had no real case to argue.

Scott's breath hissed with anger. "You still haven't explained where you were all weekend. Are you asking me to believe that you already had something fixed beforehand? If so, why the deuce didn't you tell me about it?"

"Could the reason be," she inquired witheringly, "that it isn't any business of yours?"

"Not my business?"

"That's right, Scott—not your business."

His mouth tightened. "But after Friday night . . ."

"Friday night was Friday night. This is Monday morning, and we're at the office, remember. I seem to recall you laying down the law to me about how I should separate my private life from my professional life. Compartmentalize, wasn't that the word you used?"

Scott felt a blaze of fury that almost scared him with its intensity. Friday night the situation with Kati had looked wonderfully settled. He'd accepted the way she'd suddenly bundled him out of her home in the middle of the night as just one of the unaccountable oddities of the feminine makeup. The weekend had stretched before him, radiant with promise. On his short walk back to the houseboat through the night-empty streets, he'd formulated wonderful plans for the two of them. A leisurely cruise up-river, dawdling through Putney and Richmond and on past Teddington lock, stopping off for lunch at some picturesque riverside inn, then on to the lovely higher reaches of the Thames—Windsor, Maidenhead, Henley. Finally, in the long, lingering twilight of a glorious May evening, tying-up for the night in a quiet spot. Perhaps a swim, or a stroll along the towpath; then dinner *à deux* on board—something simple to prepare but very special. And then . . . it would be a glorious repetition of the previous night, even better. They would make passionate love all night through, with only the gentle lapping of water against the hull to break the night silence, and Kati's sweet moans of pleasure. And after a short sleep they'd wake to a lazy Sunday morning, starting with a huge breakfast of bacon and eggs to satisfy their ravenous appetites. They'd continue cruising, as far as Oxford, perhaps, before eventually turning and gliding homeward on the placid river.

A fantasy. He had often fantasized about Kati, sometimes in graphic detail. But then Kati had been three thousand miles away, and unattainable. Now, Scott happily believed, they'd come together again.

Arriving back at the *Pagan* after leaving her in the early hours, he'd not wanted to sleep, so he'd put on a Beethoven sonata and sat watching the pearly light of dawn rippling across the quiet water. He had felt a deep sense of contentment with life, an inner glow of excitement. He wasn't thinking far ahead into the future; a weekend spent with Kati was enough to go on.

Scott had waited impatiently for ten o'clock, finally giving way to his taut nerves and dialing her number ten minutes ahead of time. No answer. Well, maybe she'd slipped out to the shops nearby. The next ten minutes had seemed interminable, but he'd forced himself to wait until the hour. Then he'd dialed again— and again, no answer.

After three more attempts at short intervals, he'd walked around to Kati's cottage in the mews. Hope soared when he heard the sound of a vacuum cleaner from within. Maybe her phone was out of order.

But it wasn't Kati who'd answered his ring. A middle-aged woman with an ample figure and frizzed hair peered around the door at him inquiringly.

"Is Miss Young home, please?" he asked, with a sinking feeling in his stomach.

"Sorry, she isn't here."

"When will she be back?"

"I don't rightly know. I've only just arrived. Normally I do for her just Mondays and Thursdays, but she had a party last night, so I'm . . ."

"Yes, I know." Scott spoke brusquely, and the woman frowned. He went on placatingly, "I mean, I was at her party last night. Do you mean that Miss Young just wasn't home when you arrived? Might she be back any minute?"

"No, she's gone away for the weekend." The woman dipped into the pocket of her flowered apron. "She left me this."

Whether or not she was intending him to read the note, Scott took it from her hand and scanned it rapidly. *Sorry not to be here, Mrs. Barker, but I'll be away for the weekend. I've left your money on the bureau, but if you have to spend extra time clearing up the mess, I'll settle with you next week. Kati Young.*

Scott's mouth tasted bitter from disappointment and anger. "Have you any idea where she might have gone?" he asked the woman.

"How could I have? You've seen for yourself what she said."

In his anxiety Scott took out his wallet and extracted a couple of banknotes. "I thought you might have some idea," he said persuasively.

Mrs. Barker, indifferent till now, became hostile. "I wouldn't tell you, mister, even if I did know. Miss Young is very good to me, she's real thoughtful and considerate. She doesn't expect me to go blabbing my mouth to any Tom, Dick or Harry who asks about her."

"But I'm a friend of hers."

"In that case," she said, with sudden shrewd assurance, "Miss Young would have told you herself if she wanted you to know where she was spending the weekend. I've no time to stand talking on the doorstep, so good-day to you." With that, the door was firmly shut on him.

Turning away in helpless fury, Scott saw a face he recognized at the next door window. He strolled over, smiling, and Chloe Grainger opened the casement, a yellow duster in her hand.

"Hi there. How are you this morning?" After an exchange of pleasantries, Scott went on, "Kati didn't happen to mention it last night, but I gather from her cleaning lady that she's gone away for the weekend."

"Yes, that's right. I saw her leaving at around nine-thirty, and we had a little chat."

Scott's hopes rose, though what he proposed doing if he did discover where she'd gone, he still didn't know. Guessing that Kati would take it amiss if he disclosed too much to her neighbor about their relationship, he decided to be circumspect. With something between a smile and a frown, he said, "It's one of those stupid things, but a work problem has come up and I need to get in touch with Kati right away. Do you happen to know how I can find her?"

"She's staying with friends," Chloe said. "She didn't tell me where."

"And she didn't say *which* friends? Could it have been any of the people who were here last night?"

"Sorry, I haven't the foggiest."

Concealing his disappointment, Scott gave an elaborate shrug. "Oh, well, it can't be helped. Thanks, anyway."

He'd had one hell of a weekend. There were times when he'd felt like strangling Kati; other times, more frequently, when he'd yearned for her so much that it had physically hurt. He'd grown angry and impatient with himself for letting Kati get to him like that. But anger and impatience hadn't reduced the intensity of his longing.

And neither did it now as they stood confronting each other in his office. While he burned with rage, Kati remained looking cool, poised and unruffled; he suspected that she was enjoying herself right now, taunting him by throwing his own words back in his face.

"I meant what I said about separating our private and professional lives," he said in a clipped tone. "If you'd been halfway straight with me, Kati, I wouldn't be forced to raise a private matter at the office."

At long last her cool broke. "You have the gall to claim that *I'm* not playing straight with *you*," she cried in outrage.

"It's true, you aren't. When I left you in the early hours of Saturday morning, you let me believe that we'd be seeing each other over the weekend."

"I didn't say . . ."

"You lied, by implication. You got rid of me by

agreeing that I should call you later to make our plans, when all the time you were aiming to duck out on me."

"I wasn't. I didn't know then that . . ."

Scott pounced. "So you dreamed it up after I left. Why, Kati? Was it that you saw a chance to put me in hell from some twisted idea of revenge?"

"No, you're wrong." She scooped back a strand of hair and looked at Scott puzzledly. Then she murmured in an uncertain voice, "In hell?"

"Yes, I've been through hell this weekend. That's what you intended, wasn't it?"

Kati shook her head in silence. She felt shaken by Scott's words, by the tone of his voice and the pained looked in his eyes. Revenge had been the very last thing in her mind. All she'd wanted was to get away from him, from the will-sapping strength of his virile personality.

Yet Kati couldn't bring herself to admit that. She wasn't about to confess to him that she had suffered just as keenly over the weekend as he could have done, and that she deeply regretted her impetuous flight now. To do so would amount to complete capitulation to Scott, which was out of the question. Their relationship, if it were to continue at all, had to be on the basis of free equals. And the sooner she spelled that out, the better.

"It seems to me," she said, forcing a touch of lightness into her words, "that you're exaggerating more than somewhat in talking about going through hell. Okay, so we had sex together after my party, and you decided that it would be nice to follow through with an idyllic weekend. You didn't like it one bit that I wasn't prepared to go along with your plans. But the only casualty was your male ego, Scott, which got badly dented—and it's about time it did!"

"Have you finished?" he inquired coldly, only the bright brilliance of his eyes betraying his anger.

"Just so long as you understand."

"Understand what?" he demanded. "Did something better crop up for the weekend? Maybe your married boyfriend found a way to duck out on his wife and family in order to spend a couple of nights with you. Where did you go, Kati? A hotel at Brighton, registered as Mr. and Mrs. Smith?"

"That's a shabby thing to suggest."

"Shabby would be right up Wheatley's street."

Kati was astonished at the venom in his tone. "Why do you hate Robin so much?" she demanded.

"Hate him?" Scott uttered a short bark of laughter. "Hate is a positive emotion, Kati. It implies a subject who's worthy of that much concern. Wheatley is feeble, a nothing. I'm only surprised that you can see anything at all in the guy. Or is he a better stud than he looks?"

She was shaking with anger now. "I've no wish to stop here and listen to this sort of thing."

"Good. I was just about to say that you'd better get back to your desk and do some work."

Kati raised her chin aggressively. "You can cut out that tone of voice. I'm not some kid who joined the firm as a junior last week. I'll remind you that if you hadn't sent for me—for what turned out to be a purely personal discussion—I'd have been at my desk all this time, instead of wasting it up here."

"Okay, you've made your point." Scott's voice was like chips of ice. "The interview is over."

"That's not the only thing that's over." She strode to the door and wrenched it open and strode out, banging it shut behind her. She didn't care that Scott's secretary stared at her with intrigued surprise.

Outside in the luxurious hush of the executive corridor, Kati found that she was trembling violently, and she dodged into the nearest washroom. It took several moments before she got herself together enough to continue on her way back to her office.

Chapter Nine

It was a good thing, Kati told herself repeatedly all day Monday, a very good thing indeed that the blazing row with Scott had happened. The way things had stood between them before, there was no end in sight of their personal relationship. That row had brought about a clear-cut break without days and weeks of intellectual agonizing. Their renewed affair, which had been inevitable since the first moment they'd met again, had been short and sweet. Now, the state of armed truce was on again, only even more so. She could imagine that future encounters with Scott over work were going to be highly unpleasant.

There was, in fact, one coming up the following morning, though mercifully she wouldn't be alone with him. Scott had called a conference of magazine editors, requisitioning the company boardroom for the purpose. Probably, she thought bitterly, he hoped to intimidate them all with the grandiose surroundings. It was just the sort of way he operated.

On Tuesday, when Kati arrived at the executive floor a few minutes before the designated time, she found a cluster of her colleagues waiting in the lobby outside the boardroom—all of them, she noted with surprise, women. Each one of them was the editor-in-chief of a magazine catering to women. There was considerable speculation as to what this could mean, but nobody could come up with an explanation.

Dee turned up a couple of minutes later. Though she had come by taxi straight from the airport, her grooming was as perfect as ever. She wore a flowing coat-dress in an exuberant shade of coral. She had rolled up the full sleeves, and silver bracelets jangled at her wrists.

"You look happy," Kati greeted her. "How was Rome? Can we take it that you had a good trip?"

"Fantastic. Hi, everyone! Kati, how did your birthday party go?"

"It was great, Dee. And thanks a ton for that gorgeous nightie. I feel like a million dollars in it."

"More to the point, sweetie, I bet you look extremely sexy in it—which was the object of the exercise." She raised her eyebrows in query. "So have you put it to the test yet?"

Kati evaded answering by saying, with a glance at her watch, "What are we all waiting for? Hadn't we better go in?"

There were murmurs of assent, and Dee flung open the double doors to the boardroom with a flamboyant gesture. Scott, who stood at the head of the long mahogany table, was sorting through some papers. Kati watched as he glanced up and, seeing Dee, greeted her with one of his most charming smiles.

"Lady Dorothy! So you managed to get back in time. I'm so glad."

"I wish you'd dispense with my title," she told him, laughing softly. "I'm known around here as Dee to friend and foe alike."

The women were clustered in the doorway now, listening with astonishment to this cheerful exchange. "Please come in, ladies," said Scott, "and find yourselves chairs." To Dee he added with a grin, "Which category do I fit into—friend or foe?"

Dee smiled serenely as she took the seat at his right hand. "Figure it out for yourself, Scott."

Kati chose her own position with care. Not too near Scott, but not so far away down the long table that he would know she was putting a distance between them. As he glanced around the assembled editors it seemed to Kati that his gaze lingered on her momentarily, with a chilling expression in those blue eyes.

"All here, I see. So we'll begin." He sat down himself, and adopted a relaxed posture. Kati had to concede that Scott befitted the dignity of the high-backed, leather-studded chair which would normally be Victor Channon's seat when he chaired meetings of Universal Publications' board of directors. If only he weren't so compellingly attractive, she thought with an inward sigh, then she might be able to conquer her obsessive feelings for him.

"This is an informal meeting," Scott went on, "so I haven't brought my secretary with me to take notes. The reason I've asked you all along this morning is this—I've decided to combine all the periodicals published by U.P. that are specifically aimed at women into a separate group within the organization. It's my intention to have regular get-togethers like this for us all to chew over common problems. I'm aware, of course, that your magazines represent a wide range of interests, and each has its special focus. But obviously the similarities are much greater than the differences."

"I don't agree with that statement at all." Kati was surprised to hear the sound of her own voice. So, apparently, was everyone else. They were all staring at her.

"Perhaps," Scott invited, "you'd care to enlarge on that, Kati."

"I'd have thought I'd said it all." Oh, heavens, she hadn't intended that tone of sarcasm. "You can't lump our magazines together just like that, as if women all think and act alike. Women have as many different, individual viewpoints as you'd find in the male half of the population. It's only in the very loosest sense that women's tastes and interests can be categorized, to the extent that certain women opt to read one magazine and other women another. But those 'categories' of women are poles apart in their outlook. To take two extremes, consider *Rendezvous* and *Women At Home*. I'm not knocking Elaine's readers in any way when I say that they're a totally different species from my readers. Hers are very domesticated, and their world revolves around their husbands and families. Right, Elaine?"

The editor of *Women At Home*, a brisk, gray-haired woman with a figure verging on the ample, nodded vigorously. "Right on the nail, Kati. Eighty-seven percent married, seventy-three percent with families. Far fewer than the national average have a job outside the home."

"Compare that with the readers of *Rendezvous*," Kati went on. "Mine are younger, less likely to be married with children. But even when they do fit into the wife/mother category, they also have careers to which they are dedicated, and which they expect to be taken just as seriously as their husbands' own careers."

"They're still women," Scott insisted, "with women's interests."

"Women's interests!" Kati snapped scornfully. "Would you dare to refer to men's interests in the same all-embracing way? You yourself are a highly educated man, Scott, a man who is intelligent and articulate, and who holds a top-level executive position. So would you expect to be lumped together sweepingly with bartenders, construction workers and men who drive trucks? I suggest that you share more common interests with the women readers of *Rendezvous* than with men in general."

"Kati has a point," said Dee. "Women have emerged from the domestic ghetto, Scott. First and last, they're *people*. Being a woman is almost incidental in this case."

"Not to the readers of *Style*, surely?" Scott's tone to Dee was affable, though he'd thrown Kati a sharp, nettled glance when she had intervened. "I'd have thought that fashion consciousness was a universal attribute of womanhood, Dee."

"Huh!" Kati exclaimed in disgust. "I've never yet met a man who wasn't just as anxious as any woman to project the right image of himself."

She could feel the heat of anger building between them, and it spelled danger. She knew, though, that if Scott retaliated again, she'd go right on with the battle. As it was, he said in a shrugging tone. "Those are interesting points you've put forward, Kati. What do the rest of you think?"

It emerged, with a certain amount of iffing and butting, and wary deference to the man who was their new boss, that they all agreed with Kati and Dee.

Kati, with great reluctance, had to admire the easy way that Scott capitulated. "What did I expect?" he asked ruefully. "One man amongst eight women." Fleetingly, he caught Kati's eye, and added hastily, with a grin, "No, I'll rephrase that . . . one administrative-type person among eight editors. So—let's start with a different premise. We're discussing a group of magazines, of widely differing appeal, whose single common thread is that they are aimed at women. Right?"

"Right," they murmured around the table.

"Okay, then. Now let's explore the field of operations and consider whether U.P. is ignoring a section of the potential market, or maybe overlapping somewhere in a wasteful way, to the detriment of sales. I'm also going to ask each of you to give some indication of future plans for your magazine. That way we shall all have a clearer idea of where U.P. is heading in the overall trend of the magazine market."

After that, the talk ranged far and wide, though whenever an editor started veering off on a favorite hobby horse, Scott skillfully brought her back on track. Kati kept a low profile, scared of betraying herself. Whenever Scott asked directly for her opinion, she gave it to him straight, but at the same time she tried to avoid being overly provocative.

Coffee was brought in and Scott suggested that they should take five. Everybody stood up to stretch their legs, and Kati took the chance to ask Dee more about her trip to Rome.

"So it went as well as you hoped?"

"Better!" Dee's green eyes sparkled, and she added, "Incidentally, some of those Italians are so charming and sexy, you wouldn't believe it."

Scott was coming toward them, bearing his cup of coffee. He must have caught Dee's last words, and he inquired with an ironic lift of one eyebrow, "You wouldn't be so old-fashionedly feminine as to be discussing men?"

"Why not? Equal but different, that's our maxim. Right, Kati? And *vive la différence*, I say."

Scott raised his coffee cup in a salute. *"Vive la différence!* How was Rome, Dee?"

"It went fine, Scott. In fact, Signore Bartorelli was so delighted with my visit that he's talking of stepping up his advertising in *Style* in quite a big way."

"Terrific." Kati felt the weight of Scott's eyes in a challenging look before he glanced at his watch, and said, "We'll be resuming in a few moments."

As he walked away, Dee's eyes followed him thoughtfully. "Some guy, that."

"If you go for that sort of ruthlessness."

"Which you don't?"

"No, I don't. It isn't necessary to be devoid of human feeling to run a successful commercial operation."

Dee's gaze returned to Scott. "He might be one tough hombre, but devoid of human feeling? Never!" She drank down the remains of her coffee. "Now tell me about your birthday party. I was thinking about you Friday evening. In the odd spare moment," she added with a candid grin.

Kati reflected uneasily. Dee was certain to hear about Scott turning up at the party, so it would be best to tell her now. "As a matter of fact," she said with assumed casualness, "Scott Drummond showed up, bearing roses. Uninvited, need I add."

"Good lord, that was a surprise. He must have heard some office talk about it being your birthday, and thought it was a chance to get on a better footing with you." Dee chuckled. "You showed him this morning, though, that you aren't to be won over with a bunch of roses."

"He deserved everything he got," Kati insisted. "We can do without that sort of patronizing attitude toward women."

"Men just can't help it, poor darlings. It's their way of making a final stand behind the crumbling bastions of masculine superiority. Still, Kati, I thought you exaggerated more than somewhat in denying the existence of any kind of common denominator among women."

"You backed me up," Kati protested.

"Of course I did. We women have to stick together when it comes to the crunch. All the same, I reckon that what Scott said made a lot of sense."

"Thanks a bunch," Kati said sourly.

"You'd think so too," Dee said, "if you could bring yourself to think objectively for one minute."

"What's that supposed to mean?"

"How many times have you and I condemned the slackness and sloppy thinking that goes on at U.P.? Scott Drummond is trying to do something about it, for heaven's sake. So you should be supporting him, Kati, not trying to thwart him at every turn. I don't know what's come over you, I really don't."

Put on the spot by her friend, Kati muttered, "I just find his high-handed attitude too much to take."

Dee laughed. "That's your privilege. Personally, I find him one gorgeous hunk of man."

The more Kati thought about her performance in the boardroom, the more she knew that Dee had been right. She *had* overstated her case. Perhaps one good thing had resulted from the public clash she'd had with him. No one at U.P. was going to suspect that there was any kind of private relationship between Scott Drummond and Kati Young.

All the same, Kati cautioned herself to be careful. She'd been skating on thin ice, and next time the ice might crack and she'd find herself floundering in freezing water. Scott was a formidable opponent. If ever, as a last resort, she needed to go over his head and take her fight for the future of *Rendezvous* direct to the topmost brass at U.P., her case would be substantially weakened if it were known that she'd been shooting off her mouth in an unreasonable way. Instead, she had to appear to go along with whatever changes Scott made, so long as no ethical principles were involved. In fact, it would make life altogether pleasanter if she could bring herself to acknowledge that at least *some* of Scott's innovations might be beneficial.

Kati was lunching that day with a freelance writer who'd submitted a very snazzy article on the subject of test-tube babies. Kati liked her dry humor and hoped that she would become a regular contributor to *Rendezvous*. It was almost three o'clock before she returned to the office, having tossed around half a dozen topics as the basis for future articles.

Robin was waiting in her secretary's small outer office. He wasn't talking to Sandra, but stood at the window, staring out moodily. He swung around as Kati entered, and his face looked stormy.

"I've been waiting for you for ages," he burst out in an aggressive tone.

Kati was astonished; this was so unlike Robin. But she kept her cool and said serenely, "I'm quite sure that Sandra told you I'd probably be late back from lunch."

"Well, she did. But what time do you call this?" he muttered.

"I call it three o'clock." Kati went through to her own office and motioned him to follow. She closed the door firmly behind him. "Robin," she said dangerously, "don't ever speak to me like that again in front of my secretary, or any other member of staff."

"Huh!" he sneered. "I won't be in a position to talk to you any way at all for much longer, will I?"

She stared at him, mystified. "What do you mean by that remark?"

"As if you didn't know."

"I haven't the faintest idea," she said sharply. "So please enlighten me."

Robin hesitated, frowning. "I'm referring to the fact, no doubt unimportant to you, that I'm being given the sack."

A shock jolted through her. "Given the sack? What's this all about, Robin?"

"Don't pretend," he said bitterly. "It's not some idle rumor I've picked up, Kati. I've had it from the horse's mouth, spelled out to me in words of one syllable."

Gripped by cold dismay, Kati was again reduced to echoing his words. "The horse's mouth?"

"Scott Bigshot Drummond, who else?"

"You mean . . . he's fired you?" Kati asked faintly.

"As good as. Apparently the ad manager of *The Weekly Gardener* has applied for early retirement, and I'm being transferred there. What a come-down, after *Rendezvous*."

Anger was beginning to burn in Kati. "When did this happen?" she demanded.

"Just now. I had a summons to Drummond's office at one o'clock, and he threw it at my head. He spared me exactly fifteen minutes of his valuable time. I came down to find you, but you'd already gone to lunch, and I've been waiting ever since."

"I see!" Kati drummed agitated fingers on her desk. "What reason did he give you, Robin?"

"He gave me a load of bull about my results not being good enough, which is totally unfair. I tried to point out that *Rendezvous*'s ad revenue has been improving slowly and surely, but that it takes time to generate more orders. It's a lengthy process. He just wouldn't listen, though. He tried to make out that I'm not suited to this job. He said that I'm not aggressive enough."

Kati's fury was mounting by the second. Her impulse was to jump to her feet and charge upstairs to confront Scott. But first she had to extract the whole story from Robin. *The Weekly Gardener* was one of U.P.'s hobby magazines that were published from a branch office at Ilford, in London's northern outskirts.

"Would it really be a case of demotion, Robin?" she asked.

"Not cashwise," he said sulkily. "Drummond said that my salary won't be affected. But it's a terrible slap in the face, all the same, to be chucked out of here into the backwoods. And I'll be miles away from you, Kati."

No bad thing, that last, she reflected. But only momentarily. Just who the heck did Scott think he was, throwing his weight around without so much as consulting her? She flicked the switch of her intercom and spoke to Sandra.

"Tell Mr. Drummond that I want to see him right away," she said crisply.

"Why are you seeing him?" asked Robin, eyeing her suspiciously as she switched off.

"I'm not taking this lying down, Robin," she told him. "It's time that Scott Drummond was told a few home truths."

He gave her a look of wistful hope. "Is it really true that you didn't know about this, Kati?"

"I said so, didn't I?"

He nodded sheepishly. "I guess I sort of took it for granted that you'd been involved. After all, you are the editor-in-chief."

"Maybe I won't be for much longer, if things go on like this," she muttered darkly.

"You mean . . ."

"I was just making an observation." Her intercom buzzed, and she answered. "Yes, Sandra?"

"Mr. Drummond says he can fit you in right now, Kati, if you go up immediately. Otherwise, he won't have a vacant slot until tomorrow morning."

So Scott had managed to turn her demand to see him into a summons to his presence. Darn him, she thought furiously, and felt even more determined to let him have a piece of her mind.

"Tell him two minutes, Sandra," she instructed her secretary grimly.

"Shall I wait here?" said Robin.

"If you want to."

Kati dived into her washroom to check her face and hair before setting off. Robin had become almost incidental in her mind. This was a battle between herself and Scott . . . a battle she was determined to win.

She entered the outer office of his suite with all the

fury of an avenging angel, but she was obliged to wait while Scott finished a phone call. Only then did his secretary announce Kati and give her permission to enter. Scott was seated behind his big desk jotting down some notes, and he silently signaled to her to take a seat while he went on writing. If he imagined that this off-hand treatment was going to reduce her to a state of quivering nerves, Kati fumed, he could think again.

At length, Scott laid down his pen and looked up at her. "What can I do for you, Kati? It sounded urgent."

"You know damn well what it's about—Robin Wheatley."

Scott's dark eyebrows lifted in ironic amusement. "So he ran whining to you. Typical."

Kati balled her hands into tight fists, clinging to her temper. "It's just about the meanest trick you could have played, Scott, getting rid of Robin like that. What would the board of directors think, I wonder, if they got to hear that you were misusing your authority for vindictive reasons?"

"You're amazing, Kati, you know that?" Scott subjected her to a steady, puzzled look. "How do you figure that by replacing Wheatley I'm being vindictive?"

"Okay, I'll spell it out. You've decided that Robin and I have something going, so you're aiming to bring it to an end by relocating him to another office that's miles away from me."

"Fascinating." Scott's challenging gaze held hers. "And tell me, Kati, *is* there something going between you and Wheatley? I've never been quite sure."

"Either way," she retorted, "it's entirely beside the point."

"So you still won't give me a straight answer. In which case, I'm forced to make deductions from the available evidence." Scott looked thoughtful. "What should I surmise from the fact that you've come rushing up here to fight Wheatley's battles for him?"

"I'm not . . ." she began indignantly, then paused and conceded, "well, I guess you could put it that way to some extent. But the chief issue is, I want to know what the heck you thought you were up to, Scott, making a major personnel change on my magazine without referring to me first."

"*Your* magazine? It's very touching that you should feel so intimately involved with your job, Kati. But *Rendezvous* is hardly your personal property."

"It's my hard work that has turned it into a successful magazine," she riposted.

"Granted—on the creative side. But you don't control the other aspects of publishing *Rendezvous* . . . publicity, distribution and advertisements. Or do you imagine that these things should also come under the editor-in-chief's wing?"

Kati took a deep breath to keep her anger in check. "All I'm saying is that I ought to have been consulted before a change of ad manager was made."

"I see. And conversely, if it were my intention to replace the editor-in-chief of a magazine, you consider that I should first consult with the advertisement manager?"

"Well . . . no."

"I'm relieved to hear it."

Kati brooded rebelliously for a few moments before slightly giving ground. "Perhaps 'consult' was the wrong word for me to use. But you could at least have informed me of your intention in advance."

"Your dignity was affronted at learning the news from Wheatley himself?"

"As it happens, yes. It made me look a fool, not knowing anything about it. But aside from my dignity, if you'd told me in advance, it would have given me a chance to argue Robin's case with you before it was too late."

"And you're saying that you'd have argued for Wheatley's retention on *Rendezvous*?"

"Naturally."

"Why naturally? Do you really consider him the best man for the job?"

"You'll never find anyone more dedicated," she said loyally. "Robin has given the job everything he's got."

Scott inclined his head in acknowledgment. "Unfortunately, everything he's got doesn't amount to much. That guy was a square peg in a round hole. You know it just as well as I do."

"I don't agree," she countered, wishing that her loyalty to Robin didn't go against her candid judgment.

Scott picked up his pen again and absently stabbed it on his jot pad. "The way I see it, there are two explanations for your attitude, Kati. One is that you're trying to protect Wheatley's job from purely personal motives. The other is that you prefer to have a weak man as the ad manager of *Rendezvous*—a man whom you can easily control—rather than someone with real driving force, who, by definition, would be difficult to handle." He looked at her questioningly. "Perhaps the answer is a combination of the two."

"That's ridiculous."

"Is it? Let's examine both propositions. When I asked you just now if there was anything between you and Wheatley, you refused to deny it."

"Because it's none of your business."

Scott stirred restlessly in his chair. "None of my business? You really believe that, Kati?"

"I wouldn't have said it if I didn't."

His dark eyes burned into her, and she longed to admit the truth, that Robin didn't mean a thing to her except that she had a kind of protective feeling toward him, and that anything in the nature of an affair with him was totally unthinkable. But she remained silent, gripped by a strange sense of vulnerability. The fact that Scott wasn't certain how things stood between her and Robin gave her a kind of weapon against him.

"So let's consider my second suggestion," he went

on, tossing his pen aside with a gesture of impatience. "Are you scared of the prospect of having a really dynamic salesman as the ad manager?"

"Don't be silly," she snapped.

"Is it so silly, Kati? Okay, so you're doing a damn fine job editing *Rendezvous,* I'm not disputing that. But it's been a cozy number for you, hasn't it, having the backing of a loyal team of staff who all seem to think that you're the queen bee? Plus a tame ad manager who's too doting and too weak to challenge you on any issue."

"I happen to believe in an atmosphere of harmony," she said, choosing to ignore the slur on Robin. "What's wrong with that?"

"Harmony is okay—up to a point. But it isn't harmony that makes the corporate wheels spin around, Kati. Everyone needs a challenge in their job, to keep them up to the mark. If you had an ad manager who was as good at his job as you are at yours, there'd be sparks flying every time your interests didn't coincide. Which would be often."

"And that's supposed to be healthy?"

"Definitely. Because between the two of you, each battling for your own area of interest, you'd hammer out a policy that was best for the magazine. Believe me, Kati, it works. Now do you begin to see why I'm shifting Wheatley?"

With her hostility in no way diminished, she looked him straight in the eye, and said forcefully, "If what you say about Robin is true, how come you rate him as suitable for *The Weekly Gardener?*"

Scott's lips curved in a taunting smile. "You think I'm being too softhearted giving him that job?"

"You're twisting my words. I was merely pointing out that the argument you've been putting up is just so much hot air. The reason you've moved Robin is nothing but vindictiveness, right?"

"Wrong. *The Weekly Gardener* is in a totally different category from *Rendezvous*. It's been on the market for decades, and it has rock steady sales, with the result that advertisers clamor for the available space. A forceful ad manager would be the wrong choice there. Instead it needs a man who's content to jog along quietly just maintaining friendly contact with the clients, and keeping everyone happy. In other words, someone like Wheatley. The job at *Rendezvous* is far too much of a hot seat for a timid type like him."

Kati was making a conscious effort to resist the logic of Scott's reasoning. Even so, she knew uneasily that she hadn't a leg to stand on in supporting Robin. Suppose—as it had crossed her mind on the way up to see Scott—she were to make an issue of it and appeal directly to the personnel chief of Universal Publications, or even to Victor Channon himself? The very most she could hope to achieve was a soothing apology, and the knowledge that Scott would be mildly reprimanded for not handling matters as diplomatically as he might have done. Otherwise, they would back him to the hilt in his decision to replace Robin. So she had failed; she was powerless. A sense of bitter frustration washed over her as she rose to her feet.

"There's no point my staying here arguing with you," she said stiffly. "I'd better get back to my office."

"Is Wheatley skulking there, waiting to see how you get on?" Scott hazarded.

Kati cursed herself for flushing a deep red, giving Scott confirmation of his taunt.

"I'm sorry you'll have to disappoint the poor mutt," Scott went on. "But console yourself that he won't feel disappointed for long—at least, not as far as his job is concerned. Once he's established at *The Weekly Gardener*, he'll soon discover that I'm right, and he'll probably even feel grateful to me."

"If it's gratitude you're after at U.P.," she blazed, "you'll have a mighty long wait."

Scott also rose to his feet and came around the desk

to join her. "You still don't understand, do you, Kati? Gratitude isn't important. In doing a job like the one I've been given here, a lot of unpopular decisions have to be taken. Some people are going to be pleased, a lot more are going to be resentful . . . initially. It's only when they begin to see my policies paying off—to everyone's benefit—that they'll come around to my way of thinking."

"Except for the ones you throw out on their ear," she replied caustically.

"That hasn't happened so far, and I hope it won't be necessary. When my plans are in full operation there'll be a need for *more* staff at U.P., not less."

"Sure of yourself, aren't you?"

"Aren't *you?*" he challenged. "It's a trait that tends to go with strength of character."

"I hope I have the humility to admit when I'm in the wrong," she retorted.

Scott threw back his head and laughed. "Humility from you? That's something I have to see." His voice changed. "Before you go, how about dinner with me this evening?"

"No, thank you."

"Lunch tomorrow?"

"Is that an order?" she queried icily.

"No, it's an invitation."

"Then I decline your invitation. I have better things to do with my time."

Watching her turn and walk out of his office, Scott was gripped by a mixture of depresssion and irritation. Damn it all, why did Kati have to be so hellishly difficult? Was she really incapable of seeing that he had a job to do and that it would be dishonest of him not to carry through on decisions which he knew to be right? It was blatantly obvious that Robin Wheatley was a misfit at *Rendezvous* and that to a large degree the magazine's financial problems could be blamed on him.

The man was totally lacking in drive; he didn't have that special blend of toughness and brashness and quick-wittedness that made up the persona of a successful space salesman. Had Kati been so blinded by love that she couldn't see Wheatley's faults? A shaft of pain pierced Scott's chest at the thought. But surely she couldn't be in love with such a weak man; it just wasn't possible. Half in love, then . . . infatuated? Women fell for the wrong men for the oddest reasons. Sometimes, unaccountably, they actually seemed to find weakness an attractive quality. It was supposed to bring out their mothering instinct.

Scott felt a sudden foolish longing to be mothered a little by Kati. Cosseted. Cherished. He wanted her to smile at him in the tender way she used to in the old days, to gaze at him with eyes that were soft with fondness, sparkling with humor, warm with admiration and glowing with desire. She'd been in love with him then, no doubt about it, and he with her.

For minutes on end Scott stood at the window staring out across London's jumbled rooftops to a distant view of Tower Bridge, his hands hunched into his trouser pockets.

Love? No, that wasn't the name of the game any more. He had let love dominate him once, and see where it had led him. Kati was just another woman, he rationalized, another damned attractive woman. Okay, he could let himself admit that he desired and wanted her badly. Why should he care, though, if she disliked what he was doing at U.P.? Why should he care if she clung resentfully to memories of the past? Why couldn't Kati accept the fact that work was one thing, personal relationships something else? She still found him desirable . . . that had been proved the other night at her mews cottage. It seemed a crime to throw away the highly charged response they had for one another. There wasn't so much joy to be found in this world that such a rare opportunity could be thrown away.

With an exclamation of impatience, aimed as much against himself as against Kati, he turned and strode to his desk. Just another attractive woman, that's all she was, just another woman. Scott picked up the draft of a progress report to the board of directors, which his secretary had left on his desk, and began to study it. But a disturbing thought kept nagging him, distracting his attention. There was no doubt in his mind that shifting Robin Wheatley off *Rendezvous* was fully justified. It had been vitally necessary. But what about his decision to send Wheatley to work on a magazine that was based out of town? Could he honestly state that the thought hadn't struck him—if only at a subconscious level—that banishing Wheatley from Fleet Street would make it more difficult for him and Kati to get together?

Normally, when Scott put a question to himself, he received a candid, clear-cut answer. But this one was difficult, and he shied away from it.

Kati dreaded returning to her office. But there was urgent work to get on with, so she was obliged to face up to Robin. As she entered the room he was slumped listlessly in her visitor's chair.

"Well?" he asked eagerly, pulling himself upright.

"I treated Scott Drummond to a piece of my mind," she told him.

"Did he listen to you?"

She gave Robin a pitying look. He had no conception of what made high-powered operators like Scott tick. "Not in the sense of reversing his decision, I'm afraid. I didn't really expect him to."

Robin slumped back in the chair. "You might just as well not have bothered to see him," he said gloomily.

Privately, Kati agreed with that judgment, but she

wasn't about to admit it. "Oh, I don't know," she said. "It helped clear the air a bit."

"That doesn't benefit me," Robin grumbled.

She sat down and faced him across her desk. Suppressing her feeling of impatience, she began, "Listen, Robin, it may not be as bad as you think. Scott Drummond obviously considers you ideal for the job on *The Weekly Gardener*. When you think about it, the work won't be near as tough and demanding. You won't have people breathing down your neck all the time for better results. And there'll be no drop in salary."

"My God, you're on his side now," Robin exclaimed bitterly.

"I'm not on anybody's side!" Kati objected.

"No? I thought you were supposed to be backing me."

"Of course I'm backing you, Robin. I want what's best for you, and because of that, I can see that this move is probably to your advantage. You'll have more leisure time—time to spend with your family."

Robin stood up and scorched her with a look of harsh accusation. "Okay, I get the message. You'll be glad to be rid of me. What's it all about, Kati? Did Drummond make a pass at you, or something, is that it? Maybe you fancy your chances with a high-flyer like him. Well, go ahead, and see if I care."

As Robin strode angrily to the door, Kati bit back the words on the tip of her tongue. She wanted to protest at his unfair accusation and set the record straight. But what was the use? Robin had always believed what he wanted to believe regarding her. If he'd finally accepted now that she viewed him only as a work colleague, not as a potential lover, it was all to the good.

Alone in her office, she reached for the urgent work on her desk. She felt sorry for Robin, but she knew that

Scott was right in saying that he'd been a square peg in a round hole on *Rendezvous*. She sincerely hoped that he'd be happier in the new job.

As for *Rendezvous*, it would soon have a new advertisement manager. A man who was a very different type from Robin, much more aggressive. Angry as she still felt with Scott, her judgment told her that it was what *Rendezvous* needed, and she had to hope that the change would show beneficial results.

Chapter Ten

That Friday, a glorious May evening when the whole world seemed to bask in mellow sunshine, Kati sat beside Dee as they sped en route to Hampshire in Dee's sleek white Jaguar.

"So who'll be there this weekend?" Kati asked.

"The usual crowd, by and large. You'll know most of them. The best way to get an invite to one of Perry and Syb's houseparties during the summer is to be as nutty about tennis as they are. You're in the mood for tennis, I hope?"

"Always," said Kati with a laugh. "Normally, I don't get enough chance to play."

Dee pulled out to overtake a slower car. "By the way," she said, a shade too casually, "I've also asked Scott Drummond to come along."

"What?"

Dee shot Kati a curious glance. "I know you don't think he's the world's greatest, sweetie, but you two have to be able to co-exist. Personally, I think you're crazy to dislike him so much. I think he's the dishiest man I've met in years."

Kati found her breath at last. "How come you got to invite him, Dee?"

"We had lunch together yesterday. Didn't I tell you? Scott was saying how much London has changed during the years he was in America, so I grabbed my chance and suggested that a social weekend might help him get back into the swim. He seemed to like the idea."

"I see," Kati said faintly. "Er . . . does he happen to know that I'll be there?"

"I think I did mention it."

"Well, you might have played fair with me, then, and warned *me* that *he* was coming."

"Why?" Dee shot her another swift, sideways glance. "Would you have backed out if you'd known?"

To say yes—which was the truth—would indicate to Dee that her feelings of aversion to Scott were very strong indeed. Kati didn't want that; it would be difficult to explain away. Instead, she gave a light shrug and said, "I'd just have liked to be forewarned, that's all."

"So you've just been forewarned. Anyway, you won't really need to have a lot to do with the man." Dee gave a soft chuckle. "I'll be more than happy to keep him entertained."

"For heaven's sake, Dee, don't go falling for him, will you?"

Dee smiled again, this time with a look of wistful sadness about her. "I'm not in the business of deep commitment, Kati. It's light years since I fell in love."

"You mean with your second husband?"

Dee nodded. "That's right. Dear Theodore."

"I don't believe that I've ever heard you say one word against him," Kati observed. "What caused the split up, Dee?"

"Oh, hell . . . it was my fault as much as Theo's. We were two very ambitious people, and that doesn't add up to marital harmony. We came from totally different backgrounds, too, which didn't help. Theo was a self-made man, and it tickled his vanity to have a wife who was Lady Dorothy in her own right. No, that's not fair. He was proud of what he'd achieved—and rightly so—and I was the cherry on the top. My insistence that I should have a career of my own spoiled the image for Theo. I guess the trouble was that we were basically too different—or maybe too much alike, depending how you look at it. I too had to prove that I could make the big time, despite my background."

"Do you ever regret the divorce?" Kati asked her.

"Nosy, aren't you?" Dee reflected for a moment. "No, I haven't any real regrets. That's not to say I don't sometimes sigh for the good times we shared—they were very good. But my life as a bachelor career woman suits me just fine."

Kati might have accepted that statement without question up until a few minutes earlier. As it was, she began to wonder if Dee weren't protesting a bit too much. Did the weekend invitation to Scott indicate just another of Dee's passing fancies for good-looking, attractive men, or was there something deeper there? Was she wondering, in however low-key a way, whether Scott Drummond might not make a suitable third husband for her? The thought made Kati frown.

They turned off the main highway onto quiet country lanes, the grass alongside golden with buttercups, with here and there tall, purple spires of foxgloves. At the village of Avonbury, a huddle of ancient timber-frame houses which seemed to lean every which-way, they entered a pretty valley that was a symphony in shades of green. A small river drew a winding silver ribbon through its center, and the lush meadows rose on either side to hill slopes clothed in oak and ash trees. At the farther end, visible for almost a mile before they reached it, stood the proud edifice known as Avonbury Hall. Each time she came, Kati was enraptured. Now, on a fine summer's evening, the ancient manor house looked its superlative best.

A house had stood on the site, Dee had told her, for over eight hundred years. The present building, for the most part, went back five centuries to the first days of the Royal House of Tudor. From every angle Avonbury Hall made a picture of perfect architectural balance which delighted the eye. Graceful chimneys and pointed gables soared above the red-tiled roof, and mullioned windows glittered back the light of the evening sun.

They drove through an expanse of peaceful parkland, where several magnificent Cedars of Lebanon spread their branches wide, making dark silhouettes against the blueness of the sky. Dee gave a soft sigh. Avonbury Hall had been home to her all her life, yet Kati knew that she was still affected by its beauty.

At the arched front entrance, a white-jacketed manservant came running down the steps for their luggage. Dee slid out of the car and stretched elegantly.

"Hi there, Sidney. Are we the first to arrive?"

"Very nearly, Lady Dorothy. His lordship and her ladyship aren't down yet."

"Good! We can slip straight upstairs and enjoy a nice hot bath before we need to put in an appearance. Come on, Kati."

The room allocated to Kati was one that she'd occupied before, where modern comfort and antiquity had been skillfully blended. The scrolled plasterwork of the ceiling was particularly fine, and rose-silk damask wall hangings possessed a faded elegance. The original uneven oak floorboards, which just showed around the edges of the room, were softened underfoot by a glorious Persian carpet. A towering carved fourposter now boasted a soft-sprung mattress, and a small adjoining anteroom had been converted into a luxury bathroom.

More cars arrived while Kati was unpacking. Each

time she heard one drive up, she crossed to the tall leaded window to look down, and recognized friends of the family whom she had met before. The fourth arrival, though, was the one she dreaded. Scott unwound his long length from behind the wheel of his silver blue car, glanced admiringly at the house's facade, then lithely mounted the steps. So much for her wild hope that something might have prevented his coming to Avonbury Hall. A feeling of despair knotted her nerves, and she wished that she could escape—anywhere.

A long, hot soak in the bathtub helped to restore her flagging spirits. The sight of the dress she'd laid ready on the bed for this evening gave her another lift. To hell with Scott. Donning the beautiful, softly flowing silk faille gown with a deep vee front and back was an act of defiance against him; every sweep of her hairbrush, every brushstroke of makeup was a further thrust. And finally, she applied a touch of her favorite perfume to her pulse points.

She was just about ready when Dee tapped at her door. "Wow, Kati, you look fit to kill," she said admiringly. "I love that deep neckline, and the oyster pink is perfect for your coloring."

"That's quite a compliment, coming from you," Kati replied with a laugh, even more pleased than she let show. "Needless to say, you look fantastic." She didn't resent the fact that Dee, in a shimmering black and silver, off-one-shoulder dress, far outshone her. Dee always outshone every other woman in sheer, breathtaking chic. "That dress is just about the most gorgeous creation I've ever seen. And very sexy, too."

"No accident, that," Dee responded, giving her a wink. She adjusted her spectacles, which were a different pair tonight, with silver-glitter frames. "Come on, let's go down. I'm simply dying for a cocktail. Er . . . I wonder if Scott has arrived yet."

Kati put a clamp on her tongue, and together they

descended the massive portrait-hung stairway to the green and gold salon.

"Hello there, Kati. So glad you could come."
"I was thrilled to be asked, Perry. Your weekend parties are always terrific, and I adore this lovely old house."

Dee's brother Peregrine, The Earl of Avonbury, was a tall, spare-framed man in his early forties, with candid gray eyes. The sculpted lineaments of his lean face proclaimed an aristocratic descent stretching back across the centuries to when the hall had been built, and beyond. He and his wife Sybilla, a slim, dark-haired woman with an air of graceful beauty, were standing together to greet their guests.

After welcoming Kati, Sybilla turned to her sister-in-law, and they exchanged kisses. "I had a letter from Oliver today, Dee. He asked me very particularly to talk you into coming with us to Speech Day next month."

"Good heavens! Why does he want his aunt there?"
"To show you off, of course," Peregrine said with a chuckle. "According to Oliver, his school pals have all been head over heels about the glamorous Lady Dee since you floated into their vision at the Eton and Harrow match last summer." Oliver was their sixteen-year-old son who, together with his younger brother Charles, was at Eton College in preparation for Oxford.

Dee made a face, though Kati could see that she was pleased. "So I'm expected to go on display for Oliver like some prize heifer from the Home Farm, am I?"

"Someone less like a prize heifer it would be difficult to imagine," said her brother. "Ah, Dee, I believe this must be your other guest."

Kati made herself turn around very slowly. Scott had entered the room and was coming in their direction. Kati had never before seen him wearing a white tuxedo, and he looked breathtakingly handsome. His gaze met hers for a fraction of a moment before he greeted Dee, who took his elbow and drew him toward her brother and sister-in-law.

"This is Scott Drummond," she announced, and Kati detected a note of triumph in her voice. "Scott, meet my brother Peregrine and my sister-in-law Sybilla."

They chatted easily for a couple of minutes while Kati made herself as inconspicuous as possible. "So you're the new man U.P. has brought in to put the firm back on its feet?" said the earl.

"That's the general idea," Scott agreed.

"Then I wish you every success. I hold a small block of shares in U.P., and I've been half thinking of pulling out. But having heard about you from Dee, and now meeting you myself, I think that I'll hang on for a bit."

"I hope I'll merit your confidence in me," said Scott.

"You will," Dee forecast cheerfully. "No doubt about that, Scott. Come on, and I'll introduce you around. Apart from Kati, I don't believe you know anybody."

When guests were present, dinner at Avonbury Hall was usually a very splendid affair. The Great Hall, which soared to the height of two stories, held a long oak table which could seat up to two dozen—four more than the present houseparty. The last rays of the sun slanted through the tall windows, staining the polished stone-flagged floor to a mellow golden shade. The family coat of arms adorned the wall above the massive carved fireplace, and somber ancestral portraits in heavy gilt frames covered the paneling on three sides.

On such occasions the butler, Palfrey, abandoned his usual simple black jacket and appeared in the full splendor of a long-tailed suit. From behind his master's chair at the head of the table, he supervised the service of the meal with a critical eye.

To Kati, the course after course of delicious food held little interest. Scott was placed across the table from her, next to Dee, and she could see them chatting and laughing together, though she was too far away to hear more than the odd word of what they said. She tried to keep her eyes averted, dividing her attention between her immediate neighbors, a glossy young stockbroker and a physician from the neighboring city of Winchester. As Kati turned from one to the other, she couldn't stop her eyes from straying to Scott. Each time, she had a strong feeling that she had almost caught him watching her.

When dinner ended, a couple of bridge fours were formed, Dee being roped into one of them. Kati, not in the mood for any social activity, stood at the open French doors gazing out across the terrace into the fragrant darkness of the gardens. She sensed someone approaching from behind, and Scott's rich-toned voice confirmed her sudden apprehension.

"It's a beautiful night, Kati."

"Yes, it is."

"Care for a stroll?"

"Thanks, but no."

"That was a very emphatic refusal," he said ruefully.

"I just don't feel like a stroll."

"With me, you mean?"

"With anybody." Kati hoped that he would take the hint and go away, but instead Scott propped himself comfortably against the door frame.

"I didn't realize that places like Avonbury Hall still existed," he said.

"I'm surprised you bothered to come," Kati returned, "if you're so disapproving."

"I didn't say that I don't approve. But I'd imagined that the days of running a full-blown stately home for just one family had passed into the history books."

"Actually, the earl and the countess live fairly simply in the ordinary way, and they spend quite a lot of their time at their apartment in Mayfair. Apart from the estate, he has business interests all over the place."

"Including Universal Publications."

"I didn't know that until this evening. Dee never mentioned it. Perry said it was only a small share-holding, though."

"Small to the Earl of Avonbury would probably seem large to us ordinary mortals," Scott commented dryly. "I wonder if Dee also has shares in U.P."

"I've no idea. Ask her, if you want to know. You two seem to be getting along fantastically well, judging from the way you had your heads together all through dinner."

Scott shrugged. "Dee is very good company."

"I'm aware of that; she's my closest friend. She also happens to be a very astute woman, Scott, so I advise you not to try putting anything over on her."

"Meaning?"

"Nothing in particular. It was just a friendly warning."

"Friendly?"

"Take it how you like," she said, and turned to walk away.

Deep in thought, Scott watched her go. He was a fool to bother with her, he told himself, a fool to let his intellect be swamped by emotional reactions every time he came anywhere near her. Kati was a first-class editor, with style and flair, and in her hands *Rendezvous* was a magazine with excellent prospects once he'd ironed out a few problems. With the new man he'd appointed in place of Robin Wheatley the outlook was promising for a healthier revenue from advertising, but he'd need cooperation from Kati, too. Editorial freedom was fine—he was all for it—but Kati had to be persuaded, or forced, to face the hard facts of magazine publishing in these tough, competitive days, and make *Rendezvous* more appealing to potential advertisers. And he wouldn't succeed in that aim if he continued to be obsessed by her the way he was.

He had let Kati become a fever in his blood. Nothing

else, but nothing, seemed to matter any more except somehow getting together with Kati again. All week he'd been tense and edgy, a nervous wreck. Even the smallest mental process had needed a major effort of will. Just now, talking to Kati, there'd been a crazy, frightening moment when he had nearly abandoned all restraint and turned caveman, so overwhelming had been the impulse to snatch her up into his arms and run off with her into the darkness of the gardens.

Damn her. He refused to be in thrall to any woman. Kati Young spelled danger—to his personal life, his sanity, his whole career. It was impossible to carry out the job that faced him at U.P. with his emotions in such turmoil. The answer, of course, was very simple. He should let his attention be captured by some other woman. It wouldn't be the first time that he'd entered quite deliberately into an affair as a counterweight to the pressures of work. It had happened on several occasions in America. Like a good novel, a good affair should have a beginning, a middle—and an end. As with closing a book, the end should come with only faint regret, and an overall feeling of time well spent.

He didn't have far to look for another woman to engage his attention. Dee Faulkner had indicated in a dozen subtle ways that she found him attractive. Scott stirred restlessly, still watching Kati, who had now joined a group of people by the coffee trolley. She was very beautiful, but no way could she be said to possess the dramatic eye-catching persona of Lady Dorothy. He deliberately turned his gaze away from Kati to where Dee sat at the card table. She really was a glorious specimen of womanhood, with a very definite but not overstated aura of sexiness. She would be wonderful in bed, he hadn't a doubt. He felt confident that he only had to show a little eagerness.

He was still looking at Dee when she glanced up and met his eyes. She smiled, and beckoned him over.

"You looked bored, Scott."

"Not at all. I've been soaking up the atmosphere of this lovely old house."

"Shall I show you around?" From behind her large-framed spectacles there was a subtle challenge in her green eyes.

"I'd like that."

"Just let me finish this rubber. Then I'll get Syb to sit in for me." She glanced around at her fellow players. "That is, if no one objects?"

Ten minutes later Scott and Dee were doing a circuit of the drawing room, Dee pointing out some of her family's most prized possessions—the Gainsborough painting of a seated lady, some early Chinese porcelain and the delightful painted beechwood chairs by Sheraton. Kati, pretending to be listening with amusement to the chitchat of her group, covertly followed their progress. When they reached the double doors leading to the Great Hall, they slipped through them and vanished from sight.

Okay, she thought, that's just fine by me. If Dee got him interested, it would take the heat off herself. And what man wouldn't be interested in Dee, she pondered gloomily, if given the slightest encouragement? Kati wondered where they were now. She wondered if, alone and unobserved, they had abandoned any pretense of a conducted tour of the house. Were they in one another's arms?

"I'm sorry," she said, jerking her attention back. "What was that?"

The man who had addressed her, a partner in a London firm of accountants, gave her a curious glance. "I was saying that you must be a very powerful, influential lady, Kati. I mean, having all those thousands of readers hanging on your every word."

Kati gave a short laugh. "Don't you believe it, Adrian. The readers of *Rendezvous* are a very bright lot, and not easily swayed. The toughest part of my job is trying to keep one step ahead of them, so that I'm not asking them to read about yesterday's issues."

"How are you making out with Scott Drummond?"

"What's that supposed to mean?" she demanded, going cold.

"Sorry, did I touch a nerve?" He chuckled. "I rather gathered, seeing you together just now, that he's not your favorite character."

Kati had recovered enough of her poise to laugh it off. "You can say that again! But please don't quote me. The guy's my boss, remember."

"He's Dee's boss too, isn't he? Yet she seems to get along with him just fine."

It was like a knife turning in Kati's heart. She muttered an excuse and moved away, wandering out into the cool darkness of the terrace.

They had covered the library, the small parlor and the family dining room, and they'd looked in on the men who were playing in the billiard room. Side by side, they mounted the wide stairway, going past the bedroom floor to the one above, where a narrow oak-paneled chamber ran the entire width of the house. Dee switched on lights here and there, but even so it was dim and shadowed. Looking down its length, Scott could see such incongruous items as a harp, a rocking horse and an archery target, yet the room was by no means a dump.

"This has become a sort of family museum now," Dee explained. "Relics from down the centuries, and mementos from our own childhood years. Perry thought it was better than just shoving things out of sight in a dusty attic."

Scott gazed around curiously. "What was the purpose of such a long room when the house was first built?"

"Oh, several of the early mansions had a long gallery

like this. In bad weather the family could take exercise here . . . the children could chase each other around, and all kinds of games like ninepins and shuttlecock could be played." Dee met his eyes and laughed softly. "Other types of games too, I imagine. A couple sitting in one of those window alcoves would be nicely hidden away from prying eyes."

Yet another subtle hint, Scott noted, and knew that it was his cue to make the first move. But he couldn't do it; attractive as Dee was, she had no power to arouse him.

He realized that the silence between them was lengthening, becoming awkward. He hadn't picked up his cue. He saw a puzzled, disappointed look in Dee's green eyes, then she suddenly said with a brisk laugh, "Well, I think we'd better rejoin the party, or people will think that you and I are up to something. I could do with a drink, anyhow."

Kati was immediately aware of them returning to the drawing room. Dee's face was totally enigmatic; Scott, though, looked faintly flushed and ill-at-ease. Something, she felt certain, had happened between them. But what?

For the remainder of the evening, Scott didn't join any group that Kati happened to be attached to; nor, so far as she could tell, did he once glance in her direction. Yet her skin tingled with awareness of his presence in the room.

Before there was any general move toward bed, she sought Dee out and said with an apologetic smile, "I think I'll go up now. It was rather a hectic day at work, and I can hardly keep my eyes open."

Dee gave her a look that was disbelieving, yet granted Kati the right to keep her true reasons to herself.

"How about an early morning ride?" she asked, and when Kati hesitated, she added, "Just the two of us, I mean. At these do's it's good to get away from the herd for a bit."

Kati summoned up a smile. "Yes, I'd like that, Dee."

"Great. Sevenish?"

"Fine."

Kati said good-night to her host and hostess and slipped away. Watching her go, Scott felt a desperate longing to follow her, regardless of how it might look to other people. How would Kati react if he were to knock at the door of her room? he wondered. Could he succeed in weakening her resistance until she agreed to let him spend another night in her bed? Desire burned in his groin, racking him with bittersweet pain.

It might just be possible. It might even be easy. And yet he knew that he wouldn't go to Kati tonight. Out of pride, or out of fear of failure? He didn't know the answer.

Chapter Eleven

On horseback, Kati and Dee followed a bridle path along the riverside, past lush green beds of watercress. In the early morning sunshine the grass glittered silver with dew, and there was a marvelously sweet fragrance drifting on the air. It was very peaceful, and the soft chink of harness and the snorts and whinnies of their mounts were the only sounds to mingle with the twittering medley of the birds.

"Glad you came?" asked Dee, glancing around at Kati.

"Of course. I love visiting Avonbury Hall."

"I meant for the ride. You looked so flaked out last night that I half wondered if I ought to waken you so early."

"I'm really pleased you did," Kati assured her. "The peace of early morning helps to get things into perspective." Dee didn't *look* as if she had just spent a glorious night making love, Kati had decided with relief, in her first split-second of seeing Dee. And anyway, Kati told herself now, even if Dee and Scott *had* started something, it would be nothing to cause her any distress. She herself had no room in her life for a man like Scott Drummond, however attractive she might find him.

They crossed the river by a ford, the horses stepping delicately on the flat yellow stones, over which the sparkling water bubbled and swirled.

"Want to talk about it?" asked Dee, as they took a path across a sunlit meadow.

"Talk about it?" Kati stammered, jolted out of her musings.

"Whatever it is that's bothering you. And I've a pretty shrewd idea what . . . or rather, who."

"This is a load of rubbish," Kati said, with a light laugh that she tried to make dismissive. "There's nothing bothering me. I'm fine, truly I am."

But Dee persisted. "It was your overdone performance at Tuesday's meeting in the boardroom that made me realize that you just aren't yourself these days," she explained. "You're really letting Scott Drummond get to you, Kati, and it's so silly. That guy is at U.P. to do a job that's long overdue. Who was the person who started Cifbids, for goodness' sake? There's been far too much sloppiness around in the whole organization for far too long, you and I have always said that. And Scott will crack down on it hard; he's got what it takes. But that doesn't mean that anyone who's pulling their weight needs to feel threatened by him, Kati. I know that *Rendezvous* hasn't really been making money for U.P. so far, but you've turned it into a darned fine magazine that's really going places. I can't believe that Scott, or the directors, would want to fold something with such potential. So quit worrying."

Kati shook her head, saying, "I don't feel threatened in that way, Dee. Not really."

"In what way, then?"

"Not in any way." She couldn't tell Dee the truth, so

she went on, "All the same, it doesn't mean that I have to *enjoy* Scott Drummond snooping into every aspect of my editorship and trying to find fault."

"What are you scared of? That he'll uncover something terrible? That's stupid and you know it, Kati. No editor is a hundred percent efficient when it comes to administrative details, and you rate a lot higher than most."

"Thanks for the vote of confidence, Dee. But I honestly don't need it."

"No?" Dee turned to glance at Kati, her lips pursed thoughtfully. She looked totally stunning in her finely tailored riding gear, and her easy, relaxed seat on the sleek chestnut mare, Edwina, was classic textbook. Kati, wearing jeans and a navy zipper jacket, and sometimes finding her frisky sorrel pony a mite hard to handle, knew that she couldn't compete with Lady Dorothy Faulkner in either respect. Nor did she feel any need to. She was happy just to be riding with her friend on this glorious May morning, but she wasn't happy about the direction of their conversation.

"Oh, did you see, Dee?" she exclaimed, seizing the chance of a diversion. "A kingfisher. It was like a flash of jewel-bright color skimming across the water."

"Yes, I did and yes, it was. But don't try to change the subject, Kati. Let's dig some more into your hate-thing with Scott Drummond. Is it that you just can't take criticism?"

"You have one hell of a nerve . . ."

"Yes, haven't I?" Dee grinned at her. "Some people think it's because I have a title to my name, but actually I'm just very nosy by nature. Especially where my friends are concerned."

"Huh!"

"Huh to you, sweetie. And answer my question."

"It doesn't need answering," Kati retorted. "The staffers would fall apart laughing at the suggestion that I can't take criticism. You should attend one of our editorial meetings. The air gets quite thick with insults, and a lot of them come my way."

"So you're a good editor-in-chief, who's ready to listen to her staff. How about when the criticism comes from above? Let's say, from Scott Drummond."

Kati took a quick breath. "It's easy for you to talk, Dee. You haven't come in for a scolding from him."

"What makes you so sure I haven't?"

"Well, have you?"

"Off the record, yes. On two counts. He got to hear of my plan to redo the cover design of *Style* and have it printed in eye-catching gold ink. He challenged me for evidence that the extra expense would be justified, and I couldn't give him any. I had to admit it was just one of my wilder flights of fancy. But the other case was different. Scott maintained that the prize competition we're about to run for design college students was too extravagant. I pointed out that those students will be tomorrow's fashion leaders, and we want them growing up believing that *Style* is the one right out there in front. Scott and I both conceded a little, and between us we hammered out a compromise. I never object to constructive criticism, Kati."

"Me neither. But what gets my goat is when Scott tries to interfere with my editorial integrity."

"My, we're getting into big words now."

"You know what I mean. Within days of his arrival he was trying to turn *Rendezvous* into a mere advertisement sheet—free editorial puffs traded against advertisement orders." Innate honesty made Kati add, "Well, not quite that. But he was going on about my campaign for the handicapped not being the sort of material to attract ads."

"True, or false?"

"Not you too, Dee!"

"No, not me too. But for God's sake get yourself straightened out, Kati. I presume that you have grounds for justifying that disabled campaign?"

"Of course I have."

"Then spell them out to Scott loud and clear. He'll listen. Basically, he's a very genuine, reasonable man."

"He seems to have you nicely hooked," Kati said bitterly.

"Correction, sweetie. If anyone's holding the rod, it's me."

Kati bent away from Dee, pretending to adjust a harness strap. "Then I wish you good fishing," she said in a muffled voice.

A substantial buffet-style breakfast was laid on in the small morning room for those guests who hadn't elected to have a tray in their room. Scott was the only one there at the table when Kati and Dee arrived, having cleaned-up after their ride. He was digging into a plate heaped with sausages, bacon and fried eggs. Kati's appetite was reduced to zero at the sight of him, so she just scooped up a small serving of scrambled egg. Dee, though, helped herself liberally to kedgeree, a savory rice dish that was rich with thick flakes of golden finnan haddie, and she took it to sit down beside Scott.

"I simply adore this stuff," she said with a laugh, forking up a mouthful. "It's always been my favorite breakfast ever since I was a child. I could eat piles of it every day."

"It's very clear that you don't, though," Scott remarked meaningfully. But while he spoke his eyes wandered over to Kati, who had pointedly chosen a seat as far away from him as possible.

Dee laughed off the compliment to her figure. "I'm one of those lucky gals who doesn't have to give a damn about dieting. I never seem to put on an ounce."

A flat lie, Kati knew. Dee was very cautious in her eating habits. A lavish lunch or dinner would always be counterbalanced by something more frugal at the next meal. But, as she'd once declared to Kati, men didn't want to hear about weight watching. "They expect to have the best of both worlds, sweetie—women with gorgeous figures who can tuck into steaks and french fries right along with them."

The earl came into the room, bearing a clipboard and a faintly worried expression. "Ah, good, here's some of you up and about early. We mustn't waste a minute of this perfect tennis weather, so I suggest we get out to the courts as soon as possible. I was very relieved to find that you play, Scott. Otherwise I'd have been a man short, because Uncle St. John has sprained his ankle. Thanks to you we have five pairs now, which is a nice number." He poured himself a cup of coffee from the silver pot, while he went on explaining his tournament arrangements, which he'd devised to accommodate the varying standards of his guests' tennis. "It's a fun thing really," he said, cheerfully apologetic. "Not to be taken too seriously. Each lady plays with each man in turn, and against every other male/female combination. We play minimatches comprising just five games, and each player keeps a score sheet of the number of games won and lost. I know it sounds a bit complicated, but it'll all work out. You'll see."

Peregrine asked his sister to select the first partnerings by the simple expedient of closing her eyes and stabbing a pencil at his list. When it turned out that Dee and Scott were paired together, Kati wondered skeptically if those large green eyes of hers had been as tightly pressed shut as Dee had pretended.

"Right, then," said the earl, absentmindedly making himself a sandwich of crisp bacon between two slices of toast and munching while he made a final check of his schedule. "I'll expect everyone at the courts at ten o'clock on the dot," he finished, as he departed.

Scott started on toast and marmalade. "Did you enjoy your ride?" he asked, addressing both Dee and Kati.

"It was fabulous," said Dee enthusiastically. "This weather is perfect for riding. Do you ride, Scott?"

"Put it this way, I can stay on a horse—just."

"Oh, come on! I can't believe that you aren't successful at anything you decide to do."

"Some people wouldn't agree with you, Dee," he countered, his gaze flickering over to Kati again.

"How about joining us tomorrow, then," Dee invited, "and we'll check you out?"

Scott hesitated, and Kati said quickly, "I don't think you'd better count on me, Dee. After this morning's effort I'm discovering a whole bunch of muscles I didn't know I possessed."

Both Dee and Scott looked at her in disbelief, and Kati knew that they were both irritated, but for different reasons. Scott's eyes rested on her stonily as he said to Dee in a voice that sounded eager, "I'd love to join you, Dee."

"Great. Consider it a date."

There were two tennis courts at Avonbury Hall, adjoining each other. They were immaculately kept, and sheltered from the wind by a tall yew hedge. After a good deal of hustling from Peregrine, play began at ten-twenty, watched by the two players who were waiting their turn on the courts, and a few of the nonplaying guests. Kati's opening partner was the physician, Vernon, whom she'd sat next to at dinner the previous evening.

Playing their minimatches of five games each against the other four pairs, Kati and Vernon did moderately well, winning on total by a small margin of games. Dee and Scott, on the other hand, had done poorly. Though both were good players, they'd failed to get their act together. In the match against Kati and Vernon, they had lost one-four.

After lunch came the time that Kati had been dreading, when she and Scott were partnered together. Facing him across the net, hitting back his deliveries with all her strength, was one thing. It was enjoyable, especially when she managed to score off him. To play *with* Scott in the degree of close-knit harmony needed in doubles play was something else entirely. Covertly watching him as they warmed up for a few minutes, noting the bunched biceps showing beneath the short sleeves of his white shirt, the solid thighs and muscled calves beneath his tennis shorts, she shivered involuntarily.

Yet the instant their play actually began, her fears and unease dropped magically away. It was as if the years between had dropped away, too, and they were once more playing doubles at the tennis club near her old home by Wimbledon Common. Kati and Scott had been regarded as a formidable team in those days. It had something to do with an instinctive rapport that made it possible for them to anticipate their opponents' every stroke, to yield to one another or to take a ball with no uncertainty or confusion.

"I've never seen two people play together in such sync," the club captain had once said in admiring approval. "Not nonprofessionals, anyway."

"It must be love," one of the girls had quipped.

"If that's the case," the captain returned, "I suggest that the rest of you all fall in love forthwith."

"That would be a fine thing," the same girl had muttered with a rueful groan. "The best men are always spoken for."

Kati had listened smugly. It was true that she and Scott were wonderfully in love; it was true that there wasn't another man around who could hold a candle to Scott. Glorious, ecstatically happy days . . .

"Fault!" cried the umpire, to her serve. The second serve she raised just a fraction, and it whizzed over the net with a half inch to spare. Peregrine managed to return it, but in a soft lob that Scott smashed back in a killer.

"Fifteen-love."

Yes, they were a great team. Kati was suddenly conscious that although they were playing on the court that was farther from the spectators, all attention was on them.

"Thirty-love." The point had been won after a rally in which they'd had their opponents running all over the court.

They were unstoppable, throughout the whole five-game minimatch. Then it was time for new opponents, Dee and Vernon. Once again Kati and Scott emerged with the maximum number of games to their credit, only conceding a total of eleven points to the other pair.

People crowded around them. Dee was frowning slightly, not very pleased. But from everyone else they had congratulations showered on them.

"It's hard to believe that two people who've never played as partners before could get such a degree of togetherness," said Sybilla admiringly.

Both Kati and Scott shrugged their shoulders modestly, avoiding the need to lie by keeping silent. In fact they hardly spoke, even to each other, but it wasn't necessary. Their old game-plan tactics didn't need verbalizing; they were engraved in their memories, flowing in their veins.

There was a short interval for tea, brought out to the tennis party by Palfrey and another manservant on huge silver trays. Then they played some more before finishing in good time for everyone to get changed and be down for cocktails on the terrace. The chat over drinks was all about tennis, and it was the general consensus that Kati and Scott had done so brilliantly together that it would be impossible for anyone else to overtake them and emerge as the ultimate male and female winners of the tournament.

At dinner the seating was changed around, but Kati noted that Dee and Scott were still placed together. It was a relief to be well away from them, and not be in dread of meeting his dark eyes every time she glanced up. In the drawing room afterward Sybilla, who had studied music for the concert platform, entertained them at the piano. She played a Chopin waltz, something of Debussy's and favorite numbers from some of the operettas. Scott sat with Dee on one of the long, brocade-covered sofas close to the piano. Mainly to put space between herself and them, Kati had chosen a seat near one of the French windows, open to the warm evening air. Even so, she felt so choked with emotion that when Sybilla stopped playing for a few minutes she slipped out onto the terrace.

The first stars were pricking through the dusky blueness and a faint mistiness after the heat of the day hazed the air, lending a touch of mystery to the trees and shrubs of the gardens. From somewhere distant came the trills and warbles of a lone nightingale.

Behind her, the music began again, this time from *The Merry Widow*. Kati hesitated, wondering whether she ought to go back inside, but she doubted that she'd been missed. Instead, she crossed the terrace and descended a wide flight of steps that took her to the level of the lawns.

Gradually, as she strolled a path with aimless footsteps, sounds of the piano diminished until the nightingale held solitary sway. The cool night air was balm to her flush-heated skin. She wished fervently that she hadn't come to Avonbury Hall this weekend. There was no pleasure for her here this time, thrust into such close proximity to Scott. She found herself questioning how much longer she could continue in her present job. In order to remain, she would have to discipline her absurdly vulnerable emotions, to accept Scott as just a man who was in a position of authority over her. She had to be able to argue with him, without rancor, to put her case coolly and calmly whenever she believed that she was in the right; she had to be able to accept his policies with good grace, even sometimes conceding that right was on his side. Scott had to be just her boss—that, and nothing more. But could she ever reach that point, when her skin prickled with sensual awareness each and every time he came within sight of her, every time her wayward thoughts veered to him?

She paused beneath a copper beech tree and stood leaning back against its smooth-barked trunk, gazing upward at the pattern of stars through the lacework of new-leafing branches. It was such a beautiful night, with fragrance drenching the air. It was a night for dreaming dreams . . . lovely, impossible dreams. She felt an aching sadness deep within her.

Kati became aware of a footfall on the grass, close at hand. Startled, she turned and saw a tall figure silhouetted against the faint glow of light that spilled from the house. Scott.

"What are you doing out here, Kati?" he asked.

The sound of his voice set up a violent trembling in her limbs, and she was grateful that Scott wouldn't be able to see it in the darkness. She fought for control over her jerky breath, and managed, "I . . . I just felt like some fresh air."

"Sounds like a good idea. Let's stroll."

Kati panicked at this suggestion. "But what about Dee?" she stammered. "You're with her."

"Dee had to take a call she was expecting from America. I gathered that she'll be gone some time. So come on."

Scott's fingers made contact with her bare arm and Kati flinched, wrenching herself away before he could close his grip. She heard his sharp intake of breath, but he controlled his anger.

"Have it your way," he said with a shrug. "We'll stay put right here, if you prefer." Scott thrust his hands into his trouser pockets, as if he couldn't trust them not to reach for her again. "Everyone's still talking about the way we played tennis together, Kati. It was odd, wasn't it, how the intervening years seemed to have vanished, or not to have happened? It felt to me as if we'd been playing regularly."

"Yes, it was odd," she agreed, in a low voice.

"Significant, would you say?"

"Of what?"

"You know the answer to that, Kati. Why do we have to pretend, when it's so obvious to us both that a lot remains of what there used to be between us?"

"It's . . . irrelevant, Scott."

"I've tried to tell myself the same thing," he admitted. "There's no sense in allowing anything to develop between us."

"My point exactly."

"So you consider that hard-nosed common sense should prevent us from taking, and enjoying, what we both clearly want?"

"Speak for yourself," she muttered.

"I'm speaking for both of us, since you seem determined to be dishonest about your feelings. Everything I've ever learned in life tells me that I'm being crazy, Kati, but I still want you. All the old magic was still there, wasn't it, when we made love the other night? I can't bear the thought that it won't ever happen again."

"Forget it, Scott. Forget about me."

"I can't do that," he said slowly. "I only wish I could."

"You must."

Again Kati heard him take a sharp, angry breath. "For God's sake, what is this? Some crazy exercise in self-denial? Okay, so I'm your boss at U.P., and I call the shots. It's an unequal situation and I don't blame you for not liking it. But that needn't prevent us getting together outside the office. Maybe, for your own mixed-up reasons you think you have cause to dislike and mistrust me. I'm not going to argue with you about the rights and wrongs of something that happened so long ago. You have your view of it, I have mine. But when the old chemistry is still there, as strong as it ever was, you're denying *yourself* as much as you're denying me, Kati. And that's plain stupid."

"Okay, so I'm stupid."

"You're damned stubborn."

She took a faltering step. "I'm not listening to any more of this," she said. "I'm going back inside."

Scott moved to block her path, and her determination wilted. He was standing so close that she could feel his breath warm on her cheek, could detect the heat that radiated from his magnificent, strong body, and was intoxicated by his musky, masculine aroma. She wondered if she'd make it to the house. And if she did, how could she ever face the assembled company with anything like poise?

"Please, Scott . . ." she mumbled. But she didn't know what it was she was pleading for. To be allowed to pass? To be granted freedom from any further harassment? Or was it something more subtle, something shaming? Did she, in truth, want to be convinced against her will?

The last fragments of her resistance dissolved away when Scott touched her again. His fingertips ran lightly from her wrists to her shoulders, and she heard him give a deep sigh. Then suddenly she was in his arms, and he was kissing her. Kati made a half-hearted effort to draw back, but his lips pursued hers, and with a low moan she succumbed to the clamoring need within herself. She was limp in his embrace, her head falling back in rapture as his mouth made an erotic foray over her face, touching soft, moist kisses to her closed eyes, her brow, grazing across her cheek to capture and tease the softness of an earlobe, then moving on down the line of her jawbone and skimming the smooth skin of her throat until he met the neckline of her dress. With a special shiver of delight she felt his tongue probe further into the valley between her breasts.

"You're exquisite, Kati," he murmured huskily. "Quite utterly perfect. I want you, I need you."

She molded herself against him, slipping her hands inside his jacket and encircling his waist. Savoringly, she began a tender exploration of his back through the silky fabric of his evening shirt.

"Say yes," he whispered, demanding an answer to his unspoken question.

But Kati didn't need to speak. The supple surrender of her body was evidence enough, and Scott sighed long and low. It was a sigh of joy and happiness and anticipated delight; a sigh that was born of frustration too, since what he so fervently desired couldn't happen right there and then, on a soft, grassy bank in the sweet-smelling darkness. Yet, holding Kati and feeling her tremble in his arms, he knew how fragile was his victory. To try and rush her now would be to take a fearful risk of losing her completely.

They stood locked together, their pulses pounding, thudding in unison in their ears to the exclusion of all other sound. Again Scott took possession of her lips, melding his against them, the soft pressure escalating to flaring passion with a meeting of tongues. They remained locked together, with mouth to open mouth, oblivious of everything but this intensely pleasurable sensation.

Kati was alerted by a sudden sound. A footfall near at hand, a gasp of surprise? Or had it been a silent, electric awareness reaching through to her that she and Scott were no longer alone? She tried to dismiss her slight unease, loath to break the magic spell of enchantment, but the feeling persisted. At last, she pulled back her mouth from Scott's, but gently, as if only for a momentary respite from the swirling headiness of his kiss. Opening her eyes, she blinked to focus them. Over

Scott's shoulder, outlined against the lights of the house, she saw the tall figure of a woman by the terrace steps. Dee, unmistakably. As Kati watched, gripped by a feeling of cold desolation, Dee mounted up the steps in a stumbling fashion, with none of her usual graceful bearing, and ran the length of the terrace to disappear through a side door.

"What is it, Kati?" asked Scott, his voice concerned. "You're shivering. You can't be cold."

"No, I . . ." She swallowed, and tried again. "We'd better go in now."

"Not yet." Scott tried to draw her close against him once more, but she resisted. "Just a few more minutes," he pleaded.

"No . . ." Her chest felt tight with misery, and she had to force out every word. "This . . . it shouldn't have happened, Scott."

"Are you crazy? It was wonderful, Kati, so don't pretend. We're both mature enough not to play silly games with each other."

"I'm not playing games, Scott." She made an attempt to release herself, but his grip was too firm. "Yes, it was wonderful, but . . ."

"But nothing."

"It won't work. It can't work."

"You seem to forget that it already has worked—magnificently." His sigh was more like the groan of a man in despair. "You're tearing me apart, Kati, with your doubts and hesitations."

"Scott, let me go." There was a note of warning in her voice, and he did as she said, but his resentment came to her as something tangible. Free of the mind-dizzying spell of his embrace, she tried to be calm and rational. "I'm sorry, Scott, and I blame myself as much as you, but . . . this should never have happened. It's wrong."

"Wrong!" he exploded. "You sound like some timid teenager out on her first date. We're adults, Kati, and we both know that self-denial merely for its own sake makes no sort of sense at all."

She shook her head. "Our relationship ended eight years ago, Scott. I never expected to meet you again, certainly not as my boss. But that's the way it's happened, and we ought to be able to hammer out a way of working together. Beyond that, though, there can't be anything between us." Scott started to protest, and she added sharply, "I don't *want* there to be anything."

"What shallow feelings you must have," he said bitterly, "that you can so easily deny them."

Easily?

"I'm going back to the house now," she stated in a firm tone. "Please don't come with me."

"Suppose I won't let you go?" Scott lifted a hand toward her, but Kati angrily knocked it away.

"Don't make me dislike you more than I already do," she snapped.

With that, she walked away from him, and to her intense relief Scott made no attempt to follow. She didn't glance back; her thoughts now were directed ahead. That Dee had seen something she was quite positive—but how much had she seen? Enough, almost certainly, to know that the two figures locked in a passionate embrace had been Scott and she. Dee, being Dee, would demand an explanation of how this had come about, when Kati Young was supposed to dislike Scott Drummond so intensely.

Kati too entered the house by a side door, which she found led through a corridor to the main hall. A maid was crossing to the drawing room with a tray of fresh glasses, and Kati stopped her.

"Would you please tell the countess that I have rather a headache, so I'm going straight to bed."

"Of course, Miss Young. Is there anything I can get you?"

"No, thank you."

Up in her room, Kati made no attempt to undress or lie down. She stood at the window, gazing out at the dark silhouettes of the cedar trees that graced the parkland, her thoughts a painful jumble. After a few minutes, there was a tap at her door.

"Who is it?" Her heart began to race.

"It's me, Sybilla. Jane told me that you have a headache."

She could hardly tell her hostess to go away, nor could she conduct a conversation through a closed door. Kati crossed the room and opened it.

"I'm okay, Syb. It's just a slight headache. I guess I had a glass of wine too many at dinner. I'll be fine if I can take things quietly."

"Well, if you're quite sure . . ."

"I am, really. Thanks for coming up, Syb. It was sweet of you."

Sybilla went away, and silence returned. Kati wondered if she'd better get to bed, but she knew that she wouldn't sleep, and she'd never be able to concentrate on a book. While she hesitated, there was a second knock at her door. She froze. Would Scott be so reckless as to pursue her here?

The knock was repeated, more loudly. "Who is it?" she called anxiously.

"Dee!" The one word was sharp and jagged. "I want to talk to you."

Kati wasn't prepared for this, not yet, not tonight. She needed time to fabricate an explanation that would satisfy Dee of how and why she'd come to be kissing Scott in the garden.

"Can't it wait, Dee?" she called. "I have a headache, and . . ."

"No, it can't wait."

Reluctantly, Kati turned the handle and opened the door. Dee walked straight in, pushed the door shut and swung around to confront Kati in a blaze of fury.

"I want to know what the devil you thought you were

up to with Scott," she stormed. "I never expected anything so despicable from you."

"I'm sorry, Dee—you've got to believe that," Kati said miserably.

"Sorry? I should damn well think you are!" Dee's brilliant green eyes burned into her from behind the large-framed spectacles. "I thought we were supposed to be friends, Kati. How could you do this to me? How could you deliberately go behind my back and make a play for Scott, when I'd confided in you that I was after him?"

"But it wasn't like that, Dee. Honestly. You don't understand."

"No, I don't understand. I don't understand one bit. So you'd better try telling me . . . and by God, your explanation had better be good."

Kati swallowed hard, gazing back at Dee unhappily. There was no way she could be fobbed off with a few smooth words. The only possible thing was to tell her the truth. Without yet knowing how much of the truth she was going to have to reveal, Kati cleared her throat of its huskiness.

"What you don't understand, Dee, is that Scott and I knew one another a long time ago—eight years ago, before he went to America. We . . . we were engaged to be married."

Chapter Twelve

Dee's gasp of incredulity broke through her anger. "You and Scott were engaged to be married?"

"It's quite true," Kati confirmed in a choked voice.

"But how . . . what happened? What went wrong?"

"It's a long story, Dee."

"I think I'm entitled to hear it," Dee said insistently, her eyes flaring.

"Yes, I guess you are." Kati took a long breath. "I used to be very much in love with Scott. I was crazy about him. And he about me, so I thought. Then . . . well, something happened that made me see how hard and ruthless he really was—is. So I finished with him."

"And Scott went to America?"

"Yes, soon after."

"Then, eight years later, he came back. Are you saying he was hoping to pick up with you again?"

"Oh, no! Nothing like that. Scott came back because the big job at U.P. was dangled in front of him by

Victor Channon. He heard that I was editing *Rendezvous*, but that didn't deter him."

"Why should it have done?"

Kati turned away and smoothed an already immaculate bedcover. "Because we parted on very hostile terms. Scott couldn't have wanted to meet up with me again, any more than I did with him."

"That I find hard to believe," Dee said dryly. She was beginning to recover her normal poise, though there was still bewilderment in her eyes. "Seeing you together just now, it looked like a most joyful occasion."

"That meant nothing, Dee. It doesn't change things between us."

"Nothing? You honestly expect me to accept that the passionate way you two were kissing in the garden wasn't important?"

"It *wasn't* important, Dee. And it won't happen again."

"Why did it happen at all? That's what I want to know."

"Can't you understand," Kati said, with a feeling of helplessness. "Scott and I were once in love—we were lovers. What broke us up had nothing to do with the physical side of our relationship. When you've felt like that about a person, you can't just switch off."

"You mean that the old flame still burns as brightly?"

Kati heaved a shuddering sigh. "Yes, it does."

"For him, too, apparently."

"It's just a matter of sexual chemistry."

"*Just!*"

"Yes, it is," Kati insisted vehemently. "It's true what I've always told you about disliking Scott. I *do* dislike him. More than just dislike him, I loathe and detest everything he stands for."

"But you find him irresistible?"

Kati clenched her fists tightly. "He's a very attractive man."

"Oh, I grant you that. On a scale of one to ten, Scott would score around eleven plus." Dee's face softened into lines of friendship as she went on, "You can't leave it there, Kati. Like I said, I'm entitled to an explanation. Ever since Scott arrived at U.P. you've been at pains to demonstrate how much you dislike him, but never a word about the past. Even when I told you plainly that I was hoping for an affair with him, you still kept your mouth shut. Maybe you get your kicks out of lovemaking with a man you positively dislike . . . okay, that's your business. But it becomes my business when you haven't the decency to warn me that you had a prior claim on him."

Kati felt bemused. How could she explain tonight's episode to Dee when she didn't properly understand it herself?

"I didn't warn you off him, Dee, because I haven't any prior claim on Scott. Tonight I didn't intend it to happen. I didn't *want* it to happen."

"That takes some swallowing," Dee said thoughtfully. She sat down on the bed and looked at Kati. "If it's true what you say, if tonight really did happen against your will because you got swept away, doesn't that fact tell you something?"

"What should it tell me?"

"Give me strength! An attraction that survives eight solid years of separation, and is still as strong as ever! Heavens above, Kati, it's not just physical, believe me."

"It is," she insisted. "There's nothing else about Scott Drummond that I find even halfway likable."

"This isn't just because of the job he's doing at U.P., is it?" Dee studied Kati's face questioningly. "So what happened way back to cause you to chuck a man that you still find so intensely attractive?"

"It's his whole attitude to life, Dee."

"I want something more specific than a sweeping statement."

Kati stared back at her resentfully, feeling cornered. Yet somewhere deep down she felt an urge to relate the whole ugly story. Dee, unlike Fay and Harry Pemberton, would be fully able to appreciate Scott's treachery, and she would be sympathetic.

"Okay, then, here it is, Dee. My father used to be the owner of a thriving printing business in Wimbledon —Prestige Print. After I'd graduated I went to work with him. I was thrilled about it. Dad and I had always been very close, especially after my mother died, and we'd never been at odds on any issue. I knew that our working together would pan out. The idea was for me to get a thorough grounding in the printing trade, so as to be well qualified to take over the firm from Dad when the time ultimately came. I got to know Scott right after I started working for Dad, because in those days Scott was an executive for Arlington Journals, and we did a lot of their printing on contract. I'd known Scott for about ten months, and he and I were engaged. We were going to get married quite soon; then Dad had a fatal heart attack. It was then that I made the horrifying discovery that, far from Prestige Print coming to me, the firm had been signed over to Arlington Journals. Scott had just been using me. He'd traded on our relationship to maneuver things so that Dad had to go to Arlington for additional capital. The price of those loans was control of Prestige Print, with Dad kept on as the manager on a salaried basis. And Scott's reward for that little piece of wheeling and dealing was getting made a director of Arlington."

"I just can't believe it of Scott," Dee said, shaking her head bemusedly.

"I'm telling you, it happened. The facts were there for everyone to see. I strongly suspect that what brought on Dad's coronary was worry—worry that I'd feel he'd let me down when I learned what he'd been forced to do." Her voice cracked a little as she went on, "But I didn't blame Dad, how could I? He was a wonderful man, the kindest, most sincere, genuine man in all the world. And a man like that was a mere babe in arms when he came up against a scheming charmer like Scott Drummond."

Dee's brow was creased in a frown of incredulity. "Did Scott still expect you to marry him?"

Kati felt a sting of tears behind her eyelids. "Sure he did. He seemed quite astonished when I broke off our engagement. He just didn't understand the contempt I felt for him, the bitterness. He kept saying that the takeover by Arlington was just a straight-forward business deal, and that Dad wouldn't have accepted it if it wasn't what he'd wanted."

"What was your answer to that, Kati?"

"Dad had no alternative. He wasn't the world's best businessman, I admit that, and he'd been cynically manipulated into a position where he desperately needed a new injection of finance."

Dee's glance was thoughtful. "So after your father's death you lost your career, as well as your fiancé."

"Scott kept insisting that I needn't lose either," Kati said bitterly. "He even tried to tell me that if I were absolutely determined not to marry him, I could still keep my job. Imagine it, me a paid employee of the firm I should have owned, and under the thumb of the man who had masterminded my father's ruin. I got the hell out, Dee, and I was too sick at heart to want anything to do with printing and publishing for quite some time."

"So that's your side of it," Dee said musingly. "I wonder what his would be."

"Do you think I've lied to you?" Kati flared.

"Calm down. I do believe what you've told me, so far as it goes. But obviously there's much more to it." Dee shook her head in a stunned way. "I still can't get over it . . . you and Scott knowing each other before. But it explains so much that I'd found puzzling. The way you lashed out at him at the meeting on Tuesday, for instance . . . it didn't fit with your character. You're usually so rational and balanced. Then your tennis partnership today. Everyone's talking about it, but none of us suspected that you must have played together before. And there's the way Scott acted, too. . . ."

"The way Scott acted?"

Dee hesitated, then gave a what-the-hell shrug. "Scott and I hit it off, and I flatter myself that he finds me attractive. But when I gave him a flash of the green light, he didn't attempt to follow through. I couldn't understand it, and I decided that he probably still had some kind of a hang-up about another woman . . . a woman he'd left behind in America. I never guessed for a single moment that you were the woman."

"You think Scott's hung up about me? That's a laugh. It just pleases his ego to get under my skin. Nothing more than that."

"Liar."

"I tell you it's true, Dee. All Scott cares about is himself, his ambition. He'll trample on anyone who gets in his way. I can't avoid him at the office, worse luck, but apart from that, I intend keeping plenty of space between us."

"Are you capable of doing that?"

Kati shivered, only too unhappily aware of how difficult it would be. "I must," she said emphatically. "Don't you see, Dee, I simply must. I bitterly regret what happened this evening. Thinking about it makes me feel sick with shame."

"Only because I happened to catch you."

Kati shook her head. "No, it wasn't just that. Knowing that you'd seen us together, Dee, forced me to face up to what I was doing—how feeble it is to be so weak where Scott is concerned despite what happened in the past."

Dee regarded her reflectively for several moments. Then she said slowly, "I can't imagine, if I had such a lousy opinion of a man, that I'd find him so hellishly attractive. Not to the point of getting together with him."

"That's what I mean," Kati said wretchedly. "It's so ridiculous, so feeble."

"No." Dee made a gesture of denial. "You've admitted that you *do* find Scott extremely attractive. Ergo, to my way of thinking, you can't really despise him, not deep in your soul."

"Are you in the shrink business?" Kati demanded sarcastically.

"Not me! But a few sessions on the couch might put you wise to yourself," Dee rejoined. "Life, Kati, is for living. Perfection is just for idealists and dreamers."

"I could get on with living my life if only Scott would keep away. It would suit me just fine if you took him on, Dee."

"Well, that's not going to happen, sweetie, because —contrary to all appearances—I know when I'm beaten."

"Lady Dorothy Faulkner beaten? I never thought I'd live to hear that."

Dee grinned. "Let's say that I'm beating a tactical retreat, then, in face of withering crossfire."

"You're talking riddles."

Dee's level gaze challenged her. "Think so? Let's change the scenario, then. Suppose I'd said that in spite of everything you've told me, I still proposed getting together with Scott. Suppose in a couple of weeks' time I reported that everything was just great between him and me. Would that news charge your batteries, Kati? Think about it. Mull it over in your mind."

With a rustle of her black taffeta evening skirt, Dee was at the door. Then she was gone, and Kati was left to disentangle the chaos of her emotions.

Next morning, it was clear to Kati that the horseback ride planned by Dee and Scott hadn't taken place. At the breakfast table, he spoke of having gone for an early stroll along the river bank. Dee, without appearing ostentatious about it, sat a little apart from Scott, and there was a wariness in what she said to him. Kati, too, was wary of Scott, and he of her. Though he hardly ever glanced her way, she was keenly aware of invisible threads of tension joining them.

Again the day was largely devoted to tennis. Not even Kati's poor play, due to lack of concentration, could stop her emerging as the overall lady winner, with Scott coming top of the men. Peregrine presided at a mock-serious prize-giving ceremony before tea was served. For Kati, there were two prime center court seats for the ladies' final day at the Wimbledon Championships; for Scott equivalent seats at the men's final.

"Who're you planning to take with you, Kati?" demanded Vernon, with an envious grin. "I'm available."

"I expect they'll take each other," Dee remarked, smiling blandly at Kati.

Kati was saved the need of a comeback by Scott, who said in a lazy voice, "Nice thought, Dee. But no doubt Kati will have other ideas."

A cold buffet was served for Sunday supper, and soon afterward the general exodus began. At the very last minute, with people gathered in the hall, Dee announced that she'd decided to stay on overnight and drive to London in the morning.

"No problem for you, sweetie," she said to Kati in a loud, clear tone. "You'll easily catch a ride back to town."

"I'll take you with pleasure," Scott offered at once.

"Oh, no!" she exclaimed unguardedly.

"It's no trouble," he insisted. "We live almost within shouting distance. Is your luggage down yet?"

"Yes . . ." She was desperately trying to think up a reason for refusing that wouldn't sound too lame.

"Fine!" Scott spoke to a manservant, instructing him to put Kati's suitcase in his car.

They said their rounds of thanks and good-byes, Kati's killing look at Dee being returned by a guileless smile. A few minutes later Kati sat beside Scott in the front seat of his silver blue car as they sped along the parkland driveway away from Avonbury Hall. Kati, staring gloomily ahead through the windshield, felt like sitting the entire journey in silence. But she knew that Scott wouldn't allow that to happen, so she seized the initiative herself.

"I wish you hadn't done this," she told him forcefully. "I'd have much preferred to have had someone else give me a ride home."

"Who else lives as near you as I do? I practically pass your door, Kati, so it would have been crazy to take someone else out of their way."

"I could always have taken a taxi for the last part of the journey."

"A totally needless expense."

They slipped through the country lanes in the hush of a summer Sunday evening, and the beauty of the passing scene—lush meadows with a river winding through, grazed by sleek black and white cattle—seemed like mockery to Kati's bruised and battered mind.

"We can't go on like this," Scott said at length.

"Like what?"

He gave an impatient exclamation. "There you go again, trying to dodge the issue. You have to face the situation as it is, however much you'd like things to be different."

"I *am* facing the situation."

"No, you're not," he stated. "Otherwise you wouldn't always be attacking me, always so quick on the draw. We have to find *some* way through our problems. You'd better believe it."

"Yes, sir, no, sir, three bags full, sir."

"I wasn't just talking about work, Kati."

She threw him a quick, angry look. "How many

times do I have to spell it out, Scott? Our relationship is at the office and only at the office."

"Not true, Kati. We can't ignore the strong feelings there are between us."

"That's the whole trouble," she said, with a fierce sigh. "If I could do that, I . . ."

"If you could do that . . . what?" he prompted.

"Things would be entirely different," she said lamely.

Scott swerved the car onto the grass and stopped. He pulled on the handbrake and switched off.

"How would things be different?" he demanded.

"I wouldn't have such bitter memories."

Scott swung around in his seat, an elbow resting on the steering wheel. He met her gaze levelly. "What you're saying is that if we'd never met before I started at U.P., so you had no emotional hang-up from the past, you'd be ready to have an affair with me?"

Kati caught her breath. "That's being blunt."

"I'm feeling blunt," he said. "So what's your answer?"

"I . . . I'm not denying that I find you very attractive, so I guess . . ."

"But because of some imagined injury from way back, you're denying yourself something you'd very much like to get into?"

"It wasn't imaginary, Scott."

"Okay," he said impatiently, "but it was eight years ago. That's a helluva long time; it's ancient history. Why can't you pretend that we've just met for the first time. Why in God's name can't you just take it from there?"

"It's not possible."

"It *is* possible." His voice became less harsh, almost gentle. "We proved it once, Kati, and it was wonderful. It would be wonderful again."

She shook her head vehemently. "I got carried away before."

"Isn't that exactly how it should be . . . what passion is all about? Sex that was carefully calculated and planned for wouldn't be worth having." His blue eyes held hers in a look of appeal. "I'm not asking you to tell me right here and now that you're willing to go to bed with me again. I'm just saying, why don't you let your true feelings have a chance instead of repressing them? Accept me for what I am now . . . a man who excites you as much as you excite him. Let go of the strings, Kati, and let your emotions take over."

"It . . . it's not possible," she repeated.

"Give it a try, Kati . . . please." There was a soft note in his voice, then he went on cheerfully, "How's this for an idea, why don't we stop off at the boat for a drink?"

"No!" she said, so sharply that it sounded like panic.

"You see, you won't give yourself a chance. All I'm asking is for us to spend a little time together, just to prove that we can act like civilized people instead of old enemies. Even after a war the two sides have to set aside their differences, so it ought to be possible for us. No relationship, of any kind, can ever be perfect. It's just that you and I have a few more problems to overcome than most people."

"That," she said bitterly, "is the understatement of the year."

"But then," he countered, "we're not most people, we're you and I. I've never been short on self-confidence, Kati, and you haven't either. To people like us, problems are made to be overcome."

"My point exactly. I'm trying to overcome my problem regarding you, Scott."

"Concentrate on how much you *want* me, Kati. Forget about the rest."

Kati frantically tried to formulate a line of reasoning that would demolish his argument. "There are many things I want, Scott, but it doesn't mean that I should expect to have them. I'd like a dress we modeled in the last issue of *Rendezvous*, but I accept that it's way out of my price range. There's a grandfather clock in an antique shop in the King's Road costing two thousand pounds that I covet, but I don't consider that I have the right to break the shop window and take it."

"You wouldn't have to break anything to take me, Kati," he said quietly.

"Yes, I would. I'd have to break my own integrity."

"Then your integrity must already be in shreds."

Kati was reduced to silence. It was true that she didn't regret the time they'd made love after her birthday party. Not once since it happened had she felt any real regret. She treasured the memory close to her heart.

"Let's get moving," she said at length.

"To the boat first?"

"No!" Then, before Scott could speak again, she said quickly, "Yes, all right, if that's what you want. Just for a drink."

"A drink and a talk."

"If you say so."

The *Pagan* was rocking almost imperceptibly at her moorings as they stepped aboard. The river beyond was a great sheet of hammered bronze against the setting sun. The saloon smelled a bit stuffy after two days closed up, and Scott slid back some of the windows to let in the balmy evening air.

"What can I get you?" he asked, going to the drinks corner.

"Oh . . . white wine."

Scott poured her a glass, and fixed a whisky for himself. Kati sat down on the leather banquette and looked out across the placid river scene. A white motor cruiser was passing on its way upstream, leaving a frothy wake, but otherwise it was a smooth expanse of water.

"I guess," Scott said, "that I have one of the best views in London."

"Yes, it's lovely." Her voice emerged toneless and disinterested, but she felt too nervous to act naturally. She shouldn't have agreed to come aboard.

Scott tried again to start a conversation. "What will you do with your spare Wimbledon ticket?"

"I haven't thought about it yet."

"Someone suggested that we ought to take each other," he reminded her. "Why don't we?"

Have Scott sitting beside her at Wimbledon? What bittersweet memories that would evoke.

"No," she said decidedly. "I don't think that it would be a good idea."

"Well, I can't force you to invite me on your day," he said. "But I'm inviting you on mine. You'd like to see the men's singles final, wouldn't you, Kati?"

"So would a million other people. I'm sure you'll have no difficulty finding someone to take along." A crazy impulse prodded her to add, "How about the girlfriend you took to dinner the other evening?"

Scott raised his eyebrows in query. "When was this, Kati?"

"When I was dining with Fay Pemberton and Sir Roland Maynard, after our television appearance."

Scott's face cleared, and he looked amused. "Oh, you mean Beverley Anderson. She's Jesse's girlfriend."

"Jesse?"

"The guy who's lending me this boat, remember?"

Kati remembered vividly. She'd formed a picture in her mind of a free-living man who'd chosen the exotic houseboat as a lure. "I didn't get the impression that he confines himself to one girlfriend."

"One at a time," Scott returned, with a grin. "Beverley happens to be the current one. Jesse asked me to keep an eye on her while he's away, make sure she doesn't get bored."

"What a heavensent assignment for you."

Scott's amusement deepened. "As you saw, Beverley is a gorgeous creature. But, friendship to Jesse apart, she isn't my type."

"So what is your type?" It was out before Kati could stop herself.

Scott gave her a straight, serious look. "Oh, Kati . . . Kati! Must we fence around?"

She felt threatened by her own vulnerability. She knew that she must make her escape before it was too late.

"I'd better be going." Putting aside her half-finished drink, she started to stand up.

"No, not yet . . . please," Scott said, reaching out a hand to stop her. The first touch of his fingers on her arm sent shivers racing through Kati's veins. She tried to persist in her purpose, but the urgency had gone, and she allowed him to pull her down again onto the leather banquette. His hands cupped her face and as his mouth came close to hers she tried to turn away, but it was no more than a token resistance, a faint echo from some almost-forgotten resolve.

His lips moved over hers in sweet, tender kisses, till Kati's pulses sang with happiness and she felt excitement flow through her veins like molten gold. Her mouth opened invitingly, wanting him to plunder the softness inside. She twined her arms around his neck, clinging to him in delirious response as their kissing became deeper and more intense, with a joyful mating of tongues.

"Kati," he murmured, in a voice that was passion-deep and husky. "Darling, darling Kati."

"Oh, Scott . . ."

By now the sun had set and a hazy lilac dusk had settled softly over the river. Long shadows moved across the saloon with the gentle rocking of the boat.

Scott's hands began to rove over her, probing the secrets of her body, bringing to Kati an intense awareness of pleasure in every curve and hollow, every sensitive spot, flooding her with delight and yearning. Every cell in her body hungered for him.

She felt Scott's fingers on her breast, seeking the tiny pearl buttons of her blouse. He slid the fabric over her slender shoulders and eased it from her arms. Then he unfastened the waistband of her cotton skirt and drew it down over her hips while she fumbled with the buttons of his shirt, clumsy in her haste. Pushing it aside, she laid her open palms to the heated skin of his chest as if she had for too long been starved of contact with his flesh.

Seconds later they were both naked. Scott lifted her in his arms and laid her full length on the banquette, then knelt beside her. He began a long, leisurely exploration of her body, his fingers caressing, his lips adoring, his teeth nipping her fevered flesh in tiny love bites that sent rockets of erotic sensation shooting through her. Kati's nipples were tingling, hard and peaked with need, while his hands teased her, holding the soft weight of her breasts and kissing the valley between them.

"Please," she whispered throatily. "Please, Scott . . ."

Smilingly, he yielded to her entreaty, and let his thumbs brush the swollen tips, then flicked and pinched them gently until she was moaning aloud in delicious torment.

For Scott the torment of frustration was even greater than hers. His groin throbbed with the violence of his desire, and he had to fight for mastery. He longed with a frantic urgency he had never known before to join his body with hers, to enter her velvet dark warmth and thrust in a frenzy of passion that would culminate in an explosion of savage splendor. Since their lovemaking at the mews cottage, he'd been obsessed by the need to possess her again. But every instinct warned him to go slow and make this utterly perfect for Kati. This fragile mood of unity could so easily be shattered by a selfish grasping of his own pleasure.

So, calling up every shred of self-restraint, he disciplined himself to the creation of perfection for Kati, arousing her step by step until her own spiraling need matched his, her own passion was as urgent as his. Holding her tenderly, his fingers weaving erotic patterns against the satiny smoothness of her skin, he buried his face against her breasts. Unconsciously, he groaned in the intensity of his leashed desire.

Kati felt his trembling, and her knowledge of his need brought about a new urgency to her own. She suddenly wanted fulfilment for them both . . . now, without any more delightful agony of waiting. She clutched Scott fiercely, unaware that her fingernails bit into the muscled flesh of his shoulders, urging him to her. Artlessly bold, she guided him swiftly and surely, until they were joined and could soar together toward the final crest. When Scott knew from her rapturous moans that her moment was near, he gave his passion free rein. Together they cried out their ultimate joy, then lay with limbs entwined, shaking, murmuring half-articulate endearments. Gently, Scott touched his lips to hers, and pushed back the dark waves of hair that had tumbled across her brow.

"Sweet, wonderful Kati."

"Oh, Scott!"

Far out in midstream a vessel went by, its engines purring. Moments later, the wash rocked the *Pagan* gently, and lights reflected from the rippling water danced across the saloon's ceiling. It was a gentle reminder to Kati of where they were. Stirring, she said, "I must go."

"You don't have to," Scott remonstrated, lazily caressing her shoulder with his fingertips. "Stay with me."

"No, I can't."

He gazed into her eyes, trying to read her expression in the faint, filtered light.

"You're not having regrets?" he asked.

"No." She couldn't lie. "No regrets."

"Then why go? This is just the beginning, Kati."

"You knew this would happen, didn't you, Scott?" There was slight reproach in her tone.

"Didn't you?"

She considered that. "Not consciously, but I suppose . . ."

"It was inevitable, Kati. And will be again . . . often."

A shadow crossed her mind. "I'm not sure about that."

"You can be lying here with me like this," he asked incredulously, "and say that you're not sure? That's crazy talk."

"So let me get dressed. It won't seem so crazy then."

He remained still for several long seconds, pinning her down. Then he grunted acquiescence, and rolled himself away from her. After they'd both put on their clothes, Scott switched on a shaded lamp so that Kati could see to comb her hair.

"I remember how I used to love watching you do your hair afterward," he said. "It seemed so wonderfully intimate. They were good days, Kati, darling."

"But those days are over, Scott. Everything is changed."

He nodded somberly. "You're right—everything is changed. So let's look forward, not back. We can have a wonderful summer together."

"Scott, I don't know. I'm too confused. Everything is so complicated."

"No, darling, it's beautifully simple. I want you and you want me. All the rest is unimportant, not worth bothering about. Forget it, ignore it."

Kati sighed. "How can everything else be ignored

and forgotten, even though I . . ." She had very nearly said, *even though I love you.* She hastily tried to dismiss the thought, but it was there, solid and firm. Unmovable. Despite everything, she acknowledged with a feeling of dismay, she did love Scott. Perhaps—could it be true?—she had continued to love him all through the time of their long separation.

She had paused for so long that Scott prompted her. "Even though you what, Kati?"

"Even though I find you very attractive," she said shakily. "But I really despise the things you stand for, your whole attitude to life."

A look of pain flickered across the lean, handsome features of his face. He said in a careful, level tone, "Lots of couples have differing views on all kinds of matters, Kati."

"It's not trivial differences that I'm talking about," she stated. "These things are basics. I just can't accept the kind of man you are."

There was a long pause, then Scott said slowly, "If I had any sense at all, I'd quit trying to get through to you."

"So why don't you?"

His cobalt eyes met hers in a deep, challenging gaze. "Is that what you want me to do, Kati?"

She couldn't go on meeting his eyes, and she looked down at the floor. "No," she whispered.

"So where does that take us?"

When she didn't answer, Scott let a few moments of silence go by, then said, "At work, Kati, you can fight me and my proposals all you like. That's fair, and anyway I'll win and be proved right in the end—"

"No doubt you will," she broke in, "from a strictly commercial point of view."

"That's what U.P. pays my salary for—to make money for them."

"And you think that that justifies anything?" she

demanded. "You think it gives you the right to make sweeping changes that affect people's lives as if you're merely moving pawns around in a chessgame?"

"We're talking about Robin Wheatley now, I suppose?"

She nodded. "Robin is a good example of what I mean."

"Have you seen him since he started working on *The Weekly Gardener?*"

"With him stuck miles out in the sticks," she said ironically, "there's not been much opportunity."

"Then if I were you, Kati, I'd reserve judgment on that particular staff change until you do see Wheatley. You might be pleasantly surprised." Scott shrugged the issue aside. "My point is that away from work you'd better cut out this holier-than-thou approach. I'm getting a bit tired of it. Understand?"

"I can't help showing how I feel."

"I've had my share of hiding my feelings," he said, with a spurt of bitterness.

"What do you mean?"

"Forget it," he said dismissively. "I think you're right, Kati, it's time you went home. This evening was wonderful, but it's turned a bit sour on us. I have an idea that if you stayed, we wouldn't recapture the mood. So let's go."

In less than ten minutes they had reached her door.

"About tomorrow evening," Scott began, as she thanked him for walking her home.

"No, not tomorrow."

"Are you sure?"

"Quite sure."

Scott hesitated. "The problem is, on Tuesday I have to go north for a couple of days. I'm negotiating with a print firm to handle some of our printing that's previously been done abroad. It will mean that we shan't be able to see each other—not alone, that is—until Friday evening. It seems a long time to wait, Kati."

It seemed a long time to her, also, and she almost regretted having ruled Monday out.

"Still," Scott went on philosophically, "it'll give us both plenty of time to think about what we really want from each other. I'll be here at seven and we can talk everything through."

Chapter Thirteen

Next morning, over breakfast, Kati leafed through the newspaper. In her job it was essential to keep abreast of events and personalities in the news, but for once other people's lives failed to gain her interest. She was still hopelessly confused about her relationship with Scott and where it was leading, and about where she wanted it to go.

She bit off a corner of buttered toast and turned a page. Her eyes glossed over a story about a government contract enquiry . . . details of a new air-shuttle service between London and Scotland . . . the progress of a visiting head of state from an African republic. Halfway down the "News in Brief" column her attention was arrested by a name. Theodore Caulfield . . . Dee's ex-husband. In six lines it reported that he'd been involved in a road crash, when a truck had shot the lights and hit his car broadside on. Theodore had been taken to St. Catherine's Hospital suffering from multiple injuries.

Kati's first thought was, Poor Dee! Though Dee had been divorced from Theodore for four years, Kati knew that she still harbored tender feelings for him. Possibly, since she was no longer Theodore's next of kin, she wouldn't yet have learned of his accident. Kati pondered, wondering whether to call Dee. If she were going to, she'd better do it quickly before Dee left Avonbury Hall to drive back to London. Without waiting for second thoughts, she picked up the phone and dialed. A maid answered, and went to fetch Dee to the phone.

"Hi, Kati. Something wrong?" she asked a minute later.

"Well . . . Dee, have you seen the paper this morning?"

"No, I've been talking to Perry and Syb. Why?"

"It's about Theodore . . . Theodore Caulfield. I just read that he was in a car accident yesterday."

"Oh, my God!" Dee gasped in a voice of alarm. "Is he badly hurt . . . did it say?"

"I'm afraid it doesn't sound too good. Multiple injuries, the paper said. He's been taken to St. Catherine's Hospital."

"I'll call . . . no, I'll go there right away. Thanks for phoning, Kati; I'd have hated not to know. I'll be late at the office, of course. Will you tell my secretary, and ask her to reschedule my appointments?"

"Sure, Dee. And I hope you get good news about Theodore."

"Oh, I do hope so, Kati. I couldn't bear to think . . ."

It was very unlike Dee to be emotional, Kati thought as she hung up. It gave her a warm feeling that Dee and Theodore, even though their marriage hadn't worked out, could still have respect and affection for each other. So unlike what she felt for Scott. It had been a shock to her to discover that it was possible to be in love with someone without having feelings of respect and affection for him. Or even liking.

Around mid-morning, at the office, she had a call from Dee to say that there was no real news as yet. Theodore was at present undergoing surgery.

"They told me that he has a good chance of pulling through, thank heaven, but no one will say how badly he's going to be affected. I'm going to stick around here, Kati, for as long as necessary. I want to be here when he regains consciousness."

"Yes, of course. I'll be thinking of you, Dee. Bye for now."

Dee called again in the early afternoon, with the happier news that Theo had come around after the operation, and she'd been able to talk with him for five minutes.

"He was still groggy from the anesthetic, poor love. But, mercifully, the doctors are hopeful that he's going to make a good recovery. He's got a broken leg—a complicated fracture, apparently—some cracked ribs, and his left hand was pretty smashed up. It's going to need a lot of hard work at physical therapy to get his fingers working properly again. He'll do it, though . . . my Theo's got guts."

"I'm so happy for you, Dee."

Kati pondered about that conversation afterward. *My* Theo . . . a strange way of putting it, in the circumstances. A thought crossed her mind about the two of them, but she threw it out as crazy. Dee was just feeling sorry for a man whom she'd once loved, and who was now injured and in the hospital. That was all it could be. Even so . . .

Kati was left with an odd feeling of sadness. It was almost as if she felt envious of Dee. There was nothing new about that—she'd often envied Dee's poise and assurance, her sure touch in the complexities of fashion. But this was something else. Dee had a relationship with a man which had survived the trauma of divorce, and she'd remained steadfast, ready to hurry to his bedside when she heard that he was hospitalized. Despite all that had passed between Dee and Theo, there had to be a tremendous sense of closeness still remaining.

Once upon a wonderful time Kati had believed that she'd had that sort of closeness with Scott. And it had vanished in a puff of smoke. Love was left, love without any sense of closeness, love that had only bitter memories. It was her fate to love a man who didn't deserve to be loved.

She didn't have any contact with Scott before he left to go north. Once, briefly, she saw him from a distance as he and Victor Channon were stepping into an elevator. Just the sight of Scott's lean, athletic figure set all her nerve endings jangling. Would she ever be able to get him out of her system? she wondered with a sense of helplessness.

From Tuesday onward, Kati was hectically busy. A sudden wave of summer flu had decimated the staff just as the next issue of *Rendezvous* was due to go to the printer. A crisis seemed to crop up every few minutes. There was a suspected libel in a showbiz profile that necessitated a hasty rewrite, and a last-minute order for a full-page ad, which they couldn't afford to let go, meant a reshuffling of the editorial content to make room for it. Tuesday evening Kati was at her desk until nine, and Wednesday was nearly as bad. It wasn't until noon on Thursday that things seemed to be calming down, and she was able to go to lunch with Dee at their favorite taverna.

"How're things going with Theodore?" Kati asked her as they dodged through the surging traffic.

"Very well, considering." There was an air of suppressed excitement about Dee, and the explanation was not long in coming. As soon as they were seated, she announced, "This lunch is a celebration, Kati, and it's on me. We're having champagne, and no stinting yourself on the food. Forget calories for once."

"Sounds terrific. What are we celebrating, Dee?"

"Oh . . . just that life's wonderful."

Kati eyed her friend with eager interest. "This is to do with Theodore, right?"

Dee nodded vigorously. "I'm not usually superstitious, yet I'm almost scared of tempting fate. But . . . oh, hell, Kati, I have to tell someone, and who else but you?"

"Are you two getting together again?" Kati hazarded.

Another beaming nod from Dee. "It's crazy, I know, but it took something like that dreadful accident to make us both see sense. Theo and I were just too ambitious, too darned independent. That's where we came unstuck, Kati. Then suddenly, on Monday, it hit me how much I cared about him. I began to see everything in a new light."

"How about Theodore? Does he feel the same way?"

Dee's green eyes were a little misty. "He told me that he's never been really happy since we split up. He never even thought of marrying again, and of course that's how it was with me. I kidded myself it was because I'd been put off marriage for good, but the truth was that no other man could possibly measure up to Theo for me."

The waitress came for their orders, and they hadn't even glanced at the menus. "Bring us a bottle of champagne," Dee instructed her, "while we think about what we're going to eat."

When the waitress had gone, Kati said, "I'm really glad for you, Dee. When do you plan to get married?"

Dee laughed. "Personally, I'd be happy to have the ceremony right away, in hospital. Theo wants to wait until he's on his feet again, though, and see if I'm still of the same mind then. I will be, of course, but the darling man is so anxious that I won't feel that he's taking advantage of my good nature. He insists that we see how well he recovers, and how much permanent damage there'll be, before he lets me commit myself. Still, I'll be able to talk him around before very long," she finished confidently.

The champagne arrived and was poured foaming into tall flutes. Dee told the waitress, "I've decided that we'll both have the souvlakia, Rhoda—largely because it's the most expensive item on the menu." She raised her glass to Kati. "Here's to seeing me hitched again, quickest or sooner."

"I'll drink to that," said Kati.

"So what's new on the Scott Drummond front?" Dee asked, after a minute.

"There's nothing new," Kati said in a level voice.

"You disappoint me. Mean to say that the drive back to London with him on Sunday produced nil result? Don't tell me that after all the trouble I took to organize your riding with him, Scott just dropped you off home and left you?"

"Well, not actually," Kati admitted. "We stopped off at his houseboat for a drink on the way." She'd meant to say it matter-of-factly, something of no consequence, but she couldn't prevent a flush rising to her face.

"I see," Dee murmured, grinning with approval. "And you've seen him since?"

"How could I?" Kati demanded with a shrug. "Scott's been away from the office since Tuesday, up north. Or hadn't you heard that?"

"No—pity. Still, you know what they say? *Absence makes the heart grow fonder.* No doubt you have something nice planned for the weekend?"

Kati shrugged again, unconvincingly casual. "Since you're so interested, I'm seeing Scott on Friday evening."

"Good."

Kati gave Dee a long, morose look. "I'm not sure

that it's good at all. I feel that I'm on the slippery slope to disaster."

"Maybe it's the pathway to paradise, sweetie." Dee sipped her champagne again, wrinkling her nose delicately against the bubbles. "Haven't you two wasted too many years already? Don't leave it like Theo and I did, until something bad happens to make you see sense."

A white envelope lay on Kati's desk when she returned to her office. She slit it open while scanning through the messages that Sandra had left on her pad. Inside was a note from Greg Farley, the new advertisement manager appointed by Scott who had started work on *Rendezvous* the previous week. His brash, forceful style came through in the scribbled words, the gist of which made Kati go hot and cold with dismay.

Have an appointment in Paddington and won't be back this afternoon, but I must let you know the glad tidings right away. Have extracted a fat space booking from Brand, Fieffer and Coles for their clients West Midland Industrials. Twelve center spreads in color, commencing October. How's that for my first week on Rendezvous? Greg.

West Midland Industrials, as Kati well knew, was one of the firms under the corporate umbrella controlled by Sir Roland Maynard. She also knew that space bookings of this magnitude didn't appear from the blue, but needed hard sales pressure. Products like lawnmowers and hedge trimmers could hardly be called naturals for advertising in a woman's magazine, particularly a trendy one like *Rendezvous*. Obviously, there had been maneuverings behind the scenes to secure this space order, and it wasn't hard to guess who was responsible.

She ran through the likely scenario in her mind. Scott, knowing that she was highly regarded by Sir Roland for her support of the disabled cause, had seen an opportunity for some subtle blackmail. No matter that Sir Roland's opinion of her would have sunk to zero, the important consideration was to make full use of any opportunity to bump up *Rendezvous*'s profits. Nothing else mattered when weighed against commercial advantage.

Kati was gripped by a feeling of cold despair. How would she ever be able to meet Sir Roland again after this, without seeing a look of scorn in his kindly gray eyes? He'd been imagining that her campaign in *Rendezvous* stemmed from genuine concern for handicapped people, only to discover that Kati Young was just as money-motivated as anyone else. At last anger broke through and took precedence in Kati's mind. She felt ashamed of loving such a man as Scott Drummond. At least this incident solved the problem that had been tearing her apart. If, after this, she still went on seeing Scott, she'd feel nothing but contempt for herself.

Calling Scott's office, she told his secretary, "I want to see Mr. Drummond tomorrow. It's important. What time will he be back?"

"He won't be," she was informed. "I've just this minute finished talking to him on the phone, and he said that he'll not be here again until Monday morning."

Damn, Kati thought as she hung up. This meant that she'd have to contain her fury all through the next day until seven in the evening. And then the showdown would be at her home, instead of at the office. Should she leave a message for him that she couldn't make the date they'd fixed? But that would entail waiting all through the weekend with this weight on her mind, assuming that Scott would leave her in peace that long. And she certainly didn't intend to run away from him this time, as she had weakly done before.

Fortunately, Kati didn't face an evening alone with her grim thoughts; the Pembertons were coming for dinner.

Over drinks, Kati and Fay discussed upcoming plans

for Fay's column in *Rendezvous*. For dinner, after a starter of artichoke hearts, Kati served beef stroganoff, with fluffy rice and cauliflower. Her own appetite had deserted her, a fact which didn't pass unnoticed by her guests.

"What's the trouble, Kati?" Harry asked sympathetically. "Overwork?"

Fay dismissed that idea. "Kati thrives on hard work. You're not coming down with this summer flu that's going around, I hope?"

"No, thank heaven. Not so much as a sniffle."

"So what's getting you down?" asked Fay shrewdly.

Yes, Kati decided, she wanted to talk about it. "I'll give you three guesses," she said, making a face. "Though I expect you'll get it in one."

"Scott Drummond?" Fay suggested.

"Give the lady a prize," Kati said caustically.

"We were hoping that things might have been improving between you and him, Kati."

"Forget it!"

"The past is past," Harry put in warily. "What's the sense of souring the rest of your life by constantly brooding on it?"

"As if I could forget the past," she muttered, "when I see the man in action day after day."

"What's Scott done to upset you now?" he asked.

"What hasn't he done? High-powered streamlining is the name of the game at U.P. these days."

"From what you told us previously, Kati, that wouldn't come amiss," Harry commented dryly.

"But I didn't mean it should be achieved by throwing decent standards out of the window. Did I tell you that Robin Wheatley—he was the ad manager on *Rendezvous*—has been booted out?"

"Fired, you mean?"

"Not actually fired. But Scott's shifted him to a much less prestigious job on a smaller magazine. And the man he's appointed to replace Robin on *Rendezvous* is some smart aleck. You'll never believe what those two have pulled off between them."

The Pembertons looked at her unhappily, and Fay said in a quiet voice, "You'd better tell us, Kati."

"Well . . . you remember how splendidly we got on with Sir Roland Maynard that time, Fay? He was full of praise for the good work we were doing for the handicapped cause."

Fay nodded. "Of course I remember. And he's been very generous with contributions to some of the organizations I'm involved with."

"Well, that's fine . . . making *voluntary* contributions to charitable causes. But this is something else. Scott knew how impressed Sir Roland was with our campaign in *Rendezvous,* so he put the screws on him for a big advertisement contract. Sir Roland's companies have never used *Rendezvous* before—not in my time, anyhow—and now suddenly they're going to spend a huge amount with us."

The Pembertons glanced at one another uncomfortably. "These things happen in business, Kati," said Harry.

"When Scott Drummond is around, they do."

Fay asked, "Are you quite certain that it happened the way you described? Has Scott admitted pressing Sir Roland into advertising in *Rendezvous?*"

"He didn't need to admit anything. It's perfectly obvious."

"What seems the obvious explanation isn't always the true one," Harry said with a frown. "It isn't fair to jump to conclusions without knowing all the facts, Kati."

"I know what Scott Drummond is capable of, and that's enough for me."

Again the Pembertons looked at one another, seeming puzzled and anxious. Finally, Fay nodded at Harry as if they'd reached a mutual decision, and he began, "I'm afraid, Kati, that you've misjudged Scott for a very long time. What happened at Prestige Print wasn't at all as you've always believed."

Kati stared at him in utter bewilderment. "What do you mean, Harry?"

He laid down his knife and fork. "I hoped that I'd never need to tell you this, Kati, but I think the time has come when I must."

"Yes, Kati dear," Fay confirmed. "He really must. It's not right that you should go on blaming Scott the way you have done."

"I don't understand," she said dazedly.

Harry seemed very reluctant to start explaining. "I'm afraid, Kati, that it means you're going to hear some things that you won't like."

She had a premonition of what was coming, and asked faintly, "About my father, you mean?"

"He was a fine man, a remarkable man in so many ways. When you were left motherless, no child could have asked for a better father. He was devoted to you and your welfare, Kati. You know all that, of course."

"Yes," she agreed in a low voice.

"Fay and I know what you felt about your father, Kati. We know how you adored him. I'm afraid that you might have endowed him with saintly qualities that no man could ever deserve. Stephen Young was human, just like the rest of us, and he had his share of faults and weaknesses."

"Get on with it, Harry," his wife prodded.

"As regards the printing trade, Stephen was a skilled technician. But, sad to say, on the financial side of the business he was much less able. When your father first encountered cashflow problems he tried to make his way through by speculating on the stock exchange. In that area, Kati, his understanding was hardly better than a child's. He always had a vision that the next speculative venture would get him out of trouble, but of course it only got him deeper into debt. There came a point when he was unable to meet his payroll. In desperation, he turned to Arlington Journals, who were big customers. They helped him out by making advance payments on contracts until, as time went on, he owed them a great deal of money. Finally things came to a head when one of Stephen's stock exchange gambles failed badly. Arlington told him that they couldn't advance him any more, and that they'd be forced to foreclose if he didn't get his finances straightened out. It was at that stage when Scott came up with his proposal. Arlington Journals should take over control of Prestige Print, and your father would remain as managing director on a salaried basis." Harry met Kati's eyes in a serious look. "You've always blamed Scott bitterly for that deal, but I can tell you in all honesty that if it hadn't been for Scott, your father would have gone bankrupt. Scott had to work very hard to persuade the directors of Arlington that the proposed deal would be to their benefit, also."

Shocked, stunned, unable to believe what she was hearing, Kati burst out, "Who did you get all this from, Harry? Is it what Scott told you after Dad died?"

He shook his head. "I never discussed things with Scott, not at any time. It's what your father told me himself, Kati. Stephen always confided in me; we'd been friends for a long time, don't forget." Harry smiled sadly. "Unfortunately, he'd never listen to my advice on financial matters. Not, I hasten to add, that I knew much about finance, but at least I knew enough to see that the road he was taking was the road to ruin."

Kati was silent for several moments, trying to untangle her thoughts. "I just don't understand," she said at length. "Why didn't I know about any of this? Why didn't Dad tell me how bad things were, and that he was going to have to sell out to Arlington?"

"He didn't want you to know what a terrible mess he'd made of things," Harry explained. "He hoped that he'd be able to keep the Arlington takeover from you until well after you and Scott were married. By then, he reasoned, it wouldn't matter to you so much. You wouldn't feel so hurt, and so disappointed in him. You see, Stephen always felt terrible about squandering what he regarded as your birthright—the eventual ownership of Prestige Print. It was worry over that which brought on the heart attack that killed him—I'm convinced of it."

"You could have told me the truth then, Harry," she said accusingly.

"I'd given Stephen my word, Kati. Besides, I wasn't in possession of all the details, as Scott was. It was up to him to decide, as your fiancé, how much he wanted you to know."

Fay said gently, "Harry and I were very sorry when we learned that you and Scott had broken up. We didn't know why, exactly, just that you'd had a terrible quarrel. At the time, well, outsiders shouldn't try to interfere between young people, and in any case we didn't realize back then that it was largely due to a misunderstanding about the true facts of the Arlington deal. We only came to appreciate that recently, when Scott returned to England and we saw that your bitterness against him was still so alive. And now, because of that bitterness, you're finding fault with every single thing Scott does. I can't judge him—I'm in no position to—but from what you say about the job he's doing at U.P., he sounds to me like a shrewd, on-the-ball company executive. As for Sir Roland, from what I saw of him I can't believe that he would ever allow himself to be blackmailed into anything. So don't you think, Kati, that you ought to consider that you might be misjudging Scott yet again?"

Kati's thoughts were spinning wildly, and she felt that she was losing her grip on reality. She had two guests whom she was supposed to be entertaining, but it seemed totally beyond her ability to fetch the dessert she'd prepared.

Fay, always very wise, saw her need to be alone. "I

think, Harry, that we'll cut our visit short this evening. Fetch me my shawl, please."

Kati made a half-hearted protest, but Fay was firm. Spinning her wheelchair back from the table, she came around to Kati and laid a hand on her arm. "You've a lot to think about . . . but don't think too much. It's time for your heart to take over."

"My heart?" Kati whispered.

"That's what I said. In some situations, one's emotions are the best guide."

Kati was scarcely aware of their departure. From the milling chaos in her brain one picture emerged. Scott's face. The face of the man she loved. She knew with a brimming sense of joy that her unquenchable love had been justified. At last her heart was speaking with a clear, unequivocal voice.

Chapter Fourteen

"Hi there, Kati!" A grinning face peered around her office door. "Okay if I come in?"

"Sure, Robin. What brings you here?" Kati tried to sound welcoming, but she could have done without the interruption. It was midway through Friday afternoon, and she hadn't achieved much in the way of work. Most of the time she'd just been sitting at her desk, doodling happily, thinking ahead, making lovely plans.

Robin came in and perched himself on the edge of her desk. "I had an appointment to see Scott Drummond this afternoon, but his secretary phoned this morning to cancel. Apparently he's away."

"That's right," Kati confirmed. "He'll be back this evening." And coming to see me, her heart sang.

"Anyway," Robin went on, "I'd already fixed a couple of other appointments in central London to make full use of a trip to town, so as I had some time free, I thought I'd drop by to look up some old colleagues. Of which you, Kati, are number one on my list."

There was something about Robin that Kati couldn't quite put her finger on. He had a kind of bouncy self-assurance that she'd never seen before, but there was also a kind of wariness. She suspected that he wasn't altogether happy about this meeting with her, yet felt that he had to go through with it.

"How are things going for you, Robin?" she inquired.

"Not bad, not bad at all. There's not the pressure there was here, and this gardening lark has a lot going for it. The advertisers are a whole new bunch to me. They're mostly down-to-earth characters who are straightforward to deal with. I'm even beginning to get interested in my small cabbage patch at home. It tickled Anne last weekend to see me out there digging."

"How is Anne?" Kati asked him. "And the children?"

"They're all fine, thanks." He paused, fiddling self-consciously with the corner of her in-tray. "Kati . . . well, I want you to know that things were never *that* bad between Anne and me. I guess that all marriages have to go through sticky passages, but . . ."

"It only needs . . . a fresh outlook?" she suggested. She felt genuinely pleased at what Robin seemed to be saying. He was a nice man, kind and considerate, an ideal husband for a home-loving, family-oriented woman like Anne. If Robin was beginning to see their marriage in a new light, she was fascinated to know how it had come about.

"Have you and Anne been talking things over?" she queried.

"Yes, a bit. She's a great person, Kati, and I always knew really that I was lucky to have her. But sometimes . . . oh, I don't know! Things get you down and you tend to take it out on the person who means the most to you. It's crazy, I know . . ."

"We all do it at times, Robin." Oh, heavens, she thought, how true that was. There's no anger, no bitterness, to equal what you can feel toward the person you love. And now, suddenly, the person *she* loved seemed like a magician, putting other people's problems to rights with a wave of his hand. "I gather that you're not altogether sorry now about the change in your job?"

Robin made a gesture with his hands. "I minded at the time, Kati . . . like hell I did. It seemed like a terrible slap in the face. But I realize, looking back, that I never did fit too happily into the *Rendezvous* set-up."

"So Scott Drummond was right to move you?"

Robin gave her an apologetic smile. "I know you must hate hearing me say this, but I really think that maybe he was, in my case."

Kati smiled at him warmly. "I'm glad you're happy, Robin. You and Anne will both be coming to the firm's midsummer night party, I hope?" This was a much-looked-forward-to annual event held on the rooftop of Universal House.

"Well, I'm not sure," he said, looking at her doubtfully.

"Do try and manage it. I like Anne, and I can tell her what a wonderful couple you make." Kati allowed her expression to convey more than her actual words.

The reassuring message got through that his past indiscretions were forgotten, and Robin looked immensely relieved. "You know something, Kati . . . you ought to have our sort of luck. You deserve it."

"Let's hope so." She became brisk. "Off with you now, Robin. I have a ton of work to do."

"On my way." He slid off her desk, stood hesitating for a moment or two, then swiftly leaned over and kissed her cheek. "Thanks for everything, Kati. You're a lady in a million."

* * *

Kati had decided on dinner at home that evening. If Scott had booked a table at a restaurant, he could always phone and unbook it. She had planned the menu with great care, wanting everything to be perfect —the most delectable food, but nothing that needed attention right up to the last minute. Starting with smoked salmon pâté, they'd proceed to lamb with red currant jelly and port wine, then strawberry shortcake with thick Devon cream for dessert. She'd consulted the manager of her local store about what to drink, and he'd recommended a crisp white Burgundy.

Ten minutes to seven. Kati gave the table setting a final check and shifted the centerpiece of flowers a half-inch to one side. The hands of the carriage clock on the mantelpiece moved with maddening slowness. She checked its time against her watch. She was quite ready, as ready as she ever could be. Did Scott have to be so meticulous about time? she thought, with a flash of irritation. It wouldn't hurt him to be early for once.

Nine minutes to seven. She was seized with sudden panic at the thought of the explanations that lay ahead. Would Scott make things easy for her? Why should he, when she had so badly misjudged him, and chosen to see villainy in his every action?

Five minutes to seven. Was her makeup okay, her hair? She checked in the oval mirror in the living room. Her hands shook as she poured herself a Campari and soda, which, after one swift, nerve-bracing sip, she left untouched.

Four, three, two minutes to seven. She prowled around the room, unable to keep still. The hour chimed delicately. Another minute ticked away. He was late, darn him.

It wasn't until five past that Kati began to be afraid. Had Scott had an accident? By ten past a different kind of fear crept in. Scott had said on Sunday night that these few days apart would give them both time to think things over, and decide what they really wanted from each other. She remembered some of the other things he'd said to her. *I'm a bit tired of this holier-than-thou approach,* and, *If I had any sense at all, I'd quit trying to get through to you.* Had Scott decided, after careful thought, that he'd had enough of her constant, carping criticism? Had he decided that he could do without a woman who insisted that she despised his whole attitude to life?

The remorseless ticking of the clock swept her along, second by second, closer to despairing certainty. Scott wasn't coming. Her discovery of the truth about the takeover of her father's firm, her realization of how cruelly she'd blamed Scott, had come too late.

Kati paced the carpet; she sat down, but almost at once jumped up and paced again. She lost track of the passage of time. Her eyes pricked with hot tears and her brain felt numb. . . .

The sound of the door chimes shattered the silence of the room. For an instant she stood irresolute, her heart thudding; then, in sudden frantic haste, she ran to the door and dragged it open.

Scott stood there, looking rueful, holding up both hands to show her that they were black with grease.

"Hi, Kati. Sorry I'm late. I dare not touch you—much as I want to—or it would ruin that lovely sexy silk dress you're wearing."

"But . . . but Scott, what happened?" she asked croakily.

"I'll tell you while I wash this muck off." Easing past her carefully, he headed for the kitchen. Kati followed and watched him as he stood at the sink soaping his hands.

"As I was walking here from the boat, I came across this elderly woman in one of those three-wheelers some handicapped people have. She'd broken down, and there was no one else around. I had to stop and render assistance."

Impulsively, Kati reached out and touched his arm, needing the reassuring contact. "Oh, Scott, I was so worried. I thought you weren't coming at all."

He paused in his hand-washing to look around at her. "I'm sorry, darling. I guess I should have found a way to let you know. But there was no phone box in sight, and I didn't want to leave that old lady on her own. She was a bit panicky because she couldn't walk at all without help. It seemed best to see if I could get her car started for her—which luckily I managed to."

"Oh, I'm so glad." Kati felt inordinately proud of him for his thoughtfulness, for his cleverness in understanding the mysteries of an automobile engine. "And you're here now, aren't you?"

"Yes, I'm here now." He rinsed his hands, shook them dry and reached for a towel. "So let's not waste any more time."

Kati smiled ruefully. "We've wasted too much time already, Scott."

"Agreed—eight years too much. These few days away from you have given me an opportunity to think, to get things clear in my mind. You and I belong together, Kati, whatever our differences. You'll just have to accept me, warts and all."

"I don't think I can see any warts, Scott," she said, gazing at him mistily.

"You *have* changed!" he exclaimed. "Do I get to hear what brought it about?"

"The Pembertons were here for dinner last night," she told him. "We talked."

"And?"

"Harry told me about my father, and the mess he got himself into financially."

Scott raised his eyebrows. "How much did he know?"

"Harry was Dad's old friend, remember. Apparently

they shared confidences—confidences that Dad couldn't share with his daughter."

"Yes, he *should* have put you in the picture, Kati. Still, I guess it's hard to be toppled from a pedestal. You always thought that the sun rose and set with him."

She looked at Scott beseechingly. "I just feel so terrible about the way I blamed you for what had happened. It was unforgivable of me. I should have trusted you. I should have known that you weren't capable of double-dealing, and that you'd never have cheated my father. But in a way," she added on a critical note, "the misunderstanding was your fault, too. You never tried to put me right, Scott. You should have told me the true story behind Arlington Journals' takeover of Prestige Print."

"I'd given your father my word that I wouldn't do that," Scott said, his eyes serious. "He begged me to leave it to him to tell you, in his own good time. I didn't feel that his sudden death absolved me from the promise I'd given him. Besides . . ."

"Go on," she prompted. "Besides . . . what?"

Scott hefted his powerful shoulders uncomfortably. "When you tore into me, Kati, condemning me for every underhanded trick imaginable, I felt very hurt and angry—just as much as you did. But there was something else that stopped me from trying harder to make up with you. I couldn't wholly deny your accusation that I'd worked out a deal that brought rewards to me. You see, in addition to solving your father's immediate problems I was aiming to secure your future too, Kati. I knew that you were about to lose the inheritance you'd been counting on. The substantial fringe benefit I negotiated for myself—a directorship of Arlington Journals—was something I did from the best of motives . . . or so it seemed at the time. My reasoning was that, once you and I were married, your future security was going to be largely dependent on me. I was totally shattered when you called me a trickster and a fraud. I questioned whether you had ever truly loved me, if you could think of me as being so despicable."

"Oh, Scott, I'm so sorry." The burden of past guilt weighed down on her heavily. "I suppose it was the extra shock of learning about the takeover, coming so soon after my father's sudden death, that made me unable to see straight. I just hadn't any idea how bad things were." She sighed. "You know what I used to be like when it came to understanding figures. It was feeble of me, I realized that afterward, of course, but I'd been content to leave all the bookkeeping side of the business to Dad."

Scott leaned back against the counter and smiled at her. "You were so like your father, Kati. Finance was his Achilles' heel, too. That's why the deal with Arlington would have been so right for him, and for you, after his death. It would have left you free to concentrate on what you were so good at—the technical and artistic side of printing. You were fully competent to step into your father's shoes. The job was there for you."

"As an employee of the firm I thought I owned," she reminded him sadly.

"I've been a paid employee all my working life," Scott pointed out. "You had a fine career ahead of you at Prestige Print, as I did at Arlington Journals. But it all seemed meaningless when you broke our engagement and gave me back my ring. All my ambitions and hopes were centered on you, Kati, and when I lost you, I wanted to throw in my hand and get away."

"So you went to the United States."

He made a rueful face. "It wasn't far enough away for me to forget you. Nowhere on earth would have been, I soon realized that. Despite the bitterness with which we'd parted, I could never get you out from under my skin."

"Oh, Scott!" She closed the gap between them, and his arms wrapped around her. "Nor I you. Never, for a single minute. No other man could ever compare with you."

They stood clinging together, not kissing, each content to feel the other's warmth and beating heart. Suddenly there seemed no hurry. There was so much time, days and weeks and months and years.

"I love you, Kati," he whispered.

"And I love you, Scott, with all my heart."

They kissed then, lips meeting lips. It was a kiss that restored the friendship, the respect and liking, the mutual support and deep abiding affection that had been missing from the passion they had shared so recently. Now, temporarily, it was passion that was set aside while they drank their fill of the wonderful experience of closeness.

Outside was the hush of evening. The sun's last rays, slanting low, filled the kitchen with a soft, rosy light.

"I love you, Kati," he murmured again, as if delighting in the very sound of the words. "Let's get married very soon."

Her heart raced. "Yes, Scott . . . oh, yes!"

"Meantime," he observed, "you have a starving man on your hands."

"Dinner is quite ready," she said, with a slight sense of letdown. "We can eat right away."

Scott laughed. "Not that sort of starving, darling. Do you realize, by the way, that I've never seen your bedroom?"

"A state of affairs," Kati said demurely, "that must be rectified without delay. Come on."

It was difficult mounting the narrow staircase side by side, arms about each other. On the tiny landing they paused to kiss, before she led him into her pretty, pink and gilt bedroom. Scott's virile presence seemed to fill it, marvelously, thrillingly, and Kati wondered how she'd ever imagined herself to be happy there alone.

Scott drew her to him to kiss her again. His lips were

cool, soft yet possessive, shaping the curve of her cheek and jawline. Kati's body seemed to liquefy, flowing into his, so that her trembling was his, and his was hers. Their kisses grew more intense, lips melded to lips, tongue curling against tongue. She felt Scott's quickening passion, and rejoiced. There were no barriers to be broken down, no reservations to be cast aside. This evening their coming together was not marred by a feeling of uncertainty; it would not be flawed afterward by questioning doubts. They were free to go to bed together as true lovers, happy in the knowledge that what they were doing was right and beautiful.

Scott took her clothes off slowly, pausing to savor the delights of her slender, curvy body as they were revealed to him. Kati's fingers were rendered clumsy by haste as she pushed his jacket from his shoulders and started to undress him.

"Scott . . . oh, darling Scott," she whispered, as she laid her face lovingly against his bare chest and nibbled tiny kisses.

His voice was too thick in his throat to shape any word except her name. "Kati . . . Kati . . . Kati."

Naked now, she wrestled with the buckle of his belt, but it defeated her. Scott lifted her in his arms and laid her down upon the pink satin counterpane. With quick, economic movements he threw off his remaining clothes. Standing there, he looked so wonderful to Kati, so magnificent, that she felt weak with desire and breathless with anticipation. Scott knelt beside the bed and touched her reverently, his fingertips weaving an erotic trail across her.

"Kati, I want you so much that I'm almost afraid."

"Don't be afraid. I want you too, just as much."

She reached for him and clasped her hands around his neck, drawing him up to the bed. He stretched out beside her and they twined their limbs together, both eager for fulfilment and the sweet afterglow that would follow. Their lovemaking took them to the heights of ecstasy, and there was no sadness in its wake. They lay panting, still joined, their skin moist with passion, their bodies suffused with golden glory. This time it was not like those other occasions, a doubtful step in a tenuous affair; this time, they both knew and were exultant in the knowledge that it was the beginning of forever.

"It was wonderful, Kati," Scott murmured against the abandonment of her dark hair on the pillow. "You are perfect beyond imagining."

"And you."

"You're not sending me away tonight?"

"No fear!" She clung to him more tightly, as if he might dare to escape her.

"It's Friday," he reminded her. "Isn't that perfect? We have the whole weekend before us."

"The whole lovely weekend," she agreed.

They lapsed into a contented, loving silence. It was a silence broken by tiny murmurs as echoes of their rapture rippled through them. Eventually, Scott stirred, and said, "How about sampling that dinner you told me was ready an hour or so ago?"

"Oh, heavens!" Kati exclaimed. "My lamb will be all dried up."

"Who cares? It was in a good cause."

She donned a robe, and Scott pulled on his trousers and shirt. Together, they descended to the kitchen. As she'd feared, the casserole dish was past eating, but they collected together an appetizing assortment of the smoked salmon pâté and crackers, half a cucumber and a bunch of grapes, plus the strawberry shortcake. Scott extracted the bottle of wine from the fridge and inspected the label.

"You are doing me proud."

She laughed. "Don't you think you deserve it?"

His cobalt eyes glinted into hers, and Kati was startled by the shaft of fresh desire that pierced her.

"Let's make a picnic of this," Scott suggested. "Upstairs."

"Let's."

They loaded a tray and returned to the bedroom. Scott put the tray down on the bed, drew the curtains against the fading daylight, and switched on a rose-shaded bedside lamp. Then he came to Kati, and firmly removed her robe, his own trousers and shirt following it to the floor.

"That's much better," he said, and set about opening the wine and filling their glasses. They toasted one another silently, then attacked the food. Nothing she'd eaten before had ever tasted so delicious, Kati thought. In her own deep happiness, she suddenly remembered the happiness that Dee too had found.

"Scott . . ."

"Uh-huh?"

"I don't think you can have heard. Dee's ex-husband was in an accident—a car crash."

"He wasn't killed?"

"No, but very smashed up. I think it was touch and go for a while. Dee was in a bad way about it. But what might have been tragic has turned out wonderfully well. She told me yesterday that they're going to try again."

"Get remarried, you mean?"

"Dee wants to right away, but Theodore is holding off until he sees what kind of recovery he makes. I think he can't bear the thought that she might only be taking him back out of pity."

"I can understand that feeling, Kati. But I'm glad for them. Dee is one nice lady. Why did they divorce? Was he two-timing her?"

"Nothing like that. The way she explained it to me, it was basically a case of two people who were each too bound up in carving out their own careers to have enough time left over for one another."

"That won't happen to us," Scott said fervently. "I'm an ambitious guy, Kati, darling, but I'll never let my career get in the way of our marriage."

"Nor I, Scott. Not ever."

He wiped away a small piece of pâté that had stuck to the corner of her mouth, and licked his finger. "You still have a long way to go, careerwise," he said reflectively. "You'll get offers that you'll find difficult to refuse."

"You think so?"

"I know so. I'll tell you something, darling. I was lunching with Victor Channon last week, and your name came up. He asked me if I was as impressed with you as he was."

"You told him no, of course."

"I tried to keep my yes just short of adulation."

"What brought me into the conversation?" she queried.

"Well, I wasn't planning to tell you until it's completely definite, because I don't like counting chickens too soon. But I suppose I might as well, even though it gives you the laugh over me. Apparently Victor Channon bumped into Sir Roland Maynard at some city function, and he was told of a large advertisement order that's coming to *Rendezvous* from one of Sir Roland's companies, I don't know which. And it's all down to you, Kati. Sir Roland was so taken with you when he met you on that TV talk show, and so grateful for the good work you're doing for handicapped people, that he wanted to find some way of showing his appreciation."

And she'd been all set to tear into Scott for what she'd seen as another example of his unscrupulous business ethics. Thank heaven she'd been spared that mortification.

"Actually, Scott, the order has come through," she told him. "Greg Farley left a note about it on my desk yesterday. He didn't say anything about the background, though; just that there was a big space booking from West Midland Industrials."

Scott laughed. "No doubt, like a typical smart adman, he was hoping to claim the credit for himself.

But I'll make sure that everyone knows who's to get the medal. Victor Channon has you marked down for big things, Kati—a high-powered job on the executive floor, no less. He says that a talent like yours mustn't be wasted."

It gave Kati a real lift to be rated as having top-level potential, but she shook her head decidedly. "Corporate politics aren't for me, Scott."

"Are you sure? You're not the sort of person to coast along comfortably. You'll never feel really happy if you don't stretch yourself."

"Being your wife will stretch me plenty. And editing *Rendezvous* isn't coasting—and it won't ever be. However well the magazine does, it'll still need a lot of effort to keep it one step ahead of the competition."

"I guess you're right."

Kati turned to look at him, her gaze feasting on the fascinating planes and angles of his face, the humorous, loving expression in his cobalt eyes. "Now it's time to give *your* ego a boost . . . if it needs any boosting."

"Come on, tell me. Flattery will get you everywhere," he added, not very originally; but just then they both thought it was witty and apt.

"You were right about Robin Wheatley," she told him. "So utterly and completely right that I feel ashamed when I remember how I attacked you for shifting him to that new job. He dropped in to see me today."

"And?"

"Robin is obviously as happy as a clam. It's a transformation. You're a genius to have seen what he needed."

"I'm glad to hear it's worked out for him," said Scott. "I knew it would, really, but I couldn't help feeling a tiny bit of doubt about sending him to the branch office."

"How do you mean?" she asked curiously.

"He was the wrong man for *Rendezvous*, no question. But in an organization as big as U.P. there were lots of other slots I could have found for him that would have kept him in Fleet Street. *The Weekly Gardener* struck me as the magazine that would suit him best, but I kept wondering if part of my reasoning wasn't to try and put an end to whatever was going on between you two."

"I see. But there wasn't anything between Robin and me, Scott. There never was."

"He wanted there to be."

"Yes," she admitted candidly. "But Robin hadn't a hope. Not at any time."

He gave her one of his endearing, lopsided smiles. "You'll be saying next that it was all on my account."

"Robin wasn't my type," Kati told him, "and anyway, he was married. Still . . ."—she touched Scott's nose with the tip of her finger—"you managed to get in the way of every budding romance I ever had. I never understood why they never seemed to work out, but I do now."

"Which makes us even. I never managed to have a relationship that really meant anything to me. You were always there, haunting me with your loveliness. Oh, Kati, darling, I'm so thankful that we've finally got together again. From now on you're my number one priority. Don't ever let me forget it."

"Fat chance. I'm going to hang on to you like grim death."

He touched his lips to hers in a soft, tender kiss. "You know something, Kati, you're quite perfect."

"Far, far from perfect," she said with a happy sigh. "Just very much in love."

"Aren't they one and the same thing? Let's get this damned tray out of the way . . ."

They clung together in a sudden resurgence of need. This time their lovemaking was at a more leisurely pace; they could allow their passion to build slowly, beautifully, swirling them up from crest to crest. They reached high summits of bliss that they had never quite attained before. Afterward, gloriously spent and satiated, filled with a delightful lethargy, they cuddled together in a loving embrace and drifted off to sleep.

They wakened simultaneously to the first pale flush of dawn. Scott clung to her for a long, lingering kiss, then thrust her back.

"Come on, Mrs. Drummond-to-be, we have things to do."

"Such as?"

He was already out of bed, stretching his arms above his head. Kati gazed up with love at the tautly muscled male power of his fine body, before, with a swift movement, Scott whipped the covers off her.

"Show a leg, woman. Grab yourself some suitable gear for our weekend on the river. Ten minutes, and we're off. This is where one of my fantasies gets to be for real."

"I can't be ready in ten minutes," Kati protested.

"Yes, you can. Throw something on, and chuck the rest of what you'll need into a bag. Don't even wait to do your hair. At this hour there'll be no one on the streets to see, and I love it all wild and sexy."

"A half-hour would be more like it," she stated, then leaped from the bed as his open palm descended in the direction of her rear.

"Fifteen minutes, and that's my final offer," he said. "Get your skates on."

Behind them, above the swirling wash of the *Pagan*, the eastern sky was blushed pearl pink with the promise of a beautiful day. Ahead, the bridges of the Thames were still dark silhouettes. She and Scott, Kati thought dreamily, had to be the only people in London awake and about so early. She was standing behind him as he sat at the helmsman's seat, her arms about his neck, her chin resting on his head. Scott's left hand idly coiled a strand of her hair. Steering the boat only needed one hand.

Slowly, the day came alive. There were early scullers at Putney, and at Richmond a riverside shop was open where they bought bread, butter and eggs. They made breakfast while still tied up, and never had coffee tasted better, scrambled eggs more delicious.

Then they were on their way again, slipping gently between lush green banks, with sunlit meadows stretching in a golden haze to the horizon.

Genuine Silhouette sterling silver bookmark for only $15.95!

What a beautiful way to hold your place in your current romance! This genuine sterling silver bookmark, with the distinctive Silhouette symbol in elegant black, measures 1½" long and 1" wide. It makes a beautiful gift for yourself, and for every romantic you know! And, at only $15.95 each, including all postage and handling charges, you'll want to order several now, while supplies last.

Send your name and address with check or money order for $15.95 per bookmark ordered to

**Silhouette Books
120 Brighton Rd., P.O. Box 5084
Clifton, N.J. 07015-5084
Attn: Bookmark**

Bookmarks can be ordered pre-paid only. No charges will be accepted. Please allow 4-6 weeks for delivery.

N.Y. State Residents
Please Add Sales Tax

Enjoy romance and passion, larger-than-life...

Now, thrill to 4 Silhouette Intimate Moments novels (a $9.00 value)— ABSOLUTELY FREE!

If you want more passionate sensual romance, then Silhouette Intimate Moments novels are for you!

In every 256-page book, you'll find romance that's electrifying...involving... and intense. And now, these larger-than-life romances can come into your home every month!

4 FREE books as your introduction.

Act now and we'll send you four thrilling Silhouette Intimate Moments novels. They're our gift to introduce you to our convenient home subscription service. Every month, we'll send you four new Silhouette Intimate Moments books. Look them over for 15 days. If you keep them, pay just $9.00 for all four. Or return them at no charge.

We'll mail your books to you *as soon as they are published.* Plus, with every shipment, you'll receive the Silhouette Books Newsletter absolutely free. *And Silhouette Intimate Moments is delivered free.*

Mail the coupon today and start receiving Silhouette Intimate Moments. Romance novels for women...not girls.

Silhouette Intimate Moments

Silhouette Intimate Moments™
120 Brighton Road, P.O. Box 5084, Clifton, NJ 07015-5084

☐ **YES!** Please send me FREE and without obligation, 4 exciting Silhouette Intimate Moments romance novels. Unless you hear from me after I receive my 4 FREE books, please send 4 new Silhouette Intimate Moments novels to preview each month. I understand that you will bill me $2.25 each for a total of $9.00—with no additional shipping, handling or other charges. **There is no minimum number of books to buy and I may cancel anytime I wish.** The first 4 books are mine to keep, even if I never take a single additional book.

☐ Mrs. ☐ Miss ☐ Ms. ☐ Mr.   BMS225

Name _____ (please print)

Address _____ Apt. #

City ( ) _____ State _____ Zip

Area Code   Telephone Number

Signature (if under 18, parent or guardian must sign)

This offer, limited to one per household, expires July 31, 1985. Terms and prices subject to change. Your enrollment is subject to acceptance by the publisher.

Silhouette Intimate Moments is a service mark and trademark.

MAIL THIS COUPON
and get 4 thrilling
Silhouette Desire®
novels FREE (a $7.80 value)

Silhouette Desire books may not be for everyone. They *are* for readers who want a sensual, provocative romance. These are modern love stories that are charged with emotion from the first page to the thrilling happy ending—about women who discover the extremes of fiery passion. Confident women who face the challenge of today's world and overcome all obstacles to attain their dreams—*and their desires.*

We believe you'll be so delighted with Silhouette Desire romance novels that you'll want to receive them regularly through our home subscription service. Your books will be *shipped to you two months before they're available anywhere else*—so you'll never miss a new title. Each month we'll send you 6 new books to look over for 15 days, without obligation. If not delighted, simply return them and owe nothing. Or keep them and pay only $1.95 each. There's no charge for postage or handling. And there's no obligation to buy anything at any time. You'll also receive a subscription to the Silhouette Books Newsletter *absolutely free!*

So don't wait. To receive your four FREE books, fill out and mail the coupon below *today!*

SILHOUETTE DESIRE and colophon are registered trademarks and a service mark.

Silhouette Desire®
120 Brighton Road, P.O. Box 5084, Clifton, NJ 07015-5084

Yes, please send me FREE and without obligation, 4 exciting Silhouette Desire books. Unless you hear from me after I receive them, send me 6 new Silhouette Desire books to preview each month before they're available anywhere else. I understand that you will bill me just $1.95 each for a total of $11.70—with no additional shipping, handling or other hidden charges. **There is no minimum number of books that I must buy, and I can cancel anytime I wish.** The first 4 books are mine to keep, even if I never take a single additional book.

☐ Mrs. ☐ Miss ☐ Ms. ☐ Mr.   BDS2R5

Name	*(please print)*	
Address		Apt. #
City	State	Zip
( ) Area Code	Telephone Number	

Signature (If under 18, parent or guardian must sign.)

This offer, limited to one per household, expires July 31, 1985. Terms and prices subject to change. Your enrollment is subject to acceptance by the publisher.